ALIEN EMBRACE

Tracy St.John

Futuristic Romance

New Concepts

Georgia

Be sure to check out our website for the very best in fiction at fantastic prices!

When you visit our webpage, you can:
* Read excerpts of currently available books
* View cover art of upcoming books and current releases
* Find out more about the talented artists who capture the magic of the writer's imagination on the covers
* Order books from our backlist
* Find out the latest NCP and author news--including any upcoming book signings by your favorite NCP author
* Read author bios and reviews of our books
* Get NCP submission guidelines
* And so much more!

We offer a 20% discount on all new Trade Paperback releases ordered from our website!

Be sure to visit our webpage to find the best deals in e-books and paperbacks! To find out about our new releases as soon as they are available, please be sure to sign up for our newsletter (http://www.newconceptspublishing.com/newsletter.htm) or join our reader group (http://groups.yahoo.com/group/new_concepts_pub/join)!

The newsletter is available by double opt in only and our customer information is *never* shared!

Visit our webpage at:
www.newconceptspublishing.com

Alien Embrace is an original publication of NCP. This work has never before appeared in book form. This work is a novel. Any similarity to actual persons or events is purely coincidental.

New Concepts Publishing, LLC.
5202 Humphreys Rd.
Lake Park, GA 31636

© copyright Sept. 2010, Tracy St. John
Cover art (c) copyright 2010 Alex DeShanks

NCP books are available at special quantity discounts for bulk purchases for sales promotions, premiums, fund raising, or educational use. For details, write, email, or phone New Concepts Publishing, LLC., 5202 Humphreys Rd., Lake Park, GA 31636; Ph. 229-257-0367, Fax 229-219-1097; orders@newconceptspublishing.com.

First NCP Trade Paperback Printing: December 2010

Chapter One

"You're being watched," Ambassador Vrill whispered to Amelia.

Of course I am. I'm the guest of honor and the only Earther here, the redhead thought. Still, Vrill's excited tone raised goosebumps on Amelia's bare arms. She checked the fiery red and gold gown that had been custom sewn for her there on the planet Plasius. It managed to cover her where it should – barely.

She still couldn't believe Vrill had convinced her to wear the almost non-existent dress. The Plasian must have snuck something in Amelia's drink. There was no other explanation.

The neck of the sleeveless gown plunged to below her navel. It was bad enough the fabric was whisper-thin; she had to be careful her movements didn't shift the barely-there bodice to expose her entire breasts to the crowded room. Since she was amply endowed, the meager bit of fabric was constantly endangering Amelia's modesty.

The halter of the dress would have left her entire back naked but for her hair. Her tresses were caught back from her face in glittering combs to flow in a waved auburn river all the way to her waist. Amelia found the feeling of her hair on bared flesh wickedly seductive. It was an unfamiliar if titillating sensation; she usually wore her hair in a ponytail. With a shirt on her back.

Beneath the waterfall of hair, the shadowed cleft of her buttocks disappeared into the intricately laced train, which made up ninety-five percent of the gown's fabric. It was made of heavier material that swept the floor. When Amelia walked, the drag of the train pulled at the dress, making the front stretch taut against her torso. She felt sure no one was guessing how she looked naked. Every curve of her body must be blatantly obvious.

The worst part of the dress was its scrap of a skirt. The hem in the front was barely a scandalous inch below her sex. Her long, golden-hued legs were framed by the cascading scarlet and gold fabric.

Things here were definitely different from morality-driven Earth. The seductive Plasians knew much about allure and cared little for modesty.

"Who is watching me?" Amelia whispered back to Vrill. Her eyes darted over the crowd assembled in Saucin Israla's home. High-ranking Plasians of the government and art guild swarmed the ballroom, flirting with one another. In darkened corners where overstuffed couches lined the walls, movement Amelia dared not watch too long indicated coupling had already begun for some lovers. Their soft moans provided a background hum to the other partygoers' easy conversations. An occasional cry informed anyone who cared that bliss had been realized.

The room was for public functions but still managed to create an aura of seduction. Amber colored fabric swathed the walls, and golden lighting globes drifted across the ceiling, giving the room a soft, dreamlike quality. The gentle illumination provided shadowed areas for amorous activity.

The globes also highlighted the fantastic but pornographic mural on the ceiling. Amelia had snuck many a glance at the painted figures cavorting overhead, each passionate scene more explicit than the last.

Despite the subject matter, there was no doubting the talent of the unknown artist. If Michelangelo had painted orgy scenes, Israla's ballroom ceiling might have been his work.

Amelia's scan of the room met many eyes, and all nodded in respect. The party was for her, Plasius' first Earth artist-in-residence.

Vrill's eyes, streaked like black marble, smoldered. Amelia recognized her friend's arousal with amused embarrassment. The willowy Plasian's bronze skin glistened. The thick olive mane on her head, more like fur than hair, moved as if in a breeze. Her body heat released the perfume globules woven in her scant gown's ice blue fabric. The air grew heavy with the sharp scent of spice, Vrill's preferred aroma. Her voice rose to its usual husky tone.

"You've caught the attention of a Kalquorian clan. If stares could burn, you'd be on fire now."

Kalquorians! Amelia froze. For a moment she forgot to breathe. "Are you sure it's a Kalquorian clan?"

"I'd know and want a Kalquorian if I was blind." Vrill's dark gaze ran over the Earther's face. "That puts you in a spot, doesn't it? I mean, since Earth refuses to treaty with Kalquor. Your people speak against them at every galactic council."

Amelia swallowed. Her voice sounded defensive to her own ears. "Our leaders consider them a threat, especially to Earther women."

Vrill smirked. "That's because all of your leaders are male, and they don't want their women running off to join clans. All of you would, if you had just a taste of what the men of Kalquor offer." Her expression changed to one of concern. "Would your government make you leave Plasius if they knew a clan was here?"

"Not if it's just one clan and I stay away from them." Amelia heard the uncertainty in her own voice.

"Good! I don't want you to go. And if you don't stay away from them, well *I'd* never tell." She tittered.

"Where are they, Vrill?" Amelia continued to look around but only a forest of tall bronze Plasians greeted her eyes.

Vrill pulled Amelia a few steps to one side. "Now you can see them. They're in the middle of the room, a little behind you and to your right." She pointed.

Amelia twisted her head to look in that direction. Her tensed neck muscles creaked. She saw the men staring at her immediately. Even from the distance of half the immense ballroom, it was impossible to miss the monumental differences between the Kalquorians and Plasians.

The three aliens towered over the Plasians. Where the Plasians were soft, thin beings, the Kalquorian men looked sculpted from granite. Where the Plasians were slightly curved, the Kalquorians bulged muscle. The Plasians broadcasted their readiness to receive pleasure; the Kalquorians looked capable of taking it by brute force.

Vrill whispered in her ear, "Someone's thinking naughty thoughts. Your skin is as red as your hair."

Amelia's whole body flushed with heat. Her own gown's scent wafted over her; the aroma of a summer night's breeze after a thunderstorm. Fresh, new, and somehow electric.

The Kalquorians looked like Earthers who'd eaten steroids from birth. There were numerous differences to be sure; outside of the size difference, Amelia knew from reports they had fangs that folded to the roofs of their mouths when not in use. Supposedly a Kalquorian's bite sent an intoxicating substance into its victim, leaving him or her incapable of defense.

Otherwise they were very much like Amelia's species. In fact the resemblance was shocking. It was whispered, though not around those in Earth authority, that Kalquorians and Earthers might have a common ancestry.

According to historians, an alien race had fled a doomed planet millennia ago and settled on Kalquor. Theories abounded that some of the Kalquorian ancestors had also settled Earth; too many similarities between the two races existed for mere coincidence.

Such ideas were taboo on Earth. Anything that contradicted the Church's edicts was illegal to consider, much less discuss. Earthers were God's chosen people; Kalquorians were viewed as poor copies, perhaps even emissaries of Satan.

Amelia privately prided herself on her more open views, and once off Earth she'd discussed the possibilities of Earther/Kalquorian species ties with her alien friends. Her small circle of Plasian associates had been shocked and delighted to meet an Earther willing to entertain the idea in depth.

For her part, Amelia reveled in the freedom of being away from Earth's religion-based regime. She'd seen too much corruption, too much damage done in the name of God on her home planet. While she still believed in a higher power that would punish evildoers, she felt

it was more kind than vengeful, more forgiving than damning. It was this view that allowed her to happily reside on Plasius. Despite the sexual decadence of her Plasian hosts, she tried not to judge them.

If only she could get her emotions to agree with her reason, she often lamented. She was still too conditioned by her restrictive upbringing to be comfortable around the amorous race.

In the brief glance she allowed herself, she noted all three Kalquorians had black hair, wide foreheads and strong jaws. Their skin was dark, like Earthers of Middle Eastern origin. Despite herself, she appreciated the strength of their features, too masculine to be attractive in Earth movie star fashion. Hollywood's current crop of leading men were sometimes prettier than their female co-stars and androgynous enough to pretend sexlessness.

She jerked her eyes away from the clan's penetrating stares. Her clinging scrap of a dress provided no obstacle to their evaluating gazes. She looked down to see the erect buttons of her nipples press against the tissue-thin fabric. She blushed anew at the sight of her body's brazen spectacle and crossed her arms over her breasts. How naked she felt! She shivered.

"I didn't realize Kalquorians were so...big," she said. "Are clans always made up of three men?"

"Of course. There's the Dramok, the clan's leader. That one's wearing a government insignia, so he's an official of rank. He's wearing the black formsuit with blue trim. Those formsuits are nice, aren't they? You can tell exactly what you're getting. That Dramok has a lot to offer a lucky female." Vrill licked her lips.

"He has a commanding presence." Amelia thought about the stern features and piercing gaze of the man Vrill identified as the leader. In that brief glance, his eyes seemed to pierce her very soul. She shivered again and wished she could control her body's reactions. "What about the others? What are they?"

"The biggest Kalquorian wearing the green tunic is an Imdiko, the clan's nurturer. That's an Interstellar Medical Council badge on his shirt. Only the top doctor from each planet can sit on that council. The other man is a Nobek, who's charged with the protection of the clan. He's wearing a Kalquor Global Security formsuit. Very impressive credentials," Vrill purred. "The situation must be dire on Kalquor if such an important clan is searching off-world for a Matara."

Matara? Amelia wondered. Her excellent grasp of the liquid Plasian language omitted that word. It sounded too guttural for Vrill's tongue.

Vrill fluttered alabaster eyelashes in the Kalquorians' direction. She flicked her tongue over her lips again. "It's nice to see them here scouting for a female."

Amelia started. "I thought Kalquorians and Plasians aren't compatible."

"Our species can enjoy certain pleasures together, but Kalquorian men are too big to penetrate Plasian females in regular intercourse. Of course, there's always lovely things to do that don't require the typical; I once used my mouth on a Kalquorian to..."

"No, Vrill," Amelia interrupted.

The Plasian blew an exasperated breath. "You're so repressed. Anyway, I'm betting that clan isn't here for a Plasian fling. I think they're more interested in finding out what the Earther race can do for them."

Amelia's body temperature dropped from hot to cold. "You think they're here because of me?"

Her friend smiled a long, slow smile. "Why don't you ask them, my lovely prudish friend? Here they come."

"What?" Her head whipped around. Her neck cracked, sending dull pain through her arms and hands. The clan indeed walked toward her, their intent eyes riveted on her. She turned back in time to see Vrill disappearing into the crowd.

"Vrill!"

"Excuse me, Amelia Ryan?"

She started, and not just because the man spoke to her in her own language. The voice rumbled through her very bones. Her whole body seemed to vibrate to the resonance.

She resisted responding to him. She wanted to run away, *tried* to run away, but the Kalquorian's commanding tone swiveled her body toward the men. She had always obeyed authority, even when it put her life in danger. Now was no different even though the man was not of her species. Any time she sensed someone dominant to herself, Amelia instantly complied with that person's expectations.

As she turned, the clan slid into her line of sight: the bare, muscled arm of the Nobek, his wide formsuited chest, and other arm. Then the sleeved, bulging arms and chests of the other two filled her vision. Her eyes lingered over corded necks, strong jawlines and three pairs of eyes.

She thought of the concord grapes that grew on the fence surrounding her childhood backyard. She remembered the tart sweetness that slid down her throat like liquid silk. The Kalquorians' sharp eyes were that same cool blue-violet color. Their pupils were slit like those of cats.

I should run away, Amelia thought. *Earth would not want me to even speak to them. They say the aliens are degenerate, wanting Earth women for unspeakable sexual games. What kind of games, I wonder?*

Her body, pinned by their stares, refused to move. Despite her yammering thoughts, her muscles remained locked statue-still.

The Kalquorian standing in the middle, the one treacherous Vrill identified as the leader, spoke again. "Amelia Ryan?"

Her voice floated from her, distant like a dream. "I'm Amelia Ryan."

He bowed, his sleek, shoulder-length hair swinging forward. His eyes never left hers, and she was riveted by his stare. *He's handsome._They all are*, Amelia thought with surprise. With the trimmed mustache and goatee, she decided the Kalquorian speaking to her looked like an old movie version of a Muskateer.

His voice, despite its strength, was soft. "I am Dramok Rajhir. This is my clan. Imdiko Flencik," he motioned, and the largest Kalquorian bowed as well, a smile softening his strong features.

Flencik's ebony hair fell well below his shoulders in soft spiral curls. His face was clean-shaven and not as narrow as his leader's. He was easily the bulkiest of the three, but his expression was the gentlest. His smile was one of real warmth.

"And Nobek Breft."

The Nobek echoed the others' bows. The smallest of the three, he stood a foot taller than Amelia's five feet ten inch frame. His hair swept from his face in waves. Amelia caught herself wondering what it would feel like to stroke it. His mustache and goatee were fuller than Rajhir's, softening the hard planes of his stern but attractive features. The predatory look in his feline eyes suggested he was more dangerous than his larger companions. He looked her up and down, as if wondering how tasty a snack she might be.

They watched her. She realized they waited for her to respond. She struggled for anything to say.

"Um...hello," she said.

Still they waited. Their expressions seemed polite, even patient. She took courage from that.

"I'm sorry if I seem rude." She smiled. "It's just that I've never met

Kalquorians before. You're rather imposing."

Rajhir's brow creased. He looked at Breft and spoke in staccato bursts. Breft, looking concerned, answered in the same language, his eyes darting from the clan's leader to Amelia.

Rajhir and Flencik exchanged dark looks, and Amelia's stomach turned. What had she said to upset the Kalquorians?

Flencik spoke to her in a voice deep like Rajhir's but even gentler. "Your language to us gives confusion. Says Breft our appearance you are threatened?"

Breft interjected, his tenor diplomatic but lined with steel. "Flencik's grasp of your language is not very good yet. He meant to say, our appearance threatens you?"

"Oh...well..." Amelia struggled for a tactful tone. "Threaten isn't quite what I meant. When I said you were imposing I meant I'm not accustomed to your great size. You're much taller than most Earth men."

The clan relaxed, and Amelia mentally sighed relief. If the Kalquorians found her language confusing, landmines lay waiting within any conversation.

Rajhir smiled at her. "Our people have misunderstandings, yes? Earth does no like Kalquor, but we have no harmed any Earthers."

Speaking of landmines, Amelia thought, feeling her stomach knot again. *Why am I even speaking to them? Earth would have my tongue cut out if they saw me right now.*

She couldn't seem to keep her mouth shut though. "Your culture is very different from ours. Unfortunately, Earthers have a long history of not accepting what they don't understand."

Her statement prompted another exchange between Rajhir and Breft. After this, Rajhir smiled down at her again as if about to confer a great favor.

"We will discuss Kalquorian culture with you. We will show you Kalquorian ways. When you know the pleasure we offer, you will understand and accept us. Mataras do no——" he paused and looked at Breft. "*Grolic?*"

"Fear," the Nobek said.

Rajhir nodded. "Mataras do no fear clans."

Matara again. Now Amelia realized why it sounded strange coming from Vrill; the word was Kalquorian. "What are—?"

Saucin Israla's aide slipped beside her, interrupting the question. The lithe Plasian female inclined her black-maned head toward Amelia before raking greedy eyes over the clan. Once again, Amelia felt herself flush in the presence of overt sexuality. Would she ever relax in this atmosphere of pleasure-seeking decadence?

"Saucin Israla requires Amelia Ryan," the aide purred, still looking at the Kalquorians. She glided away, casting glances over her shoulder. Her fur waved as if to beckon them to her.

The three men ignored the Plasian. Their eyes remained riveted on Amelia. She smiled an apology. "I must go for the presentation. Please excuse me."

She turned from the clan, both relieved and disappointed to be escaping. She didn't lie to herself about enjoying their attention. She was fascinated by how much they resembled her own race. And they were so unabashedly masculine. Even repressed Amelia had to admit a stab of desire. No wonder Vrill had become aroused.

She took one step when a hand slipped around her waist. Before she realized what was happening, Rajhir pulled her backwards and held her against himself. She gasped as the hard muscles of his thighs, abdomen, and chest pressed against her from behind.

Flencik and Breft moved to surround her, blocking her from the view of the other guests. She stood frozen in shock. Rajhir's hand flattened against her slender belly, his touch hot against the exposed skin. He pinned her against his own body so she couldn't pull away. His other hand stroked her throat with a feather touch. It drifted down, sliding over one round breast and cupping it. His forefinger and thumb massaged the tip of her nipple. The sensitive flesh hardened into a hungry nub and strained against the thin material of her gown. The heat of his touch shot from her breast in a lightning bolt to her sex.

The surge of desire snapped her paralysis. She gasped and reached to slap his hand away. Breft caught her hands and pressed them to his lips as Flencik stroked her cheek in a soothing manner. Rajhir switched his attention to her other breast, slipping his fingers inside the dress to pinch the naked nipple. Breft held her hands effortlessly, his lips curling under his mustache in a grin as she tried to pull free. She thought of screaming, but the thought of the Plasians seeing her being ravished by the three men made her cheeks burn with humiliation. The amorous Plasians wouldn't understand what the fuss was about; sexual play in public was as natural to them as breathing. She'd seen many at the party locked in such embraces already, some indulging in outright public sex. She doubted any would come to her aid. They'd probably cheer the Kalquorians on.

"Be a good girl," Rajhir breathed in her ear. "We know Earthers do no like others to witness sex pleasuring. Do no resist and none here will know of our little game."

He'd done his homework on Earthers; more than anything she didn't want to be seen like this. She stopped her struggles, surrendering to Rajhir's demanding touch and praying that no one indeed would see her humiliation. Her heart thundered in her chest as he rubbed each breast in turn, testing their weight and fullness in his heated palms. Flencik's thumb brushed over her parted lips, his eyes drinking in the sight of his Dramok pulling aside fabric to expose her taut nipples, which flushed rose pink from the attention. An appreciative growl emanated from Breft who brought her fingers to his lips. He sucked each slender digit into his wet, warm mouth.

Even as she trembled with fear, even as she closed her eyes in shame, Amelia's insides sent honeyed lava to creep a molten path down her thighs. Desire pulsed through her at the brazen ravishing. She tightened her legs together, willing the flow of moisture to stop. Panties had been impossible to wear; the back of the dress dipped too low and the fabric of the gown molded to her skin so smoothly that underwear would have shown with blatant lines. The Plasians already thought her ridiculously uptight. When she'd dressed for tonight, she'd been willing to go nude under the gown so she wouldn't have to endure the snickers and pitying looks. Now she regretted it. What if the men decided to explore her there, discovering the nakedness, the wetness of her sex? Would her uncontrollable desire encourage them to do more than simply explore with fingers? Would they take her right here in front of the Plasians?

Flencik caressed a breast when Rajhir held it up to him like an offering. The Imdiko licked his finger and whirled his saliva over her areola. Amelia's traitorous body responded against her will. She arched, filling his hand with her breast. Had anyone ever touched her with such gentle knowledge? She moaned. "Please..."

Rajhir's breath warmed her ear. "You are in great need. We know how your society keeps your people from pleasure."

"I – I have to go," she whimpered, wishing her voice sounded stronger. She tried to pull away again. The Kalquorians held her still as if to show her their physical power. Another bolt of desire shot through her. She trembled and quieted again, not fighting, waiting to see if they would set her free. Only when she surrendered did Flencik tug her dress back into place, hiding her breasts with a rueful smile.

"We will speak again, Amelia Ryan," Rajhir promised.

They released her and stepped back to let her pass between them. She hurried toward the still waiting aide who smiled at her as if they shared a secret. Amelia's face flamed anew; the aide hadn't seen what she'd let the Kalquorians do, but no doubt the Plasian knew something had happened. Amelia prayed the moisture between her thighs wasn't obvious because of the shortness of her skirt. It took all the pride she could muster to not run from the Kalquorians.

* * * *

Rajhir watched Amelia rush away through the willowy crowd of Plasian elite. His eyes drank in her lush body, a pleasing collection of soft, pliant curves. Her auburn curtain of hair swayed, offering tantalizing glimpses of smooth skin bared by the backless gown. The tops of her buttocks were round, the shadow between them a teasing invitation. He longed to explore her there, in all the sweet dark places a woman's body offered. To discover her with fingers, mouth, and sex organs. To uncover all her body's treasures, to decode its secrets.

He enjoyed the sight of her flesh glowing in the amber light. He thought of how his brown hand had looked in contrast to the golden mounds of her breasts and the pink of her nipples. He couldn't wait to touch her burning skin again. *Soon* he promised himself. Tonight, if possible. To bury his dark flesh in her pale sweetness, to let her light, soft flesh enclose him, consume him...

"The poor woman is terrified," Flencik said in Kalquorian, interrupting Rajhir's fantasy. The Imdiko's voice betrayed his disgust. "Her government has done severe damage to her natural instinct for sexual pleasure. She cannot enjoy what her body craves."

Breft answered. "Totalitarian regimes, especially fanatical religious ones, have a nasty habit of taking the life out of living."

Rajhir found himself unable to tear his eyes from Amelia. She stood with a group of Plasians next to a draped square suspended on a stand. She spoke to Art Guildmaster Osill, a male with languid, drooping eyes, and the Plasian Saucin herself, Israla. Amelia glanced at the Kalquorians then looked away, blushing furiously.

Rajhir said, "They haven't destroyed all her carnal instincts. They may have even done us a favor with their repression; did you notice how she immediately submits to authority? Asserting complete dominance over her may be what's called for. As an Earther female, it's all she's ever known."

Breft licked his lips. "I have no problem dominating such a lovely creature. I scented her desire. She wants to be taken."

Flencik's tone grew concerned. "There are limits to forcing someone to submit to anything, even on Plasius. Saucin Israla might draw the line at coerced medical tests."

Rajhir ran his gaze up the long, lovely line of Amelia's legs. Was it his imagination, or was there moisture glistening on her inner thighs just below her high hemline? He licked his lips. "It would depend on the manner of coercion. If we can get the Earther to let her guard down enough, we may be able to gain a sample of her eggs."

"How are we to gain Amelia Ryan's cooperation if she's too scared to even speak to us?"

"Who says either she or the Saucin have to cooperate?" Breft said, the grin on his lean face hungry. "We can take Amelia Ryan back to Kalquor easily with no one here the wiser until it's too late."

Flencik narrowed his eyes at his clanmate. His heavy brow creased. "Such action might traumatize her. Earthers are much more fragile than we are. We don't know if stress damages their reproductive abilities. You dare not kidnap this Matara."

"We don't know if she can be a Matara."

Rajhir held up his hand to quiet the argument. They fell silent and waited for him to speak.

He eyed Amelia again. The thought of the lovely creature struggling against him and then surrendering to his seduction threatened to publicly arouse him. He knew the sweetness of such a forceful seduction and felt the possibility given Amelia's reluctant but eager reaction to their touches.

He kept these thoughts to himself, determined to maintain Flencik's peace of mind. He said, "Her art has endeared her to the Plasians. To kidnap her from here would strain relations between our peoples. Plausius has been too long a trading partner to risk Israla's censure."

He thought for a moment before continuing. "We must also remember that if we force her to take Flencik's tests against her will and her government discovers it, we risk Earth not letting any more of their females off-planet where we have easier access. We must find a way to gain her trust and compliance."

Breft scowled. "What if she refuses to cooperate anyway? Then what?"

"Then we'll have no choice but to gain samples through trickery or force." Flencik opened his mouth, protest written all over his face, and Rajhir added, "Only as a last resort and with the hope it does not damage her."

"I'd rather it not be an option at all," Flencik said.

"I know." Rajhir squeezed his shoulder. "Remember, we're facing the extinction of our species if we don't find compatible females soon. Keep that in mind, Imdiko."

* * * *

Osill clasped his long-fingered hands together. "The anticipation has nearly driven me mad." He eyed the covered painting like a starving man at a feast. Then again, the reed-thin Guildmaster always looked hungry. His marbled black eyes bulged from his sharp-edged face.

Amelia managed to smile despite the Kalquorians' heated stares. She did her best to ignore them. How naked she felt in her scanty gown! "I only hope I've met the Saucin's and Guild's expectations." She inclined her head toward Israla. The Plasian leader's smooth face remained emotionless as she spoke with her aide, as if she hadn't heard the Earther's comment. Amelia's nervousness turned up a notch.

It wasn't just Israla's rank that intimidated Amelia. Despite being three times her age, the Saucin was a beautiful example of her species. She'd make any Parisian model stalking the catwalk envious with her long slender build and ideal proportions. Her clothing was scantier than even Amelia's, consisting of only a scarf-like fabric draped around the back of her neck and hanging over her small but perfect breasts and another scarf tied about her hips. The fabric was deep red and completely see-through. Nothing was left to the imagination; her hairless sex was easily discerned behind the transparent scarf.

Israla's legendary appetite for young men of all races and body types was also a testament to her disregard for her age. Tonight two young Plasian men flanked her, wearing small loin cloths made of the same fabric Israla wore. Vrill had confided these boys were young enough to be Israla's great-grandsons. Their slender penises stood at attention as they unselfconsciously rubbed Israla's back. Occasionally Israla smiled at them and stroked their eager flesh with pointed fingertips. Amelia couldn't bear to look at them.

Amelia preferred Israla's aloofness to Osill's enthusiasm, as the Guildmaster did little to quiet her fears. He practically panted with anticipation. "If this painting is like your other works, all of Plasius will fall at your feet in adulation."

She regretted the Plasians expected so much of her. Such attention could only doom her latest painting to failure. It would never live up to their hopes.

The opposite would have happened back home. Earth noticed little of her current work because her style confounded the critics. Not only that, Amelia's choice of voluptuous, sensual shapes and colors, while not explicit enough to be unlawful, still pushed the envelope of acceptable art in Earth's Puritanical society.

In contrast, Plasius embraced her art with a fierce passion, importing prints of her paintings by the thousands. Her arrival three months ago had been met with much sensation, although 'sensation' in Plasian terms was tame by most interstellar beings' standards. There had been an endless round of quiet dinner parties hosted by Plasian elite. She learned fast to leave the dinners as soon as eating was done because Plasian parties always degenerated into sex orgies that lasted well into the next day. She was sure tonight would be no exception; as soon as she finished her presentation, she planned to head straight for the nearest exit.

Outside the upper crust of Plasian society she'd received dozens of offers from both male and female fans eager to help her shed the well-known issue of Earther sexual inhibitions. She'd been kissed on the street, pulled onto turgid laps at the outdoor cafes, and on one memorable occasion, nearly undressed in the middle of an art exhibit by four amorous women. For their part, the Plasians couldn't understand how someone who painted such sensual pictures became flustered when confronted with sensuality itself.

Israla ended her conversation with her aide. She ran her fingers over chimes that tinkled over the murmur of conversation. The hall silenced at once as all eyes turned the quartet's way.

The aide said, "Attention, please. We will begin the presentation now."

The crowd surged forward, and Amelia saw the Kalquorians also approach. Their eyes devoured her, setting her skin on fire with their glances alone. It was as if they possessed her body with their stares. She looked away, fighting to maintain an aura of nonchalance. Her burning face informed her of her failure.

Osill stepped forward to address everyone. "We have not long known of Earth. Indeed, the more we learn of our new neighbors, the less we understand them."

A ripple of laughter greeted his words. He bowed his head to Amelia to indicate he meant the comment as a joke. She smiled, no offense taken. "It is only that our cultures are so exceedingly different. Art, however, speaks one language. Not in many generations has an artist spoken as eloquently as our new friend Amelia Ryan. We are honored to host her on Plasius where we hope she will find much inspiration."

He stepped back to polite applause as all eyes settled on Amelia. The bronze-skinned Plasians looked at her with as much hunger as the Kalquorians. She took a deep breath, put on a smile, and stepped forward.

"Thank you, Guildmaster Osill." Her steady voice surprised her. She avoided looking to her right where the Kalquorian clan stood.

"It is I who feel honored to have been granted the opportunity to paint the landscapes and people of your planet. In gratitude for your kindness and hospitality, I present to Saucin Israla and the people of Plasius this work." She nodded to Israla's aide.

The aide lifted the velvety drape from the canvas Amelia had labored three months over, sometimes going for days without sleep. The mere memory of her hand cramped around the paintbrush, the agony of effort slicing up her arm to her shoulder and neck, was excruciating. Only pure will had kept her going. Now she would know if the weeks of pain she'd endured to complete it on time had been worthwhile.

With a flourish, the aide swept the cloth aside, revealing the painting: the landscape of Plasius' Lisidia mountain range. As it came into view, all the tension leading up to this moment released its grip on Amelia's gut. Indeed there could be no doubt that it was the best work she'd ever done.

When she'd first viewed the seemingly endless line of mountains, the spirit of the rock and earth revealed itself to her with unguarded abandon. She instantly saw in them the undulating curves of a reclining Plasian woman, lush with invitation. Amelia painted the Lisidias in the hues of bronze and olive, the predominant colors of Plasian flesh and fur. At first glance, the mountains appeared to be a woman lounging in a languorous pose, her black marble eyes half-closed, and her parted lips curved in a provocative smile. It was not only a landscape of Plasius, it was the planet's very spirit of relaxed, graceful sexuality.

The assembled Plasians gasped as one. For a moment, they gaped at the artwork. Amelia's heart stopped.

Then applause crashed over her as the usually indolent race roared their approval. Osill shook her as he cried, "Beautiful, Amelia Ryan! Absolute perfection! Better than my greatest hopes!"

Most astounding of all, the aloof Israla embraced her, sobbing like a lost child found. "It is beyond expectation! An incomparable gift! I was born in a village in sight of these mountains, but I never saw them in truth until now. You have honored all of Plasius with your art. Thank you." She kissed Amelia with an open mouth then bowed. Her mane, dyed red to match her outfit, danced with delight.

Plasians jostled to get close to the painting and its creator. They crushed against Amelia until she gasped for air. They congratulated her with exuberant shouts and many tears. Fingers brushed against her cheeks, throat, breasts, belly and arms. The bodies pressed against hers until she couldn't draw breath. The room tilted like a funhouse, and Amelia realized she was near fainting. Black spots appeared in her vision. Then someone grasped her hand in an iron grip. She found enough air to cry out as pain shot from her fingers to her shoulder.

The pressure eased as dark muscled arms pressed the Plasians back. Rajhir's rumbling voice said in passable Plasian, "Please, good friends, give Amelia Ryan room! She needs air!"

Breft eased himself through the crowd to her side. He lifted her into the air as he cradled her in arms of steel. He hugged her close as he carried her from the knot of Plasians. "Relax, little one. I will take you to safety."

She whooped air into her chest. She lay limp in Breft's arms as her grateful lungs heaved.

Rajhir and Flencik flanked them. Israla, her aide, and Osill darted ahead to peer at her.

"Is she all right?" Osill asked. "I'm so sorry! We didn't mean to hurt her."

Flencik answered. "She well, but overwhelmed."

"We must keep her from the crowd until they have calmed," Rajhir added. "You will also want to guard the art. They may destroy it in their excitement."

"The painting!" the aide exclaimed and rushed away, presumably to save it.

Israla waved them to a closed door. "Use this private room," she said, opening the door and ushering them in. "You will care for her? She is precious to us." At Flencik's nod, Israla patted Amelia's arm. "Rest now. No one will bother you here. I will have refreshment brought to you."

She swept out, and Osill took Amelia's hand. His long fingers trembled. "Forgive our enthusiasm. You have captured the very soul of Plasius with your painting, and we cannot contain our joy. No harm was intended."

Despite her dazed response to the excitement of the last few minutes, Amelia managed to console him. "It's all right. I'm glad it was so well received."

Flencik spoke up. "She rest now must."

"Of course. I leave her in your capable hands." Osill bowed to them and left, closing the door.

They left her alone with the clan. Fear spiked through Amelia's chest, and her heart skipped a beat. She suddenly realized the Plasians' jostling had shifted her gown to expose her breasts. She jerked the bodice over her nakedness, fresh embarrassment turning her skin almost as crimson as the dress.

"Lounger," Flencik said, and Breft carried her to the seating area. The Plasian lounger looked like an oversized sectional sofa, perfect for sprawling, relaxing and sleeping.

And lovemaking, Amelia felt sure as the Nobek lowered her onto the deep red billowy surface. She clutched her arms to her chest, a self-protective gesture. The Kalquorian men had been quick to ravish her in a roomful of people. What would they do to her in private quarters?

To her relief, Breft released her and stepped back. He remained standing as Rajhir and Flencik sat beside her prone body.

She looked about the room, seeking an avenue of escape. Lighting globes drifted across the ceiling, illuminating the room in a soft golden glow. A smokeless firepit crackled in the middle of the room as chunks of scentwood burned. Aromatic fumes scented like the roses back on Earth swirled about the room.

In a corner, the Plasian version of a shower sluiced a waterfall into a bubbling basin. Amelia knew from her own apartment the roiling warm water eased tense muscles.

The room was a sensual retreat, but only one door offered Amelia escape.

She looked at the trio of men who regarded her in silence. What could she say to them after the way she'd surrendered to them earlier? Surely they believed her to be a slut, a whore, a wanton creature eager to couple at the slightest provocation.

Still, such behavior was the norm on Plasius. Many times she'd dined in a restaurant with Vrill while fellow diners pleasured each other right at their tables. Early on, Amelia learned to keep her eyes on her meals.

Had the Kalquorians really acted inappropriately? Not in the least by Plasian standards, though Plasians usually had the courtesy to ask before they grabbed.

Another misunderstanding, Amelia thought with relief. *That's all. They simply don't know how to act with an Earther.*

She tried to smile. She pretended her heart wasn't pounding. She ignored the voice in the back of her mind whispering, *You know it has nothing to do with misunderstandings. These brutes want something from you, and it's not lessons in Earther etiquette!*

She said, "Thank you for the rescue. I thought I would be crushed out there."

Rajhir stroked her shoulder, and she held back a shiver. His hands were so warm. "The Plasians are passionate for beauty," he said. "Your painting excited their senses to overwhelm. Tell us--"

A knock at the door interrupted him. Breft whirled; the next instant he was at the door. Amelia blinked. The Nobek was incredibly fast, too fast to follow with the eyes. It brought her fear of the Kalquorians up another notch.

He opened the door. A Plasian servant stood outside with a tray of goblets and a pitcher filled with azure liquid.

Amelia tensed as she heard the loud voices of excited Plasians. "They're still reacting to the painting."

"Relax," Flencik said, squeezing her hand ever so gently. "We will no enter give to them."

Amelia nodded her understanding of his halting English as Breft took the tray and shut the door, closing the servant and noise out. He carried the tray to the lounger.

Flencik nodded approval as he filled a goblet from the pitcher. "This leshella good drink is. You try it to drink," he said, handing Amelia the goblet. "It will you calmer."

"What is it exactly?" she asked, sniffing the sapphire liquid.

Rajhir and Flencik turned to Breft. He poured a goblet for himself. "Like the Earth drink called wine, I think." He drank his serving in one swallow.

"Try it, Amelia Ryan," Rajhir prodded.

"Just Amelia, please. Earth people have two names, sometimes more, but we're usually called by just the first."

"Amelia," Rajhir said. He smiled. "Easier."

She smiled back, liking how the expression softened his stern features. She took a sip.

The drink tasted smooth and buttery, and yes, similar to an expensive white wine. The knots in her muscles loosened. It went down easily. Too easily. She took the glass from her lips and noted with shock she'd drunk half of it.

"You started to ask me about my painting?" she said to Rajhir to hide her embarrassment. A slut and a drunkard. What a wonderful impression she must be making.

"I have seen the Lisidias. I know that is what you painted. The woman resting in mountains...the colors you put to paint. They are no true, but they look – correct?" He struggled. "I do no have Earther words. The painting was wrong reality but perfect. How did you know the mountains wanted to be those colors, that woman?"

She swallowed more wine without realizing it until the warmth made her tingle all over. She felt very relaxed now. The lounger beneath her was like a cloud.

"I paint subjects not how I see them on the surface but how I feel their soul appears."

"Soul?" Rajhir's brow furrowed. He looked to Breft who shrugged his own confusion.

"A soul is a person's life force. Or in my painting's case, the mountain's true inner self."

Her explanation only made them look more perplexed. Amelia gave up. "It's hard to explain. As you say, I don't have the words."

She raised the goblet and saw it was full again without her noticing one of the Kalquorians refilling it.

"Is it good?" Breft asked.

"Wonderful." Languor spread through her body like a balm. She was relaxed but not fatigued; indeed, her senses felt so alive. Her body flushed with warmth, and the lounger felt to her skin like the softest cashmere. She longed to kick her heels off and dig her toes into it, if she could summon the effort. Her limbs lay heavy, melting into the cushions. She wanted to purr. The top of her gown had shifted again; one breast was in danger of exposure. What did it matter? she thought lazily. The men surrounding her had seen the show already. It no longer seemed like such a big deal.

Rajhir leaned close, and she looked into his blue-purple cat eyes. His scent wafted over her, a pleasant cinnamon-y smell. She felt his warm breath on her lips as he spoke. "Are all Earther women so desirable?"

Fingertips -- Flencik's? -- brushed over her throat. She caught her breath. The flesh felt sensitive there. Flencik's fingers drifted down to her breastbone, leaving a trail of heat.

"You think I'm desirable?" The fingertips moved to her breasts, flattening so that his huge hands covered them. She moaned, the heat from his touch spreading to her sex. Warmth trickled between her thighs. Rajhir's hypnotic gaze held her captive as his face drifted closer. She closed her eyes as his moist lips brushed hers. "You are very desirable, lovely Amelia."

Chapter Two

Rajhir's tongue invaded her mouth, filling it. As he tasted her, the massive hands on her breasts squeezed before pinching the engorged tips.

Warmth coursed from the lips of her sex as another pair of hands parted her thighs. Fingers slid up the insides of her legs, pushing up the scant material of her dress up and over her hips. She lay completely exposed to the man rubbing her thighs. She imagined him watching the honey flow from her.

Rajhir pulled his mouth from hers and cupped her face in his hands. He gazed into her eyes as if trying to read her mind. She felt embraced by the cool depths of his blue-purple eyes. Flencik continued to massage her breasts, slipping his fingers inside her bodice. Breft's fingers slid closer to her damp naked sex, tantalizing with their nearness to her pleasure button.

I'm not supposed to be doing this, she thought and giggled at her own naughtiness. The combination of Plasian wine and insistent hands made it impossible to resist the ravishing. Rajhir inclined his head, his lips parted to kiss her again.

He plundered her mouth, his wicked tongue sweeping across her teeth, flicking the roof of her mouth, twining around her tongue.

Flencik drew her bodice away from her breasts, exposing the ripe globes to his warm breath. He kneaded one with a strong hand while his hot mouth closed over the other. He drew as much of her breast into his mouth as he could, sucking hard and scraping teeth on the tender flesh. She moaned into Rajhir's mouth, the little twinge of pain from Flencik's teeth enhancing the greater pleasure of being possessed.

Breft dipped the tip of one finger into the well of moisture pooled between her legs. He swirled the wet finger around her clitoris, sending tiny shocks of need through her belly. Her hips moved of their own accord, trying to get his elusive touch to make contact with the throbbing bud.

Rajhir finally drew back, and she gasped raggedly. Her whole body was one hungry ache, begging for satisfaction. The Kalquorians were driving her mad for release.

Bad girl, naughty girl, she thought. *What would Israla think if she knew how you're abusing her hospitality? Do you think she'd want to join in?*

Amelia giggled again, shocked at the audacity of her own thoughts. Rajhir's smile was questioning.

"What if the Saucin doesn't approve? This is her home." Amelia pretended horror.

Breft chuckled as he stroked the moist lips of her sex. She felt ready to explode down there and wriggled uncontrollably.

Rajhir stroked her hair. "You have much to learn of Plasian culture. This room and others Saucin gives to guests for use."

"And wine to lower prudish Earther inhibitions. You do know I don't usually kiss on the first date?" Amelia giggled.

Rajhir grinned. For an answer, his mouth crushed down on hers. He kissed her deeply, devouring her.

She felt Flencik gather the strips of her bodice in his fists, and he ripped her dress down the front, the fabric purring apart. The warm air caressed her body, now fully bared to the clan's exploration. His mouth and hands resumed their play on her breasts, his tongue and teeth alternating; lapping and sucking one moment, gently nipping the next while squeezing.

She groaned when Breft's fingers finally slid where she wanted them against her aching sex. He traced a wet trail over her clitoris, and she cried out into Rajhir's mouth.

Breft's fingers closed over the bud between her legs. He rolled the swollen flesh between his finger and thumb. The warmth of his rough tongue probed her sex. He pushed in and out of her, pausing from time to time to suck on her clitoris. She trembled violently and clutched Rajhir's broad shoulders as the Nobek tasted her tender pink flesh. She lay open to them all; Rajhir feasting on her mouth, Flencik suckling hungrily at her breasts, Breft devouring her sex.

A feather touch brushed her anus. For a moment she forgot to breathe. No one had ever touched her there, and the fog of arousal intensified even as she felt a twinge of fear. Breft's finger circled the tight flesh, and she flushed with new heat at the sensation. His finger slipped into her wet sex before returning to tease her anus.

Rajhir released her mouth to run his tongue across her jaw and up to her ear. "Is it good, Amelia?" he breathed.

She was at their mercy and loved being helpless, incapable of fighting the effects of the drink, their greater strength, her own desperate need. "So good," she sighed.

Rajhir's eyes darkened with desire at her admission, and his mouth settled over hers again. Breft's finger stopped tracing the edge of her nether orifice and settled on it. He pressed the tight flesh, and his finger slid inside her.

She cried out in shock. It felt strange, but Breft's fingers on her clitoris quickened their pace, and she surrendered to him without a fight. His thick finger moved within her, stirring a curious hunger, an arousal greater than any she'd known before. She felt herself softening, opening to his touch. His careful movements reassured her. Her sex grew wetter in response to the gentle violation of her anus. The hunger of her loins grew at the unthinkable but delightful intrusion. Her hips moved in rhythm with the stroking finger.

Rajhir released her, and he stood. "I will take her now," he said.

He peeled his formsuit from his muscled body. Amelia looked over the amazing physique as he bared it from the neck down. He was beautiful, as beautiful as a Greek statue, so utterly perfect with his wide shoulders, chiseled chest, tight abdomen, and...

As soon as she saw what stood erect between his legs, she nearly screamed.

Rajhir had *two* penises.

The one in front was larger than those of her previous two lovers. It was huge, in fact. Smooth like a bullet, it tapered at the end. It stood rigid as if carved of marble. It was shaded a deeper brown than the rest of Rajhir's skin.

The smaller organ, a couple of inches behind the first, had no opening for fluid release. Amelia could discern no function for the rigid member. Was it only for anal stimulation? Was that why Breft used his finger in that taboo orifice, to accustom her to the sensation? Both organs glistened with moisture; she realized through her shock that the Kalquorian males secreted their own lubricant.

Breft rose from his position between her legs, removing his hands from her aching flesh. Before she could think of what to do, Rajhir took his place, bringing his hips low to meet hers. She felt his organs prod both her openings and tensed in fear.

Rajhir felt the openings he desired tighten, and he stopped himself from plunging in. It wasn't easy; heat radiated from her sex, and he wanted to join that warmth more than anything.

The wine-induced haze was fading from her eyes, and fright appeared. "Will it hurt? I've never — I mean, Earther males don't have those — the second sex organ." Amelia struggled to rise from the lounger, to free herself of the men holding and caressing her. The three Kalquorians held her down without effort. Rajhir smiled at his clanmates, delighted that he would be the one to share new secrets of her body with her.

Flencik covered her face with kisses. "It will no hurt in bad way, little one," he said. He cupped her head in his hands and smiled gentle reassurance. "Relax. Enjoy. You discover great pleasure. We satisfy needs you are no told."

"I'm not allowed. It's against Earth law to …."

"We are no on Earth," Rajhir said, his tone no-nonsense with finality. He pressed himself against her, and his slick members inched their way into her, forcing past the tightness of her. His hands gripped her hips, holding her still for his invasion.

His breath caught to feel her so snug around him, yet still soft and yielding. Her sex and anus were tight-fitting sleeves, opening to welcome him into moist warmth.

Amelia made small cries of protest that quickly faded as the sensations overtook her. Her anus, virgin territory until now, delighted in the intrusion of the steel of alien flesh. It stretched to welcome Rajhir into her most secret orifice. The slight discomfort only excited her senses beyond control. She was being filled as she'd never imagined, and even if she hadn't been helpless to stop Rajhir, she would have allowed this wonderful violation. He took her, this commanding alien; he took her as if it was his right. She made little helpless cries, wetness pouring out to ease his passage. He took his time as he impaled her with himself. The warm tickle of her sex warned her of impending climax. She felt she must burst with the size of him, and still he pressed in more. She strained to open herself to him, hungry to be filled.

"Warm," he breathed, his face rapturous with sensation. "So warm and soft. You are a wonder, my little one."

His hips rocked against hers. He moved easily within her, the friction making her back arch. Flencik bent over her to caress her face and breasts, and she gripped his shoulders as her legs wrapped around Rajhir's waist of their own free will, giving her the leverage to buck against him, driving him into her. The Dramok responded to her need with a growl, pumping his hips harder and faster. He gripped her buttocks in both hands, squeezing the pliable flesh to hold her still as he plunged even deeper into her flesh.

Flencik shifted to watch his leader dive into Amelia's body and emerge glistening. Breft also stared, his wet lips parted. Far from being self-conscious, Amelia's excitement grew as they watched Rajhir take her, as their close-fitting formsuits betrayed their arousals.

I can't do anything to stop them, Amelia thought. The full weight of her helplessness against these creatures fell upon her. No matter how she might struggle or beg, they would do as they pleased with her because they knew she wanted it. The realization fed her desire and tipped her over the edge.

Her orgasm exploded through her, pure electric warmth. She cried out and hung onto Flencik as Rajhir rocked steadily inside her. In time with his rhythm, wave after wave of pleasure crashed over her, shattering her into a million pieces. She screamed peals of ecstasy.

Slowly she came down from the high of the incredible orgasm. Even as her body calmed, Rajhir's continued lovemaking kept her pleasure at a steady hum. She'd never come more than once during each episode of sex before and doubted she would this time either. Still, she enjoyed the sensation of having Rajhir move inside her. She glowed with the aftereffects of her climax.

Flencik shifted over her, and his tunic was pulled from him. It took Amelia a moment to realize Breft undressed his clanmate. *These Kalquorians sure aren't inhibited*, she thought, letting the Imdiko kiss her. While not as demanding as Rajhir had been, he tasted her mouth with a sweet thoroughness. His tongue was hot, the flesh pleasantly rough.

His hand grasped hers, and he pulled it to his naked sex. "Touch me," he said and wrapped her slender fingers around his thick front penis.

He was wet, and her hand slid over his organ easily as she pumped. She felt the thud-thud of his pulse in the vein on his organ's underside. He closed his eyes, his expression rapturous.

"Now the other," he said, guiding her hand. She felt for the smaller penis and rubbed it in time with Rajhir's rhythm. The Dramok's thrusts into her had been joined by his fingers massaging her clitoris. She felt a spike of intense pleasure and wondered if she would experience a second orgasm after all.

She stroked Flencik's organs with one hand and explored the contours of his chest with the other. His skin over the rock-hard muscle felt smooth and warm. His tongue slipped in her mouth to taste her.

A shadow fell over them. They looked up to see Breft standing there, his organs jutting from his groin like exclamation marks. "I need," he said.

Without hesitation, Flencik grasped the larger of Breft's penises and guided it towards Amelia's face. "Open your mouth," he encouraged her. "Taste him."

She smelled Breft's sex, the same sharp cinnamon aroma she'd scented on Rajhir. The tip touched her mouth; Flencik moved the Nobek's organ over her lips. She opened her mouth for him, and he slipped his penis into its warmth.

She closed her eyes and ran her tongue over the hot smooth flesh. He did taste of cinnamon. His pulse pounded beneath the surface of his skin. He pumped his hips, driving his sex deep into her mouth. His second penis slid under her chin along her throat, leaving a hot, wet trail. He took her orally, his eager strokes matching Rajhir's.

Flencik turned his attention to her breasts once again. He playfully slapped the heavy mounds between his hands, making them sting. She groaned with the sensation of being completely possessed.

Both her hands pleasured the Imdiko's twin sexes, keeping in time with Rajhir's and Breft's thrusts into her accepting body.

The heat in her womb rose, and she heard the three men gasping as well. Breft moaned, and he ground his hips against her face. She realized he teetered on the brink of orgasm. He was poised to spill himself right in her mouth. Her mother's strict teachings made her feel the dirtiness of the act. She tried to pull away, but his groin pinned her head against the lounger. She wriggled against him.

"No, Amelia," Flencik said. "You taste of Breft and swallow the seed of his. Make part of us you. Do no fight."

Breft's gasps grew louder. His hand stimulated his swollen shaft each time it emerged from Amelia's lips. He really meant to pump his semen into her mouth. And she wanted it. She wanted to know the flavor of this alien male, and to hell with her deceased mother's voice in her head; to hell with the laws of Earth forbidding sex outside of the marriage bed, outside of her species. God only knew how many laws she was breaking now, screwing three aliens at once.

To hell with them all.

I'm a bad girl, Mama. I'm sucking a man's penis...no, not a penis. I'm sucking his cock. I like it. I like it, do you hear me?

Knowing Breft's juices were on the verge of pouring down her throat heightened her excitement. Not even lawful marriage allowed such perversion on Earth. The alien worked himself even faster, his gasps becoming growls as he moved closer to climax. Amelia moaned as her own flesh strained towards crescendo.

Rajhir grunted as he pounded himself into Amelia, his pace frantic. The friction of his loins against hers brought her closer to the brink. Her hands pulled up and down on Flencik's organs just as desperately.

Breft suddenly shouted out. His pulsing flesh erupted and filled Amelia's mouth with his strong, sweet fluid. A heavy hand stroked her throat, massaging. She submitted to the domination and swallowed the thick seed pouring down her throat as her own hunger swallowed her.

Her orgasm filled her like a blinding white light. Its heat streamed into her entire body, suspending her in the sweetest of agonies. She convulsed beneath her lovers, wave after wave pounding through her.

Rajhir and Flencik came at the same time. Flencik's hot fluid spilled onto her belly as Rajhir's organ pulsed into her womb. Again her pleasure crested, another starburst of delight exploding throughout her body. She cried out as another tidal wave shook her. So good. So damn good...

At last her body spent itself, settling into a warm, satisfied glow. Amelia's strength was gone, and she lay still as her lovers disengaged. Her heavy eyelids refused to open. The Kalquorians carried her to the basin. Large, gentle hands bathed her with reverent thoroughness. She dozed as warm water sluiced over her utterly exhausted, utterly satisfied body.

She woke briefly as they put her back on the lounger and arranged themselves around her. She opened her eyes once to see Rajhir smiling down at her.

"No more misunderstandings," he said.

She closed her eyes again. Sandwiched between the Kalquorian bodies, Amelia fell into a deep sleep.

Chapter Three

Amelia woke to the daylight brightness of the globes and blinked at her surroundings.

Where am I?

She shifted, and the soreness between her legs reminded her of the Kalquorians' sensual assault the night before. She sat straight up on the lounger, her heart drumming.

The firepit had gone dark, the scentwood burnt out. The waterfall gurgled and the basin bubbled, but she was alone. The Kalquorians were gone.

Amelia hugged herself. Tears of shame pricked her eyes. The things she allowed the three aliens to do to her last night! All the depraved acts she performed! Worst of all, she enjoyed it. Her body had responded over and over despite the immorality of the situation.

Her mother's voice spoke in her head. "Sex is dirty and sinful." Amelia could see her as she had been before the cancer took her. Martha Ryan's wasted frame was nearly lost in a mountain of sheets and blankets, her hair pulled back in a severe bun, her claw hands gripping a worn Bible. Years of pursing her upper lip in disapproval ridged the skin above it.

"You only have sex after marriage and only to conceive. I will not allow my daughter to be a bad girl. I'd rather see you dead." She shook her Bible at Amelia.

Amelia shook herself from the memory. How many times had she heard that speech, both in person and in her head? How long had she fought to silence that judgmental voice?

"Sex is not dirty," she whispered to Israla's guest room. "It's normal and beautiful as long as it's not perverted."

Didn't sex with three aliens qualify as perversion though? How could she justify her participation in last night's orgy?

"The wine of course." Amelia sank back on the lounger with relief. "They knew it would drug me and took advantage. That's all. I did nothing wrong. I wasn't myself."

Her heart felt lighter now that her innocence proved intact. Just as it had been with her previous unlawful liaisons, she was not to blame. Even Martha Ryan's vengeful God could not find fault, though Earth's religion-crazed legal system would certainly impose harsh sentences for her unmarried, nonvirginal status.

Nevermind she'd been drunk last night. Nevermind her previous two lovers had gained access to her body through coercion, threats, and force. She was still at fault in the eyes of the law.

Her first time, she'd been fourteen. It started with a good deed, an innocent knock on her neighbor's door.

The door swung open to reveal Mr. Perkins, her neighbor of three months. He worked construction as a vocation, but the crumbling economy left him doing odd jobs to make rent. He was home more often than not, and Amelia's mother had him over for dinner twice a week. "Charity to those less fortunate," she admonished Amelia when the girl dared to venture the observation they didn't have much themselves. "God knows we can go a little hungry to keep another from starving."

Mr. Perkins didn't look like he was starving. He had arms like slabs of deeply tanned beef. His chest was wide, and his beginning beer belly didn't droop over the waist of his jeans quite yet. Amelia supposed women her mother's age would find him attractive with his shock of reddish-brown hair, heavy-lidded eyes, and full pouting lips. She even caught herself looking at him surreptitiously when he joined them for dinner, especially at his big, capable hands. When her thoughts strayed to sinful ideas, she did her best to shut them down. She prayed often for God to keep her mind pure.

From his open doorway, Mr. Perkins blinked at her. "Hey girl." His voice sounded bored, but as his avid eyes traveled her body from head to toe and back up again, Amelia felt warm all over. "What's up?"

"The mailman put your mail in our box. I thought I'd save you the trip." Amelia held out the envelopes, two of which had angry 'Past Due' stamps.

"Put it on the table there." Mr. Perkins nodded toward the battered coffee table in the middle of the living room. He stepped aside to allow her passage.

She wondered why he didn't just take the mail from her, but obeying adult authority was too deeply ingrained for her to question him. She stepped inside the dim house.

With the shades pulled down over the windows, the room existed in a netherworld shaded gray. From the cracked ceramic lamp adorned in numerous coats of dust to the sunken couch bleeding tufts of foam from multiple wounds, gray ruled the rental.

The rental house Amelia and her mother lived in was just as patched, water stained and threadbare as Mr. Perkins', but at least they kept it clean. Garbage in the form of newspapers, take-out food wrappers, and used Styrofoam coffee cups littered every surface of this house. The frayed carpet was stained and probably hadn't seen a vacuum cleaner since the man had moved in.

"Your mamma home?" Mr. Perkins' voice was close, almost directly behind her. The hair on her neck stood up.

"No sir." Afraid to look at him standing so close, Amelia carefully placed the stack of mail on the table and straightened. "She's working."

"Stay right there." His voice *was* right behind her, his breath hot on her ear, left bare by the long hair tucked behind it. Her flesh goosebumped, but she obeyed. *Always mind your elders* her mother's voice in her head sternly whispered.

Mr. Perkins' hands stroked her arms from wrists up to where her short sleeved blouse stopped them at her upper biceps. "Easy," he breathed. "That's a good girl. Pretty girl, ain't ya?"

Her whole body was frozen but for a fine tremor. She couldn't answer, couldn't speak. A man was touching her, not illegally, but the touch was intimate just the same.

His hands moved to her waist. He rubbed them up and down her ribcage. She could feel them damp through her thin shirt. She knew she was in trouble, knew she was trapped. Her heart threatened to pound out of her chest. His touch was scandalous at the best; edging ever closer to being criminal. If he did commit felony contact, she'd be just as guilty as he. Somehow, she had enticed him to touch her. Somehow, he had sensed the few illicit thoughts she'd had. If caught and convicted, her sentence would be worse than his.

Then he did break the law. His big bear paw hands, the very hands she'd imagined touching her too many times, slid up her torso and cupped her breasts. She gasped but remained frozen. She'd asked for this, hadn't she? She'd developed early and tried to keep her amply endowed bosom modestly covered most of the time, but today had been too hot to wear more than a thin tee shirt over her smallest bra.

That's what I did wrong. That's how I tempted him to break the law, by not being modestly covered. Oh God, forgive me! I didn't mean to be a Jezebel!

Mr. Perkins squeezed the soft flesh, his grip strong, stronger than she'd imagined. Amelia's body and throat unlocked enough to allow her to jerk a little and whimper. "Easy. Easy," he growled in her ear. "Don't fight me, girl. You do what I tell you, and you won't get hurt."

"Yes sir," Amelia whispered. Tears of humiliation prickled her eyes as he manipulated her flesh, molding it like clay. He grasped and squeezed, testing the weight and softness of her. She stood absolutely still, letting him maul her supple breasts. His breathing blew violently against her ear as he looked over her shoulder, watching his hands as they performed their vile dance on her chest.

He moved close so their bodies met. He was all hardness, especially where his groin pressed against her skirted buttocks. She felt his manhood pushing against her, trying to find her beyond the fabric of their clothing. A little sob escaped her throat.

God, I am so sorry. Punish me however You will for my sin, even if I must give Mr. Perkins my purity, but please don't let me get caught with him. Please don't let the police come to get me.

His breath puffed in her ear faster. He pulled at her shirt, untucking it from the skirt's waistband, allowing his hands access to the flesh of her torso. He jerked her bra up towards her neck, spilling her heavy breasts out. His hands greedily devoured the taboo flesh. He ground his hips and the hard thing between his legs against her buttocks.

A strange warmth licked through Amelia's body, starting where the man attacked her chest and sliding down into her groin. She caught her breath and unconsciously lifted her breasts up and out, her body instinctively striving for more of the ticklish sensation pulsing from Mr. Perkins' touch to her illegal regions.

"Yeah baby girl," he breathed. "We're gonna make each other feel real good."

I didn't mean to do that! I swear it!

Tears streamed down Amelia's cheeks. She knew they were being sinful — not little sins either like daydreaming during school prayers or accidentally tearing a page in her math book and not admitting it. This was a big sin — a sin of the flesh. This sin could send her to the everlasting infernos of Hell.

And if the police caught them — well, she didn't even want to think about that. Her mother had been only too willing to show Amelia the pictures of maimed, scarred men and women toiling in fields and factories, guarded by grim uniformed men holding tasers, and worked so brutally that even five months of hard labor were usually death sentences.

"There's no chance they'll ever sin for pleasure again," Martha said with a grim smile. "They're all castrated without benefit of anesthesia. The women have it the worst — all their devil flesh is burned and branded until it is useless for any temptation to wake it. They're punished at the end of every day with lashings until they lose consciousness."

Despite Amelia's shame and fear, her body responded to Mr. Perkins' heavy pawing. Indeed, the more she thought of what would happen if they were caught, the greater the heat built in her belly. The warmth spilled out of her, wetting the secret flesh between her legs and soaking her panties.

What is wrong with me? Why is my sinful flesh doing this to me?

Mr. Perkins pinched one rose pink nipple hard, as if to punish her for such evil. A bolt of electric pain shot through her from the cruel pincer, and she moaned as honeyed pleasure gushed to escape the cotton of her underpants and dampen the insides of her thighs. She groaned as he pinched the other nipple.

"You like it. I knew you would," Mr. Perkins gasped. "A girl with a body like yours has got to love it. Get down on your knees."

"Please, I didn't mean to make you do this. Please don't make me sin——" Amelia started.

He cut her off with a harsh slap to her rear. She cried out at the sting. "This is what bad girls who tease men get. You get punished." He spanked her twice more, his hand painfully warming her buttocks. "Do what I say or get worse," he ordered.

Always mind your elders. It's the same as 'honor thy father and mother'. Her mother's stern tone brooked no argument.

Amelia obeyed as she always did, dropping to her knees. Her head hung down with shamed submission. Sin or not, laws or not, there was no quarrel with an adult nor the omnipresent mother's voice buried in her brain. Martha Ryan had raised an obedient girl.

Mr. Perkins knelt behind her, his knees between hers, pressing them farther apart. She felt the cleft between her legs open, a tender bud flowering. Moisture flowed freely. Her chest hitched as she wept in shame.

He put his hands beneath her thighs where her skirt began and slid them up towards her buttocks, lifting her skirt as he went. When he reached her hindquarters, he kept going, running his hands over the thin white cotton of her little-girl panties.

"Bend over the table," he gasped. "Bend over so I can get this damned skirt out of the way."

Amelia started to cry in earnest, the only way she knew to protest the evil she was making him commit. From the waist up, she laid herself upon the table. Fast food wrappers and Mr. Perkins' mail crackled under her.

"Shut up your blubbering," he commanded as he gathered her skirt across her back, leaving her panties and legs bare. He slapped her rear a few more times to drive the lesson home, and Amelia choked off her cries. Her buttocks burned pleasantly warm from his discipline. The heat moved up to her most secret flesh, and she trembled from the sensation.

His jeans were rough against her inner thighs, chafing as he rubbed against her. "You want this. You want to know what men and women like to do together."

Yes, she did. She must for her body to respond in such an evil fashion. God help her, she wanted him to show her mysteries she had no business knowing. Mysteries that could get her maimed, imprisoned, killed. What was wrong with her that she wanted this cruel man and the filthy act he was about to force on her? She crammed her fist against her lips to muffle her sobs of shame.

Mr. Perkins slid a finger inside the leg of her panties and slipped through the wetness to trace a hot line in her crevice. Amelia jerked as the bold, thick digit rubbed flesh even she didn't dare touch. He barked breathless laughter and pushed the crotch of her panties to one side, leaving her illegal flesh completely exposed.

He was touching her *there*, where no man but her future husband might caress, and only for the purpose of making babies.

His knuckle ran up and down her slit, first lightly teasing her anus, then onward to dip into the well of her femaleness, and further up to brush against the shockingly sensitive button that gave her a trembling, melting sensation all through her belly. Then he reversed the journey and repeated it over and over until her muffled sobs mixed with moans.

He paused at the opening of her womanhood, stroking the lips. Then he pressed a thick finger into her, invading her body. Amelia gasped at the violation, of feeling something *inside* her. He pushed his finger all the way into her. Her hips, beyond her conscious control, lifted up in an effort to take in more.

He worked his finger in and out, his breathing heavy like a hurricane. God help her, it felt good. She'd never known her body could offer her this kind of pleasure. Did Mr. Perkins like it too?

Amelia peeked back once to see him watching what he did to her, looking at her naked devil flesh. His eyes were glazed as if hypnotized, his lips wet and loose. Amelia closed her eyes and laid her head on the table.

He's looking at me. At my private parts. I did this to him with my evil body. He likes it because I made him like it. And I like it too. I thought the sex stuff was supposed to hurt. Mama says it hurts because it's a sin. But it feels so good. Why would it feel good if it's a sin?

Mr. Perkins' thumb stroked the hard engorged button at the front of Amelia's secret folds. She shuddered as her pleasure intensified beyond description. Thoughts of sin fled with the waves of desire that engulfed her. Never had her body experienced such bliss! Her hips rose and fell with his rhythm. Her juices flowed heavier than before. The ache in her belly grew, and she felt something wonderful might happen if only he'd move his finger and thumb faster. She sensed it was there, just out of reach. She gripped the sides of the coffee table in her fists. *Oh, please.* She moaned, a high keening note of supplication.

Mr. Perkins gasped, and jerked his finger out of her. Amelia moaned again, this time with loss, then clamped her teeth together. Maybe if she was quiet he'd put his finger in her again. She lay still but for the trembling she couldn't control.

The leather and metal of Mr. Perkins' belt slapped against the bared cheek of one buttock as he freed himself from his pants. It stung enough for her to lift herself from the table.

"Stay right there," he grunted. One meaty paw caught her by the back of the neck, forcing her down onto the table top. "Baby, you ain't going anywhere till I'm done."

Oh yes, please, the wicked part of her mind whispered. Her buttocks rose in supplication.

He pressed his coarsely haired legs against hers, forcing her wide open for him. Moisture trickled down her thighs from her gaping sex. Then she felt his fist against the secret flesh, gripped around something hard and hot.

He was touching her vulva with his penis. His *cock.* She'd never seen one, but she'd heard the words whispered in the girls' bathroom at school. They said it looked like a sausage. They said it looked like a snake. They said it hurt when a man put it inside you to make babies, especially the first time.

Mr. Perkins was breathing in soft grunts, running the head of his velvet skinned penis through her wetness as if bathing his infernal flesh. She shivered to feel the hot maleness tracing her folds. It felt thick, heavy, too big for the tight aperture it now settled against. She wanted it anyway. She wanted it to hurt her, to punish her for her evil desires. She wanted him to drive himself into her and drive the damning pleasure out.

He pressed harder against her opening, inserting the tip into her soft center. She shuddered, squeezed her eyes shut, and bit her fist. He was going to punish her now, just as she deserved. She welcomed it.

"So wet." The words grated into her ear, and the hand pinning her to the tabletop tightened around her neck. He pushed, shoving more of the iron shaft into her. "Tight too. Damn, I love little virgin girls."

Amelia barely heard him over the roar in her ears. Her whole world was now centered on the intruder forcing its way into her reluctantly yielding flesh. Her gasps were an equal measure of sobs and moans. It hurt with a heavy ache that bloomed into deep pleasure. She couldn't help raising her buttocks to encourage him to penetrate deeper, to continue the beautiful agony.

A sharper pain, knifelike, burst through her womb, and she cried out. Over her, Mr. Perkins grunted, "Got it. I just made you a woman, baby."

The electric pain faded and the good pain, the pain that made her belly feel full and swollen until she must burst from the pressure, returned as he continued to impale her with himself. She thought he would never stop; he'd keep pushing until his sex emerged from her mouth. He would kill her with his desire, a holy justice for her own depraved lust.

Finally he reached his end, deeply rooted inside her vagina, filling her soft clinging sheath. She felt his crinkly pubic hair against her buttocks. She moaned to feel his groin pressed up to her flesh, to feel his sex immersed in hers to the hilt.

He slid back, pulling out, and she whimpered at both the relief and disappointment of being emptied of him. She, in her innocence, thought their coupling was done. She felt strangely bereft and unfulfilled. He withdrew until only the head of his penis remained inside her.

He rammed back into her, as if battering through a fortress door. She cried out in surprise and hurt as he drove himself into her belly.

Over and over he pounded his sex into hers, heedless of her wordless cries. He grunted in rhythm with his pistoning hips, and his sweat rained warm drops on her arms and back where exposed. He continued to hold her firmly by the neck. Helpless, she could only endure him working her body to his satisfaction.

Whore; evil, lustful whore, it's what you deserve, so submit to it, accept it, take your penance. Harder, do it harder, punish me!

The pain of his brutal use became less important as the continuous friction grew hot, expanding the sweet pressure that filled her womb. It built thicker and thicker until she thought she might faint on the wonderful sensation. Her moans grew throatier; she vocalized to release that monstrous pressure that her body couldn't possibly contain though it grew greater still.

He worked her faster, and the promise of something wonderful just around the corner was on her again. But now she knew she'd realize whatever it was her body was straining for, whatever it was that gave her the strength to shove against him in desperate need. The pain and pleasure mixed into a heady potion, spurring her to buck harder still, striving for something...something...

Suddenly the crescendo burst through her loins, the pleasure carrying her up and over sanity, leaving her screaming and clawing the refuse on the table. Mr. Perkins' hand clapped over her mouth even as he emitted his own hoarse cries. He jerked and spasmed against her, and she bucked as hard, riding the sensations that poured molten pleasure through her very soul.

She rode wave after wave of excruciating delight, senseless from her climax. Forgotten was the virtual stranger violating her innocence. Forgotten was the gritty carpet rubbing her knees raw. Forgotten was the filth her face was shoved in. Forgotten, the judgmental mother and penalizing religious authority. All that mattered was the delicious release pulsing from her sex. Guilt and shame would come later. Now was only an ultimate fulfillment she never imagined.

They quieted a little at a time, and Mr. Perkins laid on top of her, crushing her to the table. The iron of his flesh dwindled within her, becoming soft and blameless. She ached deep inside, the pain growing as the pleasure wore off. She cried again, cried for her immortal soul no doubt now damned to everlasting hell. She deserved to hurt. She deserved to be scarred and maimed for her wicked criminality. If the police crashed through the door right now, she would not plead for mercy. She would confess her sin and submit to the justice her evil warranted.

The weight of Mr. Perkins' body lifted, his lustful flesh withdrawing from hers. He chuckled and slapped her buttocks with a playful spank. "Damn girl, that was good. You got one sweet luscious little bod there."

All my fault. I tempted him. Amelia shuddered. She slowly rose to tug her bra and blouse back into place. Her skirt fell to calf-length, covering her reddened knees. She tucked the blouse back into the waistband.

Mr. Perkins walked into his kitchen, humming as he zippered his pants and buckled his belt. He grabbed a soda from the fridge.

"You'd better get back home before any nosy neighbors wonder what you're doing in here for so long. Good thing your mama's such a tightass religious nut; that'll keep most of them thinking nothing could be happening." He grinned and winked at her. "But you deliver the mail anytime you want, sweetheart. I'll be sure to reward you."

Never again. I swear to you, God, I'll never tempt him or any other man again if You just keep me safe from the police.

However, the next time Martha Ryan had Mr. Perkins over for dinner, Amelia was in for a surprise.

"I'm not much for keeping up a house," he informed the elder female. "I could use someone good at cleaning. P'raps your little girl here would like to make a coupla dollars to come in once a week? I'm sorry I can't pay more, but you know how my situation is."

"Amelia would be glad to clean once a week for free." Martha's voice was grim, but her daughter knew right away she was pleased with the idea. "She has too much free time during summer holidays, and that invites trouble."

Amelia listened to this with a sense of unreality and mounting horror. She kept her head down, her eyes on her chipped and scratched plate of gravy-covered mashed potatoes and chicken, praying her mother wouldn't sense her guilt.

Every Wednesday, as soon as her mother left for work, Amelia entered Mr. Perkins' rental and submitted to his lust. The sex was always rough, and there was not even the pretense of tender feelings from her lover.

He began their relationship by teaching her outrageous methods of pleasuring him, first by showing her illustrations bought on the black market. Amelia nearly fainted when she saw the pictures; surely people didn't really do such things as that! He gave her wine to drink, to help her steady herself, he said. The cheap, overly sweet liquid made her head swim even worse, but it relaxed her. She felt warm and languid. Then he began touching her in the sinful, illegal ways that felt so good. Once she was tipsy, wet and aching, he cajoled her to "just try this one thing, baby girl". And she tried the one thing. Then another. Then another. Any time she hesitated, he begged. If begging didn't work, he threatened. He always got what he wanted.

About a month into Amelia's 'cleaning service', they had established a routine. He often liked to start by using her mouth. Ordering her to her knees, he'd take his penis out and have her lick up and down the shaft with long, lingering strokes. He stood over her, holding her hair back so he could watch her little pink tongue wet his devil flesh. She pleasured him in this manner for several minutes, feeling the throb of the vein on the underside of his cock pulse against the silk of her tongue. A flick over the tip often rewarded her with a drop of salty liquid. Then she'd lave the top smoothness of him, feeling how hot and hard he was and knowing she'd soon be filled with him. She learned quickly not to let her impatience take over; if she worked him too fast he'd humiliate her by slapping her cheek hard enough to sting but not mark.

Finally she'd hear him say, "Suck it." And only then was she allowed to take the profane organ into her mouth, to move her head back and forth so that he slid back into her throat. She moved so that he felt her tongue working him, rubbing that pounding vein. Soon he'd take her head in both his hands, holding her so he could drive himself hard and fast. He grunted obscenities as he did this, ugly phrases like, "Suck that cock" and "You love getting your mouth fucked, doncha?" And she kneeled quiescent, letting him have his filthy pleasure as her own desire grew. Somehow, the perversion of having a man's unclean flesh in her mouth excited her passion more than anything else they did.

Usually he pulled out, panting hard and pushing her to all fours so he could mount her from behind like a dog. Never did he take her facing him, only like a lowly beast. He drove her hard, bringing her screaming with pleasure and pain as he grunted his own release.

Sometimes though, he continued using her mouth until he fountained within. He didn't care that she was left wet, unsatisfied, and spitting his seed into the kitchen sink. He'd only wink and grin, "Catcha next time, baby."

Hiding the bruises and scrapes from her mother was a constant fear-driven task. Once a month, she begged God's forgiveness and promised to be good if only her period would show up on time, which it always did. But Amelia couldn't seem to help herself where having sex with Mr. Perkins was concerned; the sinful sensations that must surely damn her to hell were like an addictive drug. So she risked everything with a man who used her selfishly for six months until he was arrested for raping another girl her age. Both Mr. Perkins and his victim were sentenced to castration, scarification, and hard labor for life.

Amelia would not commit the sin of fornication for another seven years.

* * * *

Looking around Israla's guest room, Amelia tried to figure out how to get back to her own apartment while preserving her modesty. The scraps of her gown would cover nothing now. She remembered the sound of Flencik ripping it open to expose her defenseless body. She shivered. How easily the behemouth had destroyed a dress that barely existed in the first place.

She looked about the room for something to put on. To her relief, a simple blue sheath lay folded by the vid.

She blinked at the vid. *Message Waiting* flashed in Plasian characters on the screen. Nervous, she fumbled the dress on and stared at the two ominous words. Her stomach flopped at the thought of seeing one or all the Kalquorians, even on a pre-recorded message.

The message might not be from them. It could be from Israla or, more likely, Osill.

"Play message," she croaked in a voice barely her own.

Identify.

"Amelia Ryan."

Rajhir's face filled the screen, and she dropped onto the nearby chair. Her whole body seemed to melt. Even pre-recorded, his purple cat's eyes seemed to drill into her very soul. His soft black hair framed his handsome smiling face, a face she had kissed over and over. She thought of how he had looked the night before, his nude muscled body magnificent as he stood over her. She heard his voice in her mind.

I will take her now.

Her body flushed with heat, and her sex tickled to life. She clamped her legs together. Perhaps the effects of the wine had yet to fully wear off. She should return to Earth with a case of it to sell on the black market as a marital aid.

Despite his gentle smile, Rajhir seemed grave as he spoke. "We hope your sleep was restful, Amelia. Our apologies we cannot stay. We want to watch you wake and be lovemaking together more, but our duties we attend." He sighed ruefully. "Work is continue even off Kalquor. We will locate soon your quarters and visit. Good health, Amelia."

The vid went dark. Amelia bit her lower lip and burst into disbelieving laughter. "In other words, don't call us; we'll call you. I guess our cultures aren't so dissimilar after all. Apparently 'wham, bam, thank you ma'am,' is the same on every planet."

She was flooded by disgust, relief and -- could it be? Yes, disappointment. Right or wrong, sex with the Kalquorians had been incredible. They gave her sensations she'd never imagined existed. They had even insisted that she achieved the same pleasure they sought for themselves. No man had ever troubled himself with her sexual satisfaction before.

Just reliving last night's events and the way they'd ravished her made her sex throb. Of course, the wine had a lot to do with it, she reminded herself. Under the influence of such a potent drink, she understood why the uninhibited Plasian females desired the Kalquorians so.

They'd stolen away before she'd wakened, done with their curiosity about Earther women. She didn't have to worry about them kidnapping her to become a sex slave after all. They could have done it; she'd given them complete control. She shivered thinking about that. She'd submitted to the Kalquorians in everything after only token resistance.

Three men at once and doing things to her that she'd never imagined! Had that really been her, prim and proper Amelia Ryan, obedient daughter of Martha Ryan?

What if she'd wakened this morning to find the clan still with her? What if they had tried to have sex with her again? With her faculties now intact, she'd surely have resisted. Would they have respected her choice?

I will take her now. The command in Rajhir's voice left little room for debate last night. She shivered.

No matter now. They had left her alone. "It's time for me to go too," she said to the empty room. Her own work waited.

In the great hall where last night's presentation was held, a breakfast buffet waited for Israla's overnight guests. Most of those who had slept over consisted of young males. Israla's enjoyment of youthful men was legendary, and the less experienced the better. Some looked as shellshocked as Amelia felt.

She stayed long enough to eat some fruit before summoning a shuttle to return her to her apartment. Stepping outside left her blinking in the midmorning glare. The unnamed capital city of Plasius was a balmy, tropical paradise, never too hot or cold. Only the glare of the double suns bothered one, blinding the eyes for the six hours they shared the sky. Few ventured out at this time of day.

The capital city hugged the planet's one ocean, a narrow oasis bordered on its western side by the vast barren desert that made up the bulk of the planet.

To the north of the capital was a temperate zone, so lush with growth and wildlife that the Plasians never tried to tame it. They let its fertility run rampant, only cutting back what encroached on the city itself. A river cut through the forest and the middle of the city, emptying itself into the pink-tinged ocean. The source of the river was an immense glacier which never saw the light of the double suns. Like the Plasians themselves, the planet was an object of extremes.

To the south were the farmlands that provided the people their food. Small villages ran all the way up to the Lisidia mountain range, the subject of the painting that had started all the trouble last night.

Amelia climbed into the shuttle and typed the location of her residence into the computer. The shuttle took off, whisking her quickly and safely to her temporary home. She didn't have to worry about piloting; all Plasian shuttles were tied to a central computer that controlled the transportation grid. Unless one programmed a leisurely trip, the computer always selected the quickest route. Amelia had no doubt the Plasians had developed such technology for the sole purpose of allowing their decadent pleasure seeking to continue uninterrupted as they rode to and from rendezvous.

The trip home was predictably uneventful. The moment Amelia stepped into her quarters she kicked off her heels. She sighed as her feet sank into the plush padding of the floor cover.

Amelia turned in a circle, taking in the view. Of the apartment itself, just a lavatory, kitchen, and great room made up the whole of her quarters. The only furniture the apartment possessed was a lounger, three chairs, a small dining table, and her easel along with the ever-present waterfall, basin and a firepit.

What commanded her attention came from outside the glass walls. A lake, shading from the lilac of the shallows to the plummy purple of the depths, shimmered under the green-blue sky. Mountains draped with cascades of alabaster flowers stretched across the distant horizon like the backbone of an exotic beast.

The vista never failed to stop her breath. She often wondered how she dared to paint it. To try to duplicate it felt like blasphemy. Yet she had embarked upon the project. How could she not? Capturing even the smallest fraction of the view's magnificence would give her life credibility.

She wandered to the easel. After a dozen false starts, she'd begun what she believed to be her definitive work. If her fingers maintained their ability to wield a paintbrush for the next six weeks, she'd complete it. Just six more weeks.

She looked from the canvas coated with its first layer of paint to her hands. She held them out in front of her. Slender fingers splayed like the arms of a delicate starfish. No scars, no swollen joints, no physical evidence of damage whatsoever.

Nothing to show that her days as an artist drew to a close.

Amelia lowered her hands. She had to get to work, but first she needed to change out of the sheath.

She traded it for her favorite outfit of sweatpants and tee shirt. She glimpsed herself in the mirror and laughed.

All alone and wearing more clothes than when I was in a room full of people! The absurdity struck her as funny. *Maybe if the Kalquorians had seen me like this, I'd have come home last night instead of this morning.*

The thought drove the hilarity away. The memory of the three men ravishing her made Amelia shiver.

She still felt the humiliation of her body's uninhibited response to their touches, its wanton abandon to their commands. The more helpless they'd made her, the more uncomfortable their demands, the more desire she'd felt.

The violation of her nether orifice. The insistence she take Breft's semen into her mouth and swallow it. Despite her determination to leave behind her mother's teachings and the prudish judgments of a government fallen into mindless zealotry, she viewed such activities as dirty. The worst of it was the knowledge that the more perverted the acts were and the more dominating her lovers, the wilder her body's response. All one had to review was the effect of the overwhelming Kalquorians on her inhibitions. They had molested her in repulsive ways, and her body thrilled to the assault.

Amelia had realized years before that she was what criminal psychological texts described as sexually submissive. She might even have masochistic tendencies. The dominance of the Kalquorians the night before had certainly left her in a haze of desire. The ripping of clothes, the demanding mouths and hands, their uncompromising insistence she pleasure their alien flesh...

Her breath came in gasps and her sex moistened. Just thinking about the clan aroused her.

"Enough!" she told herself. She marched to her easel, determined to forget the Kalquorians.

Before she picked up a brush, the vid beeped, warning her of an incoming call.

Nervous, she walked over to it. What if the clan wished to pursue her after all? "Answer," she whispered.

The monitor flashed to life, and Amelia restrained a groan. "Hello, Jack," she said.

Jack Frank, the official Earth liaison for off-planet humans, also ranked as an unofficial jerk in Amelia's opinion. The prematurely balding twenty-eight year old resembled a toad, especially when he puffed up with his responsibility as the government's 'link' between offworlders and Earth. Amelia took great delight in bruising his ego by calling him by his first name rather than his title.

His tone reflected his sense of self-importance. "Amelia, there's a situation developing there on Plasius. A Kalquorian clan has arrived."

"I know. I've met them."

"You--" Her calm words momentarily deflated him. He blinked muddy brown eyes at her. As the full import of what she'd said broke over his consciousness, he swelled again. His bloodshot eyes bulged. *God, he looks like one of those huge bullfrogs that eat each other,* Amelia thought. She suppressed a shudder.

He nearly shrieked his next sentences. "What did they say? What did you let them do to you? Why haven't you made a full report?"

"Calm down, Jack. They did nothing out of context with Plasian norms. They seem quite comfortable with this planet's customs." She hoped Plasius' 'norm' remained a mystery to Liaison Frank. Besides herself, only a handful of government officials had met with Saucin Israla and her advisors. Amelia doubted even the Plasians got amorous at treaty negotiations.

To her relief, Liaison Frank seemed to know nothing of the seductive leanings of the Plasian people. "Did the Kalquorians approach you?"

"They were guests at a party I attended last night. They seemed eager to clear up misunderstandings between our peoples."

He wagged a thick finger at her. "You have to be careful around those creatures. They have questionable intentions. They are, in fact, the most depraved of beings."

"I didn't perceive any threat. In fact, I doubt I'll ever see them again." Only the first sentence was a lie.

"If you do, if they approach you again for any reason, let me know right away. Avoid them as much as possible. You're not to stay on that planet if you're in any danger."

His words caused her heart to double beat. Her eyes strayed to the view outside. Leave Plasius before painting that spectacular scene? She'd slit her wrists first.

That toad wouldn't understand. Thugs like him never see--really see--the splendor that's before them. He'd look at this and see nothing more than big rocks and an oversized puddle. He's blind to anything that diminishes his own importance.

Her voice came out cold and clipped. "I'm quite sure I'll be fine, but I'll let you know if they contact me again." There, she'd damned herself yet again. She'd told another outright lie to Earth government.

"Do that. Your virtue is at stake. Frank out."

The vid went blank. Amelia stumbled to the lounger and sank into its softness.

She refused to leave Plasius before she finished her painting. Even if Rajhir's clan pursued her every second of the day, even if a whole platoon of Kalquorian clans showed up on Plausius to ravish her, her last work of art demanded completion. Her virtue was long gone anyway.

Despite her determination, she shuddered at the thought of her own people forcing her from Plasius. As ridiculous as it seemed, she feared Earth more than the Kalquorians.

Mataras do not fear the clans.

Good for them, whoever they were. Did Mataras fear Earthers? What was a Matara anyway?

Amelia looked at the vid, then at her easel. She looked at the vid again. She gave up and said, "Call Ambassador Vrill."

As she waited for an answer, she picked up a pencil and doodled on a sketch pad. Vrill wasted little time responding.

"Amelia! How are you this morning?"

She smiled at her friend's delight to see her. Vrill often shocked her, but Amelia knew the goodness of the Plasian's heart. "I'm fine."

A glint appeared in Vrill's eyes. "How were the Kalquorians last night?"

Amelia felt the guilty blush creep over her face. "What do you mean?"

A throaty laugh. "I saw how their Nobek rescued you from that mob." Her mouth dropped open, and she seemed to forget the clan. "Oh, your painting, Amelia! I wept when I saw it! Many Plasians believe you must be a divinity to have created such beauty. I almost believed it myself. All were eager to touch you, to touch the one who created such glory!"

Amelia squirmed with embarrassment. "It's just me, Vrill. You know better."

"But your art..." She closed her eyes. "It's magnificent. I can still see that mountain as you painted it." She opened her eyes and smiled. "You are far too modest, my friend. I'm glad you're all right. You appear to be anyway. You weren't hurt?"

"I escaped unscathed."

Vrill's wicked grin reappeared. "If you had been injured, that luscious Imdiko would be attending you right this moment. That would be worth a little pain. Did you enjoy your new friends?"

Amelia feigned innocence. "They're not at all what I expected. I found them to be interesting."

"Interesting!" The Plasian laughed and shook her head. "You're insufferable. Put away those silly Earth inhibitions and admit you had the most amazing sex of your life last night."

"I never said a word about having sex with them!"

"Sweet, innocent Amelia Ryan went into a room with a Kalquorian clan last night and didn't come out until the next morning." Vrill licked her lips. "Everyone who went to the party saw it, and we know the Kalquorians aren't men who closet themselves with a woman to simply talk."

Horror crept over Amelia. "Everyone knows?"

"Of course they do. You're the envy of all the women now, so stop your blushes. We're all so happy for you, and the consensus is that no one will breathe a word to any other Earthers about your..." she giggled "...indiscretions."

"Are you sure? On Earth, women are blamed for having sex even if they're raped. If my people knew..."

Vrill rolled her eyes, an expression she'd learned from Amelia. "Israla has issued orders of protection for any Earther who wants to enjoy pleasure on Plasius. No one is to speak of it to outsiders. I think she went that far specifically for you. She worries about you, you know. And how could you even speak the word 'rape'? The clan honored you. They are incredible lovers, aren't they?"

Amelia dug deep for her pride and found enough of it to look her friend in the face. "Not only did they amaze me, but I amazed myself as well. You'll have to be content with that because I'm not saying another word about it."

Vrill squealed her delight. "I knew it! I'm so happy for you. When will you see them again?"

"We haven't set a date," she replied dryly. She switched the subject to the reason she'd called. "You mentioned they were looking for a Matara. What is that?"

"You don't know? The Matara bears the clan's children. It's a permanent arrangement, like Earther marriage, but Kalquorians never divorce. The Matara is the clan's beloved, the fourth member of the group when one can be found. They're in short supply these days. I've even heard rumors the Kalquorians might be in real crisis. "

"Three men to one woman?"

Vrill shivered, her black marbled eyes darkening with desire. "Delicious, isn't it? Kalquorian women who are fertile only ovulate once a year, and they have more male children than female. Even with the men grouped in threes, there still aren't enough of their own women to go around anymore."

At the mention of ovulation, Amelia realized she'd lost track of her own cycle. She calculated, silently berating herself on her

stupidity. Why hadn't she thought of this last night? She tried to imagine herself explaining to Liaison Frank how she'd gotten pregnant by a Kalquorian clan. Knowing how that would end, she tried to imagine begging Israla for sanctuary. She relaxed as her hasty adding revealed such conversation unnecessary.

She asked, "So they're looking for another compatible species? Have they found any?"

Vrill smirked. "I don't know. Have they?"

"How should I know? I doubt Earthers are, rumors of common ancestry aside. The Kalquorians are more...endowed than Earther men." She thought of the double penises and crossed her legs.

"Really! Describe the differences," the Plasian invited.

"Vrill!"

She rolled her eyes. "Silly girl. It's a relief to know the Kalquorians will cure your prudishness. Did they teach you anything new last night?"

Amelia shook her head. "I have to go. I haven't painted at all today."

Sigh. "All right. We'll meet soon for dinner. I'll get you drunk and drag every luscious detail from your reluctant mouth."

"Goodbye Vrill!" Amelia broke the connection and stared at the sketch she'd made. All three Kalquorians looked up at her from the pad. She'd captured their personalities: Breft's somehow sexy predatory smile, Flencik's gentle but intense eyes, and Rajhir's easy confidence. She licked her lips and wondered how much longer they'd remain on Plasius. Long enough to confirm they'd failed to get her pregnant?

"You'll be very disappointed, boys," she told the drawing. "But that's not what you were after at all, is it? Just scratching an itch, that's all you wanted to do."

She put the pencil down and stood. She stepped to her easel, putting the clan to the back of her mind and drinking in the landscape outside.

Before she began to paint, a gentle chime announced a visitor at the door.

She groaned. "Now what?" It was probably the guild master, still pumped up over the night before. Or maybe even Israla, no longer so aloof now that Amelia's painting had touched her. Whoever her guest, she would send him away. She'd frittered enough time away with trivial matters.

Her curt greeting died on her lips the moment she swung the door open. Rajhir filled the entrance, a smile covering his face. Behind him, Flencik and Breft looked over his shoulders at her.

Her mind groped for something to say; in the end she managed a weak "Hello."

As if given a signal, the men entered. Before Amelia could back away, Rajhir swept her into his arms and engaged her mouth in a demanding kiss. Her senses ignited. Amelia trembled, overwhelmed by Rajhir's strength and the sudden stab of desire.

As he held her against him, eager hands pulled at her clothes. Her sweatpants were tugged off. Rajhir's lips left hers. He loosened his grip on her just enough to allow Flencik to remove her shirt. Breft undressed Rajhir.

Her shock at the unexpected caresses wore off enough for her to start a protest. "Don't--"

Rajhir stopped her with another penetrating kiss. He lifted her up and carried her to the lounger, where he removed her undergarments. Her breasts flattened against the smooth skin of his chest as he covered her with his body. His dual sex lay against her thigh, slick

and ready. His hardness pulsing so close to her own secret flesh made her legs part, allowing him access. The attack was so sudden, so thorough, she had no opportunity to defend herself.

His prodding fingers found her wet. He slid one in, then two. He pumped her hard, his palm rubbing her clitoris. She moaned and her thighs slid wider apart. Warmth pulsed through her groin, melting the bit of resistance left to her.

Her body refused to obey her inhibitions. She wanted Rajhir to take her as he had the night before. She wanted him to fill her once again.

Besides, he'll probably do as he wishes whether I give him permission or not, she thought. She sighed at the idea, unconsciously arching against him. Her arms were heavy, too weak to push against him. Her whole body conspired to leave her helpless in his arms.

His fingers left her sex, and she ached with emptiness. It lasted only a moment before she felt the twin prods at her orifices. He stopped kissing her to stare into her face. His eyes were purple pools, dark with desire.

Now I tell him to stop. Now I tell him I don't want this.

Even as she opened her mouth to obey her dignity's dictates, her traitorous legs wrapped themselves around his hips. "Wait," she said, her voice weak. "This is wrong. I can't."

Rajhir answered by lowering himself into her. Her flesh opened to him, taking him in. Again came that wonderful fullness, that devouring pleasure of him inside both secret openings. Her breath came in gasping sobs in time with his slow thrusts. The pleasure drove the last of her inhibitions into submission. Through it all he watched her, his face mirroring her arousal.

"Beautiful Amelia," he whispered. He licked her lips with the tip of his tongue.

He increased the speed and power of his thrusts. His breath quickened. Amelia felt the warmth, the blazing light growing within her, overwhelming her. Her head tossed from side to side, and she made small animal cries. Here it was, the blinding whiteness filling her, shaking her, taking her over the edge. She heard Rajhir's bellow over her own cries as he filled her with his passion.

Rajhir lifted from her. Still vibrating with desire, she whimpered at the void he left. Only then did she remember the others. They stood close, both naked and aroused. As Rajhir left her, Flencik moved to take his place.

She recalled her duty to resist him, but she ached to have him fill the emptiness the Dramok had left. As she argued with herself he entered her, solving the dilemma.

He held her close to himself and lifted her up, still impaled on his maleness. He knelt on the lounger with her sitting on his lap. Her sex spasmed, dissolving her better judgment yet again. She wrapped her legs around his waist. Using his powerful arms he pistoned her up and down over his organs. Their position allowed her clitoris to rub against him with delicious friction. He drove his groin up and her down, pounding hot moist flesh into hot moist flesh. She hung onto his wide shoulders, feeling her senses rushing toward that precipice again. It was happening already, so soon, she was going to fly apart, here it came...she screamed her ecstasy to the ceiling, her head thrown back in release.

Flencik's climax overcame him moments later. He crushed her to him as if desperate to meld their bodies together. For a moment she forgot to breathe as his seed emptied into her womb. She felt its warmth coat her insides. His moans lessened. They clung together, their breath mingling. He kissed her, the movement of his lips and tongue a gentle counterpoint to his earlier frenzy.

She saw Breft approach. His stare seemed the most intense of the three, his features almost cruel. He moved like a predator stalking prey. He carried an aura of barely restrained ferocity. Her stomach fluttered as Flencik handed her to the Nobek. A shiver of apprehension tickled down to her sex.

He frightened her but excited her at the same time. She remembered how his seed tasted, and she trembled as he bore her down on the lounger. He saw her shiver and smiled. The smile told her any resistance she might offer meant little to him.

"You will give me entrance as well, Amelia," he said. His tone brooked no argument.

She whimpered, resigned to her fate. She'd given herself to the other two without a fight; it made no sense to deny the third. Breft's body, though not as large as his clanmates', was just as muscled. She admitted to herself the delight of his body against her skin.

"Open yourself to me." His voice sounded soft but left little doubt of the command in it. "Guide me to you."

She obeyed, wrapping her fingers around his smaller organ and tugging it to her nether orifice. Her other hand positioned his larger sex so that he could thrust it into her flesh.

He pressed against her, slipping the tips of his penises in her. He stopped and stared into her face, letting her feel how good his full penetration would be when he granted it. Instead of impaling her, he said, "Beg me for it."

Her skin flamed hot with embarrassment. Tears of humiliation sprang to her eyes. "I can't," she said, her voice wavering. She shoved against his chest.

Breft's smile grew at her refusal and her attempt to fight. He gathered her wrists in one hand and held them over her head, pinning them to the cushions. She gushed honey on the alien flesh teasing her, and he chuckled, the sound so very masculine and powerful. His free hand rubbed her breasts. "I know you desire it. You want to feel me thrusting inside you. Your body betrays you, so it's no use denying it. Beg me."

"Don't." She tried to yank her arms free, but his grip held like iron. He slapped her heavy breasts playfully, the sting more arousing for the pain. Moisture flowed in a thick river from her core. He mastered her utterly, and heaven help her, she wanted him. The feeling of him at her threshold drove her crazy. To beg however...her face burned with humiliation. Embarrassment warred with the desire his commands invoked. She sobbed.

"Please," she moaned, thrusting her hips forward, trying to take more of him in. He laughed and withdrew almost all the way.

"You can do better than that," he said in a fatherly tone, but the hungry look in his eyes told a different story. He wanted total domination, mental as well as physical.

She looked at Rajhir and Flencik and knew no help existed there. They watched with rapt attention. Rajhir even nodded his head in approval.

Breft pinched her nipples. She squirmed at the pleasure his touch gave her. She cried harder. Why was she so weak in her morals? Why did she want his domination, his complete control over her?

"Tell me what you want from me," he said. His hand drifted from her breasts to her clitoris. He brushed the straining bud with a feather touch. Amelia wailed at the cruel pleasure. He gave her no mercy; instead he teased the swollen flesh by drawing slow circles against it with his fingertip. She writhed beneath him, desperate to be pleasured by him.

"Why do you fight?" he asked. "A few simple words will give you all the pleasure you desire. Speak them, little one. Speak them so we may both have release. Say 'please make love to me'."

Despite the humiliation of begging him in front of the others, her resolve crumbled to dust. She never knew such great need existed. Her voice tore from her in hitching sobs. "Please...Breft...make love to me."

"Say, 'I need you to take me now'."

She cried even harder but knew escape wasn't possible. Begging was only intensifying her desire. She had to be possessed by this alien. "I need you to take me now," she managed through the torrent of tears.

"I surrender my body to you."

"I surrender my body to you...please..."

"You may do with me as you wish."

"Oh God...please...you may do with me as you wish...Breft..."

His grin widened. "Now wasn't that easy, little one? Such a good girl," he said and slid easily into her. Her sobs trailed into gasps of pleasure. He rode her hard and fast, bringing her to the brink. Then his pace slowed, making her wait a little longer. He did this a few times before allowing them both the most intense of releases.

As their breathing slowed, Rajhir and Flencik joined them. The men held and caressed Amelia. Exhausted and defeated by their quick but thorough lovemaking, she allowed their touches without resistance.

Flencik laughed, a deep, wonderful sound. "No much time for climax. All ready for the pleasure."

Breft grinned at him. "It was all I could think of this morning. I am glad the lovely Earther needed little foreplay."

Rajhir asked Amelia, "The pleasure excuses us for no being present when you wake? We visited as soon as possible."

She blinked. "Actually, I wasn't expecting you at all."

His heavy brow furrowed. "I messaged we would visit soon. You receive no the message?"

She thought of telling him how on Earth saying and doing were two different things. She decided he'd probably not understand. Instead she spoke with chagrin. "I got it. You're very truthful."

The clan exchanged nervous looks. Flencik spoke first. "You are with us angry?"

She shook her head. "I'm just trying to think of a way to make you understand that on Earth, men can't take what they want from women the way you do. If they act like that and get caught, they get in a lot of trouble. My culture considers this very wrong."

Rajhir's eyes narrowed. "We give you pleasure."

"It's not just about pleasure. It's also about respect."

Breft answered that one. "It is a sign of respect to give you pleasure."

The Kalquorians were frustrating, but she felt sure they meant well. "On Earth it's a greater sign of respect to first ask a woman if she'd like to receive pleasure. After the man has married her, of course."

"Ask?" Rajhir looked mystified. He glanced at his clanmates, but they seemed every bit as confused. He turned to Amelia again and

spoke carefully as if explaining to a child. "On Kalquor we know women
  deserve sexual pleasure, as much to give as the clan can. It is wrong to require her the asking."

"Unless we make a game of it as you and I did," Breft added, a mischievous glint in his eye.

Rajhir grinned. "Games are good. We will play more." He glanced at Flencik to include him in the threat, and his smile dropped off. "What is wrong?"

Amelia looked at the frowning Imdiko who stared at her.

"Stand, Amelia," he said, waving the other two back. He helped her to her feet. She stood before him, aware of her nakedness. However, his eyes rested on neither her breasts nor sex. He studied her neck and shoulders. Rajhir and Breft looked from her to their clanmate and back again.

"What?" Rajhir demanded.

Flencik ignored him. Instead, he asked Amelia, "Why this shoulder is higher than the other? You are all out of line."

"I have severe nerve damage to my shoulders, arms, and hands. That arm's the worst."

He walked behind her. He lifted her curtain of hair from her back and rubbed the bunched shoulder. His large hand felt warm on the stiff flesh.

"There was an accident, and I suffered a lot of soft tissue damage in my neck and shoulders. My doctors told me the muscles spasmed in an effort to protect the damaged nerves, then atrophied in that position," she told him. "Now they cause even more harm to the nerves."

"There is pain? It is bad?"

Her answer was hesitant. "It's not too bad right now. Sometimes it's worse." Her eyes strayed to her work in progress. "That will probably be my last painting."

Rajhir and Breft stepped to her easel while Flencik's gentle fingers continued to probe the knotted muscles. She watched them examine her work.

Breft surprised her by saying in a reverential tone, "For such talent to be lost would be tragic."

She started to thank him when Flencik responded. "No loss for to paint. I can cure this."

She looked up at him. "The doctors say it's inoperable."

He shrugged. "Earth, they have no the correct skills. No good medicine for injury such to this. Easy on Kalquor I can cure this injury."

Hope sparked, but she hid her excitement. "How would you cure me?"

He opened his mouth to speak then closed it again with a frown. He looked at Breft and spoke in the guttural Kalquorian tongue. Breft listened and nodded. "He would regenerate cells. Grow new ones and rebuild the nerves."

Her hope grew. "Are you sure you could do it?"

Flencik's expression showed confidence. "I have cured on Kalquor the same injury. Mostly the injury to our Nobeks, but I have cured too other species. You come to Kalquor. I will make you will still paint."

The Imdiko's nonchalance over her career ending injury stunned Amelia. He acted as if the devastating nerve damage was no worse than a paper cut.

Could he really fix the damage? Would Earth even allow me to go to Kalquor for treatment?

A buzzing noise startled her. The sound came from Rajhir's clothes piled on the floor. With an apologetic smile he rummaged through the fabric and pulled out a small, silver box. He spoke briefly in Kalquorian and the buzzing ceased. The other two began to pull on their clothes.

"We must go," Rajhir said, also dressing. "I am in new talks for trades with Saucin Israla. Breft and Flencik in their areas of work meet with Plasians. You are no to be angry we must leave you again?"

Amelia yanked on her own clothes. "Not at all. I really need to paint." An idea occurred to her. "In fact, I need a lot of time alone to paint. I require absolute silence to concentrate."

He seemed to accept that. "You come to us when you to are no painting. We lodge in Sector Sarras."

They headed towards the door, but Flencik stopped to pat her back. "Come for medicine for the bad pain grows. On Plasius, I can no cure here, but I can help you pain less."

"Thank you," she said. The three smiled at her. Each kissed her goodbye as they left.

She didn't paint that day after all. She had too much to think about.

* * * *

As the balmy Plasian night descended, the Kalquorian clan returned to their quarters. They gathered on their curved lounger, enjoying the warmth and musky aroma of burning scentwood. Rajhir accepted a glass of dlas from Flencik. Day's end gave him a sense of relief. Despite the meeting with Israla yielding productive results, his mind kept wandering back to Amelia. He thought of her full breasts and rounded buttocks. He mused over how her skin flushed pink when she became aroused.

Apparently, Breft's mind dwelt on Amelia as well. He said, "Her excuse that she needs to be alone to paint is probably untrue. I think she is trying to postpone further contact with us. Must we really stay away?"

Rajhir sipped his dlas and sighed as the tension in his muscles unknotted. "Patience, clanmate. Flencik is sure she'll come to us on her own soon."

The Nobek's gaze turned to the Imdiko. "How soon?"

Flencik drank his own dlas without concern. "The damage to her arms and hands is severe. Her work aggravates the condition. The more she paints, the worse the pain becomes."

Rajhir nodded his agreement. "She's racing to finish that last work before she can't paint any longer."

"I spoke to the doctor she's been seeing since she got here. He can't relieve the pain when it becomes unbearable, which is every few days. She'll come to me next time it flares up, and I will help her." Flencik drained his glass.

Breft smiled. "That's a perfect time to run your tests."

All three men looked towards a closed copper-colored door which hid Flencik's examining room. The Imdiko's air of confidence grew. "Everything's prepared. If she's not compatible, she'll never know I did anything to her. Still, our physiology is so similar to the Earthers that I think there's a very good chance we can reproduce with her."

Rajhir finished his drink in a single swallow. "If you're right, we'll soon have a Matara."

Breft's grin was that of a predator closing in on his prey. "Whether she wants to be or not."

Chapter Four

Amelia sobbed as she huddled on her lounger.

Two days had slipped by since the clan's visit. During that time creative inspiration reached a fever pitch, and she painted almost nonstop.

She knew the consequences of prolonged work to her injured hands. Still, inspiration's siren song rendered her incapable of stopping. Her life depended on artistic creation just as it depended on her heart beating. Only three two-hour naps interrupted the grip of her obsessive painting.

What fatigue couldn't stop, excruciating pain did. Last night, what felt like a lightning bolt shot from her right shoulder down to her fingertips. The agony shocked her out of the hypnotic trance of painting. Her brush fell from her hand as it hooked into a claw. Paint splattered the floor. In pain's electric haze, she barely noticed.

As it almost always did, Amelia's left arm joined the clamor in sympathy with the right. Her tortured limbs held merciful sleep at bay all night. Amelia sat on the lounger, her arms folded in her lap as if cradling a baby. She had to keep them supported; she couldn't stand the weight of her own arms straining the damaged nerves. She cried, she wailed, she cursed the universe as her world shrunk to one of unceasing torment.

Dawn was an hour old, and still she moaned her agony to the walls. Lances of pain stabbed her from shoulders to hands. She her Plasian doctor's inability to offer relief. Just as on Earth, waiting out the pain until the damaged nerves recovered from overuse was her only option.

Or did she have another choice? Flencik said he couldn't cure her on Plasius, but he could relieve the pain. She tried to remember his exact words, but the combination of pain and exhaustion kept her memory from achieving clarity. All she was sure of was his invitation to visit should she have problems.

Did she dare to go to him now? Her excuse that she needed privacy to paint had worked; she'd heard nothing from the Kalquorians in the last two days. Would they take it as an invitation to resume relations if she showed up on their doorstep?

Flencik's a doctor, she reasoned. When he saw how she suffered, indulging in a sexual romp would be the last thing on his mind. Even calculating Breft wouldn't be so callous.

The promise of help beckoned, negating her distrust of the Kalquorians. The pain ratcheted up another notch, bringing her to her feet.

She went to the vid and signaled for a shuttle to pick her up immediately.

* * * *

Amelia knocked on the clan's door and cried out as the innocent action sent fresh waves of pain through her hand and arm. She hoped the Kalquorians answered; knocking again was impossible.

The door opened, and Flencik's bulk filled the entrance. He blinked to see Amelia standing on his doorstep then grinned with delight.

"Hello, Amelia."

Despite the agony of her hands, she answered his infectious smile with one of her own. Her heart leapt at his obvious pleasure to see her. "Hello," she said.

He stepped back to let her by. "Come in. Your visit brings pleasure. Good surprise."

"Thank you."

She stepped out of the blinding Plasian glare into the softly lit apartment. The windows were dimmed to an amber glow, giving the sitting room a golden hue. A fountain burbled soothing conversation to itself in one corner. A supersized lounger took up most of the rest of the room.

"You're alone?" she asked.

"Rajhir and Breft are no here. I apologize."

"Actually, it's you I need to see. It's my--" Her throat closed, and the sobs of pain she'd fought all morning burst from her lungs. She held her hands out to the Imdiko. "They hurt. Please, Flencik--"

He scooped her up and cradled her in his arms. She buried her face in the safety of his broad chest as he carried her to the lounger and sat her down.

"Stay here little one," he said, wiping her tears with gentle fingers. His voice rumbled reassurance. "I make the medicine to stop pain."

He patted her cheek before striding into another room. A copper door shut behind him, leaving her alone. Amelia settled into the billowy lounger and composed herself. She felt embarrassed to have lost control.

She heard the thud of the Imdiko's tread in the other room. The door swung open, and his bulk kept her from seeing the room behind him. The door closed again as he swept to her side and bent over her, lifting a cup to her lips.

"Drink, Amelia. It will away take the pain."

The intensity of his gaze frightened her for a moment. He exhibited an eagerness that seemed to have nothing to do with relieving her pain. He looked at her the way he did the last time they'd made love.

"This is safe for Earthers?" she asked.

Flencik's smile wiped the strange gleam from his eyes. "Very safe. I have studied Earther anatomy and biological functions. Your people much are like Kalquorians. This will no harm you."

She hesitated but saw nothing threatening about his demeanor. Her hands throbbed with the grinding pain. He pressed the cup to her mouth, cupping her chin and tilting her head back. Thick liquid flowed over her tongue, coating it with a flavor similar to vanilla coffee. She gulped it like a woman dying of thirst. Flencik took the empty cup and set it on the floor.

"Good, Amelia. You will feel better quick."

"Medicine never tasted that good on Earth." She flexed her fingers. Was the worst of the pain dissipating already? The tension in her body melted away. She snuggled against the lounger.

"Your English is better," she observed.

He smiled. "I much practice with Breft. I wish to well talk to you."

"You're much improved. Where are the others?" she asked.

"Diplomatic meeting. Too boring for me." He rolled his eyes in such an Earther fashion that Amelia giggled. "Your hands good are now?"

A huge yawn kept her from answering right away. "The pain is getting better fast." She yawned again. Her eyes wanted to close. "I feel so sleepy all of the sudden."

His heavy brow creased. "I forgot to say. This medicine can tired to make you. I apologize."

Her own voice sounded far away from herself. "That's all right. Anything's better than the pain, and I didn't sleep last night anyway. I should go back to my quarters before--"

"No, stay to rest," Flencik interrupted. "You take a small sleep...nap...here."

Amelia had no strength to respond. Her eyes slid shut, and she felt his large hands cradle her and lay her down on the lounger. His fingers stroking her cheek lulled her unprotesting into slumber.

Chapter Five

Flencik waited until Amelia's breath became deep and steady. Once he felt sure the sedative he'd given her had taken hold, he carried her to his lab.

The stark room accommodated an examination table, surgical instruments and a mini-lab. All were on loan from the local Plasian medical center. He hadn't even needed to explain why he wanted the equipment. He was the top doctor on Kalquor and chaired several intergalactic health committees. Rank had its privileges.

Flencik laid Amelia on the table, putting a pillow beneath her head despite her being unconscious. He injected a long-term pain relief agent into each of her hands and into the bunched shoulders. *That takes care of that,* he thought. *Now for the real work.*

He slipped off the shapeless garments masking her body and stood motionless, admiring the lush figure, laid before him like an offering. Earthers were small, fragile creatures, but this one really was quite beautiful. It was impossible to be professionally dispassionate when looking upon Amelia Ryan.

He brushed her hair back from her breasts and shoulders. Her skin beckoned his fingertips to stroke it, and he gave into the compulsion. He traced the pink circles of her nipples, feeling the flesh grow into hard pebbles. From there, his hands slid to her tiny waist and over the swell of her hips.

He brushed his fingertips over the soft swirl of her auburn pubic hair. Her skin flushed pink. Was she responding to his touch despite her drugged sleep? He probed at the furry vee of her sex and discovered moist curls. Amelia sighed, her lips curving into a slight smile. More moisture coated his fingertips. What a wondrous being this Earther was, Flencik marveled. Despite the strict laws governing her sexual expression, Amelia's body retained its natural hungers. He brought his fingertips to his nose and inhaled her musk before licking the wetness, rolling her flavor around on his tongue. How delicious it would feel to plunge his hungry flesh into hers right now and feed her dreams with the sweetness of lovemaking!

The agreeable ache of his loins warned him of the danger of forgetting his purpose. He straightened with a grunt and turned to his lab.

After mixing a formula, he raised and parted her legs to allow him entry. He inserted a flexible hollow tube into Amelia's sex. He sent the fluid through the tube into her womb and waited for it to work.

If all went well, the concoction would stimulate instantaneous egg release within the lovely girl's uterus. Theories on Earther female biology suggested she might respond to such treatment, unlike Kalquorian females.

Flencik gave the process a few extra minutes than required, assuring himself of thoroughness. He parted the pink petals of Amelia's sex and slid the tube out. In its place, he inserted the harvester.

The slender metallic tool, developed to gather precious fertilized eggs from at-risk Kalquorian women, went to work. It sent thin fibers into Amelia's reproductive tract, searching for eggs. Flencik held his breath as he watched the scanning monitor.

One...two...three...his mouth dropped open...four...five...six... still the egg count rose until the scanner displayed the incredible number of ten.

Ten eggs! Flencik rubbed his eyes, blinked, and looked again. Despite his disbelief, the scanner remained at ten. The harvester expelled itself from Amelia's body, and he rushed to freeze it and its valuable contents.

He returned to her side and lowered her legs. He checked the time and smiled with satisfaction. She'd sleep a little longer, innocent of the tests he performed. No heartless coercion, no force had been involved. His conscience was clear.

Flencik dressed her, his normally steady hands trembling. This tiny, wonderful creature had produced ten eggs before his very eyes. If only one of them proved viable to Kalquorian fertilization, hope would be returned to his planet's future. For a moment the possibility overwhelmed him. He touched his forehead to Amelia's, willing the miracle to happen.

He carried her back to the lounger and arranged her in a comfortable position. He kneeled next to her and watched her sleep, his expression that of stunned worship.

* * * *

Amelia emerged from sleep, her senses coming to life one by one. First came the sensation of lying on yielding softness, as if she rested on a cloud. Next, her ears detected the burble of water and the

pops of fire. The sounds, usually enemies to each other, blended in a sweet auditory spiral.

Then she smelled musky scentwood, deep and enticing as it wafted into her nostrils. It wasn't the kind of scentwood she kept in her apartment. She slitted her eyes open to light filling her sight with featureless gold. She opened her eyes a little more to recognize her surroundings as an unfamiliar Plasian apartment appointed with oversized furniture.

As a gargantuan shadow moved into her view, she woke fully with a gasp.

"I apologize. I did no intend to frighten you." Flencik sat next to her on the edge of the lounger.

"It's all right." Her initial fright over now that she remembered where she was, languor stole through her limbs once more. She smiled sleepily at the Kalquorian.

"Are you better to feeling?" he asked.

She remembered the brutal agony that brought her to Flencik. She flexed her hands, tensing for pain. "It's gone," she said in a wondering voice. She tightened her hands into fists and showed them to the Imdiko. "You really did it. They don't hurt at all!"

"I am to help glad."

Amelia sat up and stared at her widespread hands. Tears trembled against her lashes. "You don't understand," she whispered. "Even on my best days, it hurts."

Flencik stroked her splayed fingers, his touch as gentle as ever. "Only it is a relief of temporary. On Kalquor the cure is permanent."

"To have even a moment's peace is more than I hoped for." Amelia blinked back the tears. "Thank you, Flencik. Thank you so much."

He smiled and patted her cheek. "You are hungry?" He stood and went to the kitchen area without waiting for her reply.

Despite the stunning miracle of pain-free hands, Amelia's famished stomach had concerns of its own. It rumbled at the mention of food, especially when she saw the platter of succulent Plasian fruits Flencik carried. He sat next to her again, the tray balanced on his knees.

She reached for the red berrylike nellus, a delicacy that grew on one island on Plasius. Flencik withdrew the platter from her seeking fingers.

"I feed to you," he admonished her. "Your hands should rest more. Time is to give the medicine to penetrate fully."

He plucked a nellus from the platter and brought it to her lips. She ate from his fingers while stifling an urge to giggle. A Kalquorian man fed her as she lounged like a queen; all she needed was Rajhir rubbing her feet and Breft fanning her. Wouldn't the officials of Earth's government just soil themselves to see such a spectacle!

The medication lingered in her limbs. She felt relaxed, luxurious with barely a twinge of self-consciousness as Flencik fed her. Warm languor, similar to how she'd felt after drinking *leshella* at Israla's party, bathed her in contentment.

"You like nellus?" he asked.

"It's my favorite." She allowed him to place another red pearl on her tongue. The juice of the berry tasted like liquid sunshine. She closed her eyes to concentrate on its flavor. *If only Vrill could see me now, spoiled and pampered by one of the most desired creatures in all the universe,* she thought. Her Plasian friend would feel dizzy from envy.

Amelia stretched and burrowed deeper into the overstuffed lounger. She opened her eyes to see Flencik smiling down on her, enjoying her enjoyment. "How long before my hands hurt again if I paint right away?"

"To rest all of today for you. You paint tomorrow and can ten days more with no pain, I think." He added, "If to come you Kalquor, I permanent can cure you."

"That certainly has its appeal."

His blue-purple eyes riveted on her face as he fed her more. His intent gaze gave her a thrill of fear. "Why are you looking at me like that?"

"You are beautiful."

His response, so guileless and direct, startled her. He spoke it as if it was the greatest truth he'd ever told. She warmed to the compliment.

"Am I as pretty as the women on your planet?"

His gaze softened. "Their look I forget. Your beauty sends memory away of other women."

She shook her head at the morsel he offered her. She teased, "You're a charmer, Flencik."

He placed the tray on the floor. When he looked at her again, he wore a puzzled frown. "No a charmer. I am an Imdiko."

She thought to explain her meaning but decided it would be too much effort. "Yes," she agreed. "You're an Imdiko. The nurturer of your clan and damsels in distress." She knew she flirted, but what was the harm in that?

He stroked her hair, her face, and traced her lips. Her heart sped up. Damn, why did she find these Kalquorians so desirable? How did she keep getting herself into these situations?

His breath warmed her mouth as he spoke. "I would nurture you. I would care to take you all your life. I would fill all your needs."

His arms slipped around her and held her close. She inhaled, drinking in the cinnamon scent of him. He was aroused. The medication he'd given her still gripped her in its languid aftermath. She felt soft, pliant to both his and her own desire. Amelia let Flencik kiss her with a deep thoroughness that warmed her entire body. His mouth gently devoured hers, and she twined her tongue around his. She pressed upward in his embrace, wanting his hard strength against her. Moreover, she wanted him *in* her.

Besides, she owed him. He'd taken the insanity of pain from her, a miracle she'd gladly sell her soul to the devil for. *Screw those worthless fools on Earth. He can have anything he wants*, she thought. Her sex throbbed in enthusiastic agreement as he tasted her mouth.

He lowered her onto the lounger and sucked one sweatshirt-covered nipple until it stood aroused. As he moved the heat of his mouth to her other breast, she felt the trickle of her sex. "Anything," she whispered, unaware she'd spoken aloud. She shivered as he nipped at her breast with bared teeth. She raised her arms in unspoken surrender. Flencik obliged her by pulling her shirt off to nuzzle at the soft mounds of flesh. He suckled hard as if he'd devour her. Amelia moaned as he feasted.

He moved farther down, kissing the soft flesh of her belly, licking the cup of her navel. She moaned and giggled, at once turned on and tickled. The laughter ended as his mouth latched onto the fabric over her crotch. He ran his tongue over the seam of her sweatpants, teasing the swollen bud that ached to be naked to his attention.

"Wet," he grunted, looking up at her face with half-lidded eyes. "I wish taste to you deeply. You need to me satisfy you."

Oh yes, how she desired his mouth on her eager flesh. "Please Flencik," she moaned, forgetting right or wrong; needing him the way he wanted her to.

His smile turned almost cruel, and he stood. His fingertips curled into the waistbands of her pants and panties. He peeled them off her in one sweeping movement.

Flencik looked down at her, his broad chest moving with deep breaths. She lay still on the lounger, silently offering him her defenseless body. His eyes raked over her as he pulled his clothing off. His two penises stood revealed, glistening with lubrication. She ached to take him in her mouth.

"Anything?" he asked.

"Anything." Amelia's heart pounded.

He grasped her ankles, pulling them apart, and kneeled between her spread thighs. His head darted down with the speed of a striking rattlesnake, and he drank from her sex with her legs draped over his shoulders.

The feeling of his mouth closing over her clitoris made her back arch. A tiny cry flew from her lips. He sucked on the pink button, and she arched again. Flencik's tormenting left her helpless against the bucking of her own pelvis. Her breath sobbed through her parted lips as he fed from her womanhood. His tongue probed, flicking in and out of her, stopping now and then to suck at her freely flowing moisture. Then he battered her swollen clitoris with his wicked tongue again. She gasped and moaned and cried out at the varying intensity of the contact.

Her orgasm was rushing upon her when his mouth left her. She whimpered in need, her hips thrusting shamelessly at his retreating face.

The cruel smile returned. "We go now slow."

She wailed. The release had been so close, and he'd denied her. She reached for him, and he swatted her hands away as if flicking a fly. "Obey, Amelia. I command you. Be obedient for to your pleasure come."

His face drifted towards her sex again, so she quieted, enjoying the rush of anticipation.

His fingers spread the soft petals of her sex, opening her completely to his scrutiny. He stared at her secret flesh, his breath warm on her. He slowly lowered his head, and Amelia sighed in anticipation. His rough tongue lapped her juices, keeping away from her pleasure bud. After each lick, he swallowed with deliberate slowness, his expression telling her he relished the taste of her. Her desperate need for climax settled into steady pulses of gentle pleasure. She sighed again as the tip of his tongue probed her anus and flattened out to sweep a path to her sex's lips.

His tongue narrowed to press an entrance into her sex. In and out it pushed into her center. She closed her eyes, wanting only to feel him.

His mouth and tongue left her. She opened her eyes. He straightened until her ankles rested on his shoulders. His penises probed at her secret flesh.

His sudden thrust buried him to the hilt in her softness. She cried out from mingled surprise and pain.

The brief burst of hurt disappeared in the delicious friction of his strokes. He held her legs against his chest, pulling her close as he drove himself into her. He watched his length drive into her over and over. His upper lip wrinkled back, displaying long, needle-thin fangs half hidden behind his blunter, more human teeth. *Like a vampire,* Amelia thought, watching the fangs with a combination of desire and fear. Did he want to bite her? Did Kalquorians drink blood? What would it feel like if he plunged those fangs into her skin?

The liquid sounds of his sex sliding through hers was punctuated by the heavy slaps of his body pounding against her with greater and greater force. She grunted with each blow as he drove her hard. The delicious fullness that bordered on pain grew in her belly as he took her powerfully. She willed the explosion to come.

He rocked against her and the ticklish heat built to an inferno. She struggled to keep quiet so Flencik wouldn't know. He must not deny her this time. Her efforts were to no avail, however. Her pleasure demanded a voice, and she cried out as it grew beyond the bounds of her belly. "Please let me, please Flencik, please don't stop..." her begging became incoherent. In response, the Imdiko rode her harder and faster, pushing her over the brink. She came, her lungs bursting with ragged cries.

Flencik howled and drove his face against the side of her neck. She felt a quick sting as his fangs sank into her throat. She crested with fresh orgasm, feeling his mouth clamped over her skin, the teeth sunk deep in her flesh.

His sex pulsed as he emptied his seed within her. Amelia screamed her ecstasy as Flencik rode her mercilessly, bringing her to orgasm after orgasm. He pulled his fangs out, and sucked at the wound he'd made. She heard him swallow. As he drew on her blood he growled against her neck, a devouring beast. With each pull of his mouth, Amelia's sex spasmed in helpless pleasure.

He could rip out my throat, kill me right now, and I wouldn't care, was Amelia's only coherent thought. Being possessed by this biting, snarling alien who rutted like an animal made her strangely euphoric.

Flencik pumped his hips against her with a final shudder. He rolled over on his back, taking her with him so that she lay on top of him. She rested her cheek on his heaving chest as they quieted. She felt like her limbs were made of spaghetti, but the languor was sweet. In fact, all of life seemed sweet. Quiet joy pulsed through her entire being.

At last she lifted her face up and saw the scratches she had left on his skin. Angry red welts lined up in ragged rows across his shoulders and chest. She blinked slowly and traced her fingertips over them. "Did I do that to you? Flencik, I'm so sorry."

He rumbled laughter and kissed the top of her head. "Marks of honor, little one. They will jealous make Rajhir and Breft."

"Does it hurt?" As she asked, she was aware of the irony of her inflicting damage on the brute.

"It stings. It gave much me excitement." He grinned at her. "I am no can wait to make you do it again."

"You *want* me to scratch you?"

"Small pain, more pleasure. Like my biting your neck you made excited. You climaxed many times."

Amelia expected to feel embarrassed, but her relaxed euphoria persisted. *What's wrong with me?* she wondered, not really caring.

"I don't like to hurt others," she sighed.

He smoothed her hair back. "Tender Amelia. It is no real hurt. It to pleasure you so makes me happy." He grinned, deviltry filling his expression. "How do you feel?"

"So relaxed and happy. I don't want to move." She watched his humor deepen. "What? Did you do something to me?"

"It is the bite." He opened his mouth wide. She watched fascinated as his hinged fangs descended from the roof of his mouth. Slowly they folded back up, like a rattlesnake's. "The teeth are hollow. When a Kalquorian bites, we our victims inject with substance to intoxicate. It produces euphoria."

"Am I a victim?" Amelia snuggled against his warmth.

"I hope you do no so feel." He stroked her hair. "Kalquorians also use it when love making on each other. It enhances the experience. I did no bite to you make victim. I wanted to only you give pleasure."

"Mission accomplished." She giggled.

He laughed and sat up, placing her in his lap. "I wish I did no to need send you away, but you must rest. I have too much work do."

"Why can't I rest here?" Amelia wanted to stay. She felt too lazy and content to leave.

"Because Rajhir and Breft return soon. They give you no rest if they to see you." He leered at her to imply how his clanmates would keep her busy.

Amelia had no will to protest. "All right."

"Good girl. You will quiet to be the rest of today, and you can paint tomorrow."

He cleaned, medicated and bandaged her bite wound, promising the pinpricks would be healed by the next day. He tried to help her dress, but made the mistake of stopping often to kiss and caress her. She clung to him, her desire growing.

"Don't tease unless you're ready to make good on it," Amelia cried, rubbing up against Flencik's powerful body. He chuckled indulgently and laid her back on the lounger. He kissed her, his searching hands finding her wet and ready again. She groaned as he pressed fingers into her sex and anus, expertly stroking inside her while his thumb flicked her clitoris. His free hand kneaded her breasts, gentle one moment, cruel the next. She sobbed as he easily brought her to climax once more.

After that, he quickly pulled her clothes on, denying himself further access to her silky flesh. "You must to go now, before the others return. I already have tired you too much." He picked her up as she whimpered a protest. It felt so good to be held in his strong arms. She wanted to remain the rest of the day. Perhaps even all night.

His excuses notwithstanding, she couldn't figure out why Flencik seemed anxious for her to leave. Surely Rajhir and Breft were capable of keeping their hands to themselves for a change. Was Flencik angry with her? Had she done something wrong?

She supposed once the intoxication of his bite wore off she would be grateful he had sent her home. She sniffled her disappointment.

"Please do not upset be, little one," he whispered as he opened the door to the outside. "I do what is best you for."

He carried her to her shuttle and kissed her long and deep before setting her inside to lie on the cushion. He sighed. "So much work. When I am finished, you will return." He entered her apartment address into the shuttle's computer.

"Thank you again for making my hands better. You can't imagine how good it feels to not hurt anymore." She meant it with all her heart.

He smiled and kissed her goodbye. "Remember, rest today. No painting. You for wait tomorrow."

"I promise."

* * * *

Under the glow of floating globes, Rajhir and Breft sat in their quarters after a long day of meetings. They drank kloq, a Kalquorian spirit that burned the guts as it went down. It relaxed them without dulling their senses or slowing their responses.

Too well trained to fidget, Breft sprawled on the lounger, appearing to be relaxed. Still, Rajhir sensed an aura of impatience from his clanmate. He understood it. He felt it himself but fought to display the same outward calm as the Nobek.

Breft drained the last of the kloq from his cup and stared into the empty vessel wistfully. At last he gave voice to a hint of his feelings.

"I wish he hadn't sent her away."

"He did what he had to. If he ran the tests while she remained, she'd become suspicious."

Breft smirked. "I could have kept her distracted, especially after seeing the marks she left on Flencik. The thought drives me mad for her."

Rajhir chuckled, remembering the shallow scratches striping Flencik's sculpted torso. "Her heart is unwilling, but her flesh is eager."

The Imdiko had serviced her well indeed to drive her so wild. As he showed off the marks of passion, he'd assured them the intoxicant his fangs had sent into Amelia's body had not had a chance to truly affect her before she'd lost control. Rajhir and Breft demanded details of the encounter; Flencik was delighted to provide them. He'd taken her in a way that some would have found to be more punishment than pleasure. Flencik was gentle for his species, but his natural strength was still a force to be reckoned with. He'd allowed himself to unleash as much as he thought their maybe-Matara could handle, then he'd pushed the boundaries a little further. He had no doubt he'd bruised her tender inner flesh a little, but she'd responded with her strongest orgasms thus far.

"I didn't send her home just so she wouldn't know I tested her," he'd admitted. "If she had stayed, I wouldn't have been able to resist taking her savagely again. She brings out my instincts to dominate, and I didn't trust myself to not inflict serious injuries."

The clan was realizing Amelia enjoyed being dominated to the point of pain. If Flencik's tests went their way, Rajhir wanted to know how much non-damaging punishment the lush little Earther liked.

As if thinking about his clanmate summoned him, the door to Flencik's lab swung open. Rajhir and Breft stood at once as he emerged.

Unable to rein in his impatience, Breft said, "Do you have the results?"

Flencik looked from one to the other, his eyes wide. His mouth worked soundlessly, making Kalquor's leading physician look idiotic. Despair crashed against Rajhir's heart.

Another incompatible species. Our people are doomed. And Amelia is lost to me.

His life had always revolved around the wellbeing of his clan and Kalquor, so he was surprised to find the worst blow came from his feelings for Amelia. He realized he cared for the Earther despite having only two encounters with her. Something about her incited a strange mix of urges: wanting to protect her from harm, yet wanting to take her with ruthless strength at the same time.

Knowing he had no valid reason to ever touch her again left Rajhir aching for the feel of her soft skin, for her warm, yielding body. Regret made his voice sharp.

"Don't make us wait. Did our seed fertilize any of Amelia's eggs?"

Flencik blinked at him. In a disbelieving voice he answered, "All the eggs are fertilized. Cell division is normal. We have actual viable embryos."

Rajhir stared speechless. When his voice came back, it roared from his guts. "ALL TEN OF THE EGGS?"

Breft sat back down on the lounger hard as if his legs had given out beneath him, a rare display of weakness for the fearsome Nobek. "You are absolutely sure?" he whispered.

Flencik nodded, his shocked expression giving way to a wondering smile. "All her eggs responded to our seed. Earthers are not only compatible with us, they're more suited to our needs than our own women."

Joy so extreme that Rajhir thought it might kill him filled his entire body. A compatible people had been found. A Matara for his own clan had been found! With Earthers, his civilization could ensure the continuation of Kalquor and its culture. A doomed race would survive.

What made him truly happy was knowing his clan could claim Amelia. She belonged to them to keep and cherish.

His voice husky with emotion, he turned to Breft. "Send a message to Kalquor. Tonight our people celebrate."

The Nobek sped to the vid to carry out the order.

Chapter Six

Amelia awoke refreshed the next morning. She stretched her hands towards the ceiling and flexed her fingers. Not even a twinge of pain remained.

She laughed out loud. At the same time, tears sprang to her eyes. Not since the day a black Cadillac jumped the sidewalk and slammed into her body had pain retracted its dagger claws. Even on her best days her hands hummed with a steady ache.

The pain was utterly erased. Flencik's medicine had plucked the threads of agony from her nerves. *Freedom*, she thought. *This is what being without pain is like. I'd forgotten how it felt.*

She rose from the lounger. She pirouetted in the first morning sun's golden ray that beamed through the window. She moved as awkward but uncaring as a child dancing her first recital. She laughed again, ringing peals that celebrated life itself. Tears ran unchecked in a steady flow down her cheeks. She jumped up and down on the lounger, ran the length of her apartment to hold her hands aloft to the bright sky outside the window, ran back to the lounger and jumped up and down on it again.

When the giddiness subsided, she cooked herself breakfast, marveling at how effortlessly her hands accomplished routine tasks. How had she taken such ease for granted before? Lifting the fork and cup to her mouth, washing and drying the dishes -- each mundane step was a miracle.

She caught sight of her reflection in a mirror as she moved about her apartment. The bandage on her neck was a reminder of her liaison with Flencik the day before. She'd almost forgotten in the wake of his successful treatment. She pulled the bandage away, wincing in anticipation of the two holes she was sure she'd see.

True to his word, the wounds had healed completely. Amelia grinned at herself as she tossed the dressing away.

She felt too happy to settle down to paint right away. She wanted to luxuriate in the absence of pain. She delighted in the fantasy that she lived a normal life again. She piled scentwood into the pit and lit it, inhaling the floral aroma. Then she shrugged off her clothing and stepped into the wash basin.

She tilted her head back to let the waterfall sluice through her hair. She shampooed, trailing painless, languorous fingers through her thick mane to release the tangles.

She soaped her body, delighting in the softness of her own skin. She rarely acknowledged the lushness of her flesh, her body that recalled an era of voluptuous and proudly sinful women like Marilyn Monroe. Personally, Amelia preferred her own shape to the modern twig-thin, androgynous models venerated on magazine covers. Her body was blatantly female, a fact that had always secretly thrilled her despite the problems it had invited too many times.

The one naughty indulgence she'd given herself over to without guilt since leaving Earth was the enjoyment of her own touch. Now, without pain to mar the experience, she surrendered to sensual pleasure. She lavished extra attention on her full breasts. She cupped them in her hands, enjoying their weight and firmness. They filled her hands to overflowing; they'd been comfortable handfuls for the Kalquorians' massive paws. She traced the rose-colored tips, sighing with the pleasure her own touch gave her. Her hands, so long her tormentors, fondled her with loving strokes.

One drifted over her ribcage, across the soft down of her belly, and lower to the pleasant ache of her sex. She brushed the tiny pleasure button with a fingertip and felt a melting in her core. The sensation reminded her of Flencik's lovemaking the day before. She closed her eyes as she stroked herself, her hips swaying in rhythm with her fingers.

This won't take long, Amelia thought as her sex came to life. As she drifted closer to climax, she imagined Flencik's adept fingers stroking her clitoris with such assurance. Her wonderful Flencik who took away the pain; he prodded her on to pleasure. One moment gentle, the next, forceful.

And commanding Rajhir; what would he do to her if he were here?

He'd take her, pressing his penises deep into her as Flencik continued to massage her pleasure bud. She felt the Dramok forcing her open to receive him, his determined thrusts burying him in her yielding flesh over and over...yes...how sweet.

Standing over her, Breft prodded her lips with his larger member. His intense stare, the unspoken command excited her. If she refused to obey, would he punish her? She hoped so. This time however, her desire overwhelmed the temptation to defy him. She opened her mouth to allow his hot flesh entrance. Her tongue licked the silky skin covering the iron of his erection, and her lips closed over it, making it tight for his pleasure. He grunted approval. She inhaled his sharp cinnamon scent as he pumped his groin against her face.

She opened herself fully to them, a grateful receptacle to their hungers. The four of them were a single, heaving beast, hurtling toward the precipice.

Rajhir and Breft came. The sweetish spice of Kalquorian seed flowed over her tongue and down her throat. The warmth of their juices filling her belly from both directions sent her over the edge.

Amelia's head snapped from side to side as she made small animal cries of release.

Amelia opened her eyes and awoke from the fantasy. She withdrew her thumb and forefinger from her still quivering sex and her pinky from her anus. Despite the intense climax, she felt empty. She wished the Kalquorians surrounded her in reality. She wanted their strong limbs tangled in her own. *If they were here right now, I'd fuck them until my vagina went numb. What do you think about that, Mama? It's wrong, and I don't care.*

She finished bathing and emerged from the basin. She dressed and approached the easel, determined to put the alien clan from her thoughts. The painting progressed well, better than she had hoped. In the absence of pain, she dared to hope to achieve a true masterpiece. She picked up a paintbrush.

She marveled at how sure her grip on the brush felt. Minutes later, she painted in an entranced fog. No pain, no effort, as if an invisible hand guided her. The painting seemed to emerge from beneath the brush, as if the layer of canvas fell away to reveal a finished work underneath. *It used to be like this before the accident*, she thought. *Wrong*, she immediately amended. Before, she took the freedom from pain for granted. It took ceaseless agony to appreciate the lack of it.

A knock at the door intruded upon her senses. She struggled to escape the spell she'd fallen under. She noted the first sun's position in the middle of the sky and saw the second sun had risen some time ago. Surprise left her gaping. She'd painted for several hours without realizing the time passing. Still, her hand remained pain free.

Life has its share of miracles, she thought with real gratitude. She set her brush down. Wiping her paint-smudged fingers on a nearby towel, she hurried to the door.

The appearance of the Kalquorian clan failed to surprise her. What surprised her was her heart's swell of delight to see them. The three men smiled down at her, and she unselfconsciously smiled back, especially at Flencik.

"Hello," she welcomed them, opening the door wide to allow them entrance. They came in but stopped just inside.

"Your hands do no hurt?" Flencik asked.

"Do NOT hurt," Breft corrected his clanmate with a gentle tone.

"They're perfect. Not one bit of pain." She opened them for his inspection. Dried paint streaked her fingers.

"You have painted?" Rajhir said, tracing a green smudge on her thumb.

She laughed. Had she ever! "I've been painting all morning. It's unbelievable that it's so effortless."

With visible pride, Rajhir said, "Our Imdiko is the best of doctors on Kalquor. Perhaps of all the universe."

"You'll get no argument from me. Can I get you anything? Something to eat, to drink?"

Rajhir looked toward her kitchen. "If you painted all morning, then you have not eaten your second meal. Will you eat with us? We invite you to what you call a picnic. We will eat by a lake. It is nearby. Very beautiful surroundings."

His invitation startled her. Painting beckoned, yet the day outside beamed glorious, perfect for a picnic. Failing to enjoy it must rank as a sin, she reasoned.

Past dealings with this bunch indicate eating food may not be all they're planning on, an inner voice warned.

The delight of a painless day made her reckless. Giddily, she thought, what if they did get her in another compromising position? Who was she kidding anyway; she'd hand Flencik her very soul for the freedom from agony he'd given her, however temporary. Her gratitude for this day knew no bounds. Besides, she still felt a yawning emptiness from her earlier self-pleasuring. To hell with her mother's morality. Mama was dead. And to hell with Earth morality. When on Plasius, do as the Plasians do, right? No one on this planet thought ill of such adventures. In fact, they thought one mad to not indulge in them.

What Earth's government doesn't know won't kill it, or me for that matter.

"I'd like a picnic very much," she said, grinning at the pleasure that brightened the Kalquorians' faces.

* * * *

The lake, as beautiful as Rajhir promised, shone under the Plasian sun like an oval amythyst. It shimmered in the heat of midday. Amelia wished for a bathing suit. The lake's cool depths invited her to take a plunge.

She sat on the ground, inhaling the aroma of the grass that grew by the lake. Plasian grass had a lilac-type aroma, drowning her in its sweetness. Rajhir and Breft stood on either side of her. They too

contemplated the lake while Flencik unpacked a container full of food. She looked over her shoulder to see what they'd brought for their meal. She hoped for more nellus. When he brought out a platter covered with golden brown meat, she gasped. Of all foods to see on Plasius...
"Is that what I think it is?"

He smiled. "Chicken fry. You like this?"

"That's 'fried chicken', big guy, and I couldn't claim to be a true Southerner if I didn't like it. How in the universe did you get this?"

Breft answered. "Earth transports land here and trade with Plasius. They sold the meat to us and instructed us on how to prepare. Flencik says it is not healthy to cook this way, but it smells good."

Her mouth watered at the heavenly aroma. She experienced a pang of homesickness that startled her. Was it spring on Earth yet? Would the front yards of Georgia be exploding with the pink fireworks of azaleas now? Or was it summer already, the air so thick with humidity that one felt wrapped in a hot wet blanket even at midnight?

The clan watched her, aware of her mood change. She smiled. "What else did you bring?"

Flencik opened containers to show her their contents. "Grul from Kalquor," he said pointing to fiery red chunks. Amelia wondered whether it classified as animal, vegetable or mineral. "The desrel grows local. The nellus just imported this morning."

The sight of the nellus delighted Amelia, but Flencik picked up a piece of grul. "Taste," he invited, putting it to her lips.

She opened her mouth for his offering. A delicious spicy flavor filled her mouth, and then—

"Hot! Hot!" she squealed, waving a frantic hand before her mouth.

All three men dove for the carafe of Plasian wine. Flencik grabbed it first. He tipped it into her mouth, quenching the fire set by the grul. It overflowed her lips, streaming down her chin to her throat and beneath her blouse.

"I made you mess," he said in a soft voice, leaning close as he took the wine away. His breath wafted over her face. She closed her eyes against his nearness and felt the rough silk of his tongue lick the moisture from her chin. His mouth followed the stream until her collar blocked further progress. Then it travelled up the side of her neck.

His fangs bit into her skin. Amelia cried out at the twin pinpricks of pain. Her eyes flew open, but Flencik's black curls blocked her sight. He held her close as he injected her with the intoxicant that sapped her will to resist. She felt him grow hard against her thigh. Her own sex ached agreeably.

He drew back. Rajhir and Breft knelt on either side, their eyes dark as they looked down on her. Flencik's hands spanned her waist.

He pushed her blouse up to her collarbone and lapped at the wine that ran between her breasts. The warm breeze teased her bare nipples erect.

"This isn't how Earth picnics usually go." Her halfhearted protest sounded weak to her own ears. She allowed Flencik to tug her blouse off without resistance.

Breft twined his fingers in her hair, pulling her head back. "We make new rules for the picnic. We will have a Kalquorian picnic instead," he said. His mouth closed over Flencik's bite and drew on the bleeding wounds. Amelia groaned from the sweet sensation of him feeding on her.

Rajhir joined the wonderful assault. He pushed down her sweatpants and underwear. His lips sucked the lips of her sex, pulling moisture from her craving body.

She melted under their mouths, every muscle pliant to their whims. Her fingers found the coarse waves of hair that grew to Breft's shoulders; she stroked it as his mouth moved from her throat to press its demands over her lips.

Rajhir's mouth left her sex. Her legs fell further apart, inviting him back. Instead of his tongue, cold sluiced down her sensitive crevice. She yipped her surprise into Breft's mouth. He withdrew, startled. She looked down. Rajhir grinned at her, righting the wine bottle he'd tipped over her pubic curls. Liquid sapphire beads sparkled in the swirls of hair.

"Sweet wine," he said and sampled his work. Amelia moaned as his tongue lapped at her sex. Her juices flowed freely with the wine. She wondered how she tasted.

Breft grabbed a nellus berry and put it to her lips. "Flencik says you like these much."

She moaned, delighting in the juicy fruit exploding in her mouth, Flencik sucking on her breasts and Rajhir feasting between her legs. *I'm in heaven*, she thought. *Surely this is worth all the fires of hell.*

Breft sprinkled sprigs of desrel into the hollow of her throat and retrieved them with his lips and tongue. She shivered at the heat of his mouth and the scrape of his teeth on the sensitive area.

Flencik seemed to approve of his clanmate's choice of serving platter. He scattered an assortment of food over her belly and breasts. Then he drizzled wine over the works. After Breft popped a bite of chicken into her mouth, he joined the other two in gobbling food off her skin.

Now erotic places blossomed to pleasurable life under the voracious Kalquorian mouths. The creases where her breasts ended and ribcage began, the cup of her navel, the hollows of her shoulders, the tops of her knees; these areas tingled under the attention of her companions.

"Now the other side," Rajhir said. He stripped off his tunic. His muscles shone with perspiration. If Amelia's drugged body had possessed the strength, she'd have licked him from head to toe. He looked delicious. Flencik and Breft followed his example, baring their equally yummy torsos. They rolled Amelia over on her belly, depriving her of the view. She sighed a protest.

The splash of wine on her naked back and buttocks relieved the worst of the twin suns' heat. She closed her eyes as the Kalquorians resumed lunch on her flesh. Occasionally, they fed her a morsel and helped her sip wine from the rapidly depleting bottle. Her earlier fantasy in the washing basin was nothing compared to this slow pleasuring, a pleasuring Flencik's bite and the wine had left her happily defenseless against.

Amelia lay still, feeling every lick, nuzzle, nibble, and touch. The attention continued well after the food disappeared. A callused finger traced her spine. Strong hands kneaded her buttocks. A tongue slipped a wet path down the crevice to her anus. Another pair of hands slid beneath her to cup and squeeze her breasts. Lips kissed the nape of her neck, bringing gooseflesh.

"Don't be afraid," Rajhir whispered in her ear.

A strip of silky cloth was tied over her eyes, blindfolding her. Another bound her wrists behind her back. The bonds felt soft, but tight. The sudden domination brought every sense alive. She lay still wondering what they planned to do to her. Her juices flowed like a river between her thighs.

Take me. Force me. Make me obey. She tensed her arms and found her bonds held her firm. The Kalquorians had rendered her completely helpless. She moaned. Her breath quickened with anticipation.

They lifted her from the ground and made her straddle a pair of kneeling thighs. Her breasts flattened against a smooth chest. She felt the twin sets of a Kalquorian's erection pressing up beneath her. She wriggled her hips, desperate to get him inside.

She sighed as the larger of the two penises pressed its way into her. The smaller prodded at her anus.

Hands from behind adjusted the rectal penis so that it slipped into her sex with its companion. It filled her to bursting. Incapable of struggle, she submitted with a whimper that was more pleasure than pain. Her sex gushed its delight at the double invasion.

The Kalquorian behind her pressed close, and she felt his larger sex pressing against her anus. She shuddered, knowing the impossibility;

he was too large to enter her that way. She also knew impossible or not, he'd take what he wanted, what she wanted him to take. *Make me do this. Take my helpless body in ways no Earther man would dare.* She waited unprotesting for the pain that must come.

Slippery from its own lubrication, the thick member invaded her nether orifice, pressing into her without mercy. The hurt felt tremendous and glorious at once. The sweet pain stabbed into her, and still more of him slid into her, tearing her in half. She lay quiescent against the male in front of her, her sobbing breath her only concession to the wondrous agony of this possession. She accepted the Kalquorians as her masters; she, their slave, must submit without complaint.

Enfolded between the massive bodies, the pain disappeared a bit at a time. Pleasure took over as her lovers began their thrusts within her. They held her still between them as they rocked their hips in tandem. She groaned, a flesh vessel made only to accept their passion.

A hand gripped her chin and turned her head to the side. The aroma of cinnamon teased her nostrils. She parted her lips, and her third lover's sex glided into her mouth. Hands held either side of her head. The penis drove in and out, pumping her mouth and throat. Her lips clamped over the silky shaft while her tongue flicked against its driving length.

The three aliens pressed into her, their animal growls mingling in the air. They drove hard into her accepting flesh, the last of the pain blossoming into all-consuming pleasure that engulfed her entire body. She screamed her release around the cock pumping her mouth.

The Kalquorians grunted as one. Hot semen fountained deep inside her anus and womb. The third penis pulsed its juice into her mouth. Her orgasm heaved within her as the thick fluid slid over her tongue and down her throat. She screamed around the organ as fast as she could draw breath as the men's strangled cries joined in.

Afterward, they lay naked on the cloth, catching their breath beneath the glare of the two suns. The Kalquorians removed Amelia's blindfold along with the cloth binding her wrists. She lay still, relishing the ache of rough lovemaking. She had no doubt her secret flesh must be bruised. The thought made her smile. Never had she been so satisfied sexually.

Flencik grinned with a little boy's delight. "I like picnics. We should picnic every day."

Amelia giggled and wiped sweat from her forehead. "Not if it gets any hotter. The suns are almost too strong today."

Rajhir rolled over to face her, propping himself up on one arm. "Can you swim? The water would cool you."

She stretched, wincing a little. "That's a wonderful idea, but I don't have the strength."

"I will take you in." Rajhir stood and cradled her to his chest. Breft ran ahead and dove in. He disappeared beneath the surface and reappeared some distance away moments later.

"Swims like a fish, doesn't he?" Amelia said as Rajhir waded into the lake. Flencik flanked them.

"Fich?" Flencik's brow furrowed.

"Fish. A creature that lives in Earth's oceans."

As the men reached chest-deep water, Flencik leaned forward. Rajhir rested Amelia on the broad expanse of the Imdiko's back. Rajhir let her go and floated, his long black hair fanning in the water. He closed his eyes, letting the water support his dark body. He looked like a god giving himself to the elements.

Amelia clutched Flencik's shoulders as he paddled out to deeper water. The water cooled her parched skin as he towed her closer to Breft.

She splashed the Nobek as she rode by. He growled playfully, lunged at them, and pulled her off Flencik's back to dunk her. Before she rose to the surface on her own, he yanked her back up.

"Are you all right?" he asked.

"Yes."

"Good." He dunked her again.

Rajhir joined their laughing group. "Do something with your Nobek," Amelia said.

"As you command." Rajhir leapt halfway out of the water onto Breft, bearing the startled man under the water. Breft came back up snorting and sputtering.

"That'll teach you to pick on a lady," Amelia teased. He grinned at her in response then yanked Rajhir underwater.

The water had chilled her, and now the twin suns beckoned her to lay on the shore to warm under their power. Refreshed but tired, Amelia struck off for the shore, her strokes lazy and slow. She didn't worry about drowning in her euphoric state; no doubt the Kalquorians were keeping a protective eye on her. When she reached land, she stretched out on the lilac grass to let the sun dry her body.

Cavorting with three aliens sure wears a gal out, she thought sleepily. She knew self-recrimination would come later, as it always did. The thought made her more tired than ever. She hated that she had to be drugged to enjoy sex as it was meant to be enjoyed.

It bothered her to realize that the perceptions of others meant more to

her than her own beliefs that sex was a natural part of being human.
Up until now, her reluctant relationship with the Kalquorians had been
based on what Earth, what her dead mother would have thought. How
they would condemn her if they knew. What she wanted had never
entered the equation.

*But no one's getting hurt, and I'm having fun. Where's the harm in
that?*

Her eyes closed. A breeze stirred the air. It caressed her naked body,
diminishing the heat of the day. She felt herself dozing off.

The clan had other ideas. Their shadows blocked the suns as they
surrounded her, their bodies dripping onto hers. She opened her eyes.
All three men knelt by her.

Breft reached for her and clasped her so her back was against his
chest. His cool wet body was like a shelter she could hide beneath. He
slipped inside her easily, her body a ready sheath for his thick sex. He
held her close, moving his hips with slow gentleness. His smaller penis
rubbed against her clitoris with each forward swing. With one hand he
held her belly, pressing her against him. His other arm wrapped around
so he cupped a breast in his warm hand.

His lovemaking was slow, steady, sure. He seemed to be making up
for the earlier bestiality she'd enjoyed at his clan's hands. The effects of
the bite and wine kept her pliant, and her body responded to the
thoroughness of Breft's caresses. Her orgasm didn't shatter her into a
million pieces this time; it rolled in large waves through her, bringing
her shuddering from head to toe.

Breft handed her to Rajhir. Again, she was loved with care. Rajhir
cradled the back of her head, holding her so he could kiss her deeply.
His other arm supported her buttocks as he guided her onto his
kneeling thighs and lowered her onto his maleness with precision. He
rocked back and forth. The motion of his sex inside Amelia was small,
but the angle rubbed his groin against her clitoris with excruciating
pleasure. He brought her twice that way before realizing his own
climax.

Her lax body passed over to Flencik. For all his immense size, his
was the most delicate of touches. Amelia closed her eyes and
luxuriated in his butterfly caresses, in his soft kisses raining on her skin.

He even managed to enter her in a delicate manner despite his above
average endowment. He used his surgeon's fingers to part the folds of
her sex with care. He inserted his penis by increments, allowing her
body to take him in. She adjusted to him easily, as if made for him.

She lost all sense of time as he rose and descended above her. For a
blissful eternity Flencik made love to her, yet when they cried out

together, spending themselves in sudden violent contractions, Amelia felt as if it had only been an instant.

Exhaustion was claiming her, sending her into the deepest abyss of sleep where even the Kalquorians couldn't pull her free. She gave in to the fatigue with sadness. Every moment of pleasure with the aliens seemed precious in her intoxicated state; she hated to waste time sleeping when she could be making love.

As she fell into slumber, she thought, *I wish I could have this always. I wish I could stay with them.*

A tear escaped to roll down her cheek as she succumbed to sleep.

Chapter Seven

Amelia woke in a beam of golden morning sunlight. Rajhir curled behind her in spoon-fashion on the clan's velvety lounger. In front of her, Flencik wrapped his arms around her waist. *A Kalquorian sandwich with Earther filling,* Amelia thought, feeling snuggly warm between the two men. She had no memory of them bringing her to their quarters. She must have slept right through the shuttle ride, through dinner, through the night. They had exhausted her, all right.

She yawned, fighting the urge to consume herself in shame. *I'm going to do what I like while I'm on Plasius. I'm going to have amazing sex with these men. As long as Earth doesn't find out, it will be okay.*

Behind Flencik, Breft propped himself up and looked down at her. He blinked sleepily, but he wore an aura of someone fully awake and ready to strike.

"Are you always such a light sleeper?" Amelia asked.

He reached over his clanmate to touch her hair. "I am always ready to protect the clan."

She shivered at the hard light in his eyes and the steel in his voice. Flencik's more affectionate purple eyes opened, and Rajhir moved behind her. She felt him grow hard behind her, his penises pressing against her buttocks. He buried his face in her hair, inhaling deeply. "You will spend the day with us," he murmured.

With real regret she replied, "I'd love to, but I have to get back to my quarters to paint." She looked over her shoulder to see him frowning. She turned towards him and brushed his mouth with her fingertips. "It's very important to me."

His face softened. "Then you must continue your work. If it makes you happy it is important to us too."

A sudden idea struck Amelia. "Would you like to come to my apartment for dinner tonight? I'd love to cook some Earth food you might enjoy."

Breft and Flencik flicked their gazes to Rajhir. Both nodded. "We will come," Rajhir said.

"Great." Amelia stretched. "I'd better get going before you distract me too much." She wiggled against the erections Rajhir and Flencik sported, giggling.

"You will before refresh you go," Flencik said.

Breft shook his head. "You are mixing up the order of the words again. You should say, 'you will refresh before you go'."

Flencik huffed with frustration. "The language confuses me."

"You're doing very well," Amelia reassured him. "Plasian is supposed to be a simple language, but it felt like forever before I could carry on a conversation. English is much harder."

He smiled at her as he gathered her in his arms like a child. She didn't bother to argue about the delay. She wasn't really in that big a hurry. He carried her to where the waterfall chuckled into the basin and lowered her into the water.

A bath would feel great, she thought. The water's warmth seemed to seep into her pores. As the clan surrounded her, she realized they planned to bathe her.

Sinner! Whore! Her mother's voice was horrified.

"Leave me alone," Amelia whispered back.

"Amelia?" Rajhir's look was quizzical. "What is wrong?"

"Nothing." She smiled. "Everything is great."

"Good."

Breft and Rajhir soaped her arms. Flencik tilted her back to let the waterfall sluice through her hair. She sighed as the powerful but gentle hands kneaded her scalp and the muscles of her arms. Usually her arms' damaged nerves screamed with pain at such intense contact, but Flencik's medicine continued to work its magic. She felt only bliss as Breft and Rajhir coaxed knots of tension to evaporate from the muscles. Her arms felt as liquidly pliable as the water swirling around her.

After washing her hair, Flencik turned his attention to scrubbing and massaging her back. Rajhir and Breft moved their focus to her legs. Amelia lost all sense of time as they kneaded her to new depths of relaxation.

Only when they felt satisfied that they'd eradicated all tension from her body did they stop. Flencik wrapped his hands around her waist and lifted her to a kneeling position in the basin. Breft soaped her torso, moving from her trim waist up to her ribs. He lathered her breasts, his hands sweeping in circles around the mounds. He squeezed her erect nipples between his forefingers and thumbs, smiling as her breathing quickened.

She responded to more than his touch. Flencik slipped a bar of soap into the crevice of her buttocks. He glided it back and forth over the sensitive flesh. The sensation of the hard yet smooth soap sliding against her nether orifice was the most erotic thing she'd ever felt. She

remembered the day before, how they'd taken her there with such
ruthless desire. She shivered, and her heart quickened. Her hips rocked
to the slow rhythm of Flencik's hand.

Rajhir's soapy hand plunged into her pubic curls, shampooing them
with the same care Flencik used on her scalp. He rinsed her sex with
palmfuls of warm water. His big hand covered her secret flesh,
rubbing her, making her moan with sensation. She thought how she
could let the clan satisfy her forever.

You could, a voice inside whispered. *If you're compatible, you could
be their Matara. You could go to Kalquor. Flencik would heal the
nerve damage. You'd go on painting and being pleasured like this for
the rest of your life. You'd never have to worry again about Earth's
overbearing morals and laws.*

Rajhir and Flencik slid their fingers inside her. Breft's mouth warmed
her breasts in turn.

I don't dare consider this.

Rajhir's other hand stroked her clitoris. The heat down there
overwhelmed her.

I don't dare...do I?

Her climax burst through her.

* * * *

Back at her quarters, Amelia lost herself in the mesmerizing drone of
painting. The pre-programmed alarm woke her from her artistic trance
at late afternoon. She flexed her fingers, still amazed by the absence of
pain.

She cleaned herself up and went to the cooking area. She tapped her
electronic cookbook for some recipes. Judging from the grul they'd
served at the picnic, Amelia decided the Kalquorians might like a spicy
Mexican dish -- toned down for her own comfort, of course.

She scanned the list, comparing ingredients with her supplies.
Suddenly, the vid beeped for her attention. Probably Flencik
wondering if he should bring anything, she thought. She walked to the
vid and said, "Answer."

She started to see Jack Frank's wide-eyed, sweaty face fill the screen.
"Amelia! Thank God. I've been trying to reach you since yesterday
afternoon."

She gaped at him, momentarily without the wit to answer. Had he
somehow learned of her indiscretions with the Kalquorians? Dear
God, he knew *something.* Discovery was written all over his frantic
expression. She fought a rush of nausea as fear twisted her stomach.

"Are you all right?" he pressed.

"I'm fine," she said, feigning innocence. "What's going on, Jack?"

"The Kalquorians are what's going on. They're showing up on the planets we have exchange policies with, the ones where our women are located."

Amelia regained control of her senses. Liaison Frank knew nothing of her adventures. Her heart slowed from its frantic pace. She mentally cursed his hysterics. Really, the man performed like a drama queen! "That's all? Honestly, you had me scared for a moment. It's probably just coincidence."

"We doubt that. Some of the women have gone missing. No Earther men; just the women."

Amelia's heart quickened again, thudding hard enough to hurt her chest. If Rajhir's clan showed up now..."How many?"

"We've lost contact with about fifty percent of our female exchanges. That's over 1500 women in the last 48 hours."

Amelia's knees threatened to buckle. She lowered herself into a chair. "You're sure the Kalquorians are behind this?"

Frank glowered. "Those deviant freaks made it clear they wanted to use our women for their own sinful lusts. They're animals."

"But why all those women at once? Why not just one or two? They'd have to realize Earth would get suspicious if they kidnapped so many."

"Maybe they did test one and found out our races are somehow compatible. We know they want to breed with us." His look pierced her through the vid. "That's classified information, by the way. You are not to repeat that to anyone. Have you allowed that clan visiting Plasius to take any kind of samples from you? Blood, hair, anything?"

Amelia felt her face flush. They'd sampled her all right, though not in the manner Frank thought. "Of course not."

"Are you sure? Not even against your will?"

Furious, she yelled, "Don't you think I'd have reported something like that? What are you saying?"

"Calm down." Now his face turned red. "There's no need to get so emotional."

"How would you like to be accused of helping a bunch of innocent women disappear?"

"No one's accusing you of anything." A whine insinuated itself in his voice. "I'm just concerned about your safety. Those alien freaks can't be trusted. Your virtue is in grave danger, as is your very soul."

"I've had no problems with the clan here." An outright lie given her initial reluctance to enjoy the Kalquorians' attentions, but he didn't need to know the particulars. "As you can see, I'm not being held against my will. They're here engaged in trade talks with Saucin Israla. From what I've heard," she hastily added. *Stupid! If I give him too much information, he'll realize I've had more than casual contact with them.*

"Stay away from them. Do what you have to, to protect yourself. Check in with me every day." He recovered some of his poise and irritating condescension. "An Earth transport is scheduled to arrive at Plasius in two weeks. I'm sorry we can't get you out of there sooner."

Amelia's breath nearly stopped. "Two weeks?" She glanced at her canvas. The colors pulsated at her, as if the painting lived. Her child, on the verge of birth. "I'm not sure my painting will be done by then."

Frank snorted disbelieving laughter. "Your painting! Haven't you heard what I've said? Earth women in the vicinity of Kalquorians are disappearing!" He grew stern like a father confronting a recalcitrant daughter. "There will be no discussion about this. Earth has formally recalled you, and you will be on that transport in two weeks. Liaison Frank out."

The vid went blank. Amelia stared at it with growing anger.

Two weeks! As long as her hands remained pain free she might complete the painting by then. Still, she might not. Unfortunate circumstances and Earth's paranoia threatened to destroy her opportunity to complete the greatest piece of art she'd ever created. Damn Earth's religious radicalism!

"That sniveling creep did all but outright accuse me of letting the clan test me for compatibility!" she fumed out loud. She stormed her quarters like an angry caged animal.

She'd allowed Flencik to treat her nerve damage. The medication was the extent of anything approaching scientific experimentation. The Imdiko took no samples. He'd only relieved her pain.

She stopped pacing the length of her quarters.

The medicine had knocked her unconscious.

She gasped. She *had* been sedated by Flencik's medicine. Judging by the position of Plasius' suns, she'd slept for at least two hours. Had he left her on the lounger all that time? Or had he taken the opportunity to do other things?

She'd allowed him to administer the drug three days ago. Kalquorian clans had arrived on other planets the next day, and the Earther women on them began disappearing in the last 48 hours.

Had Flencik tested her? If so, had he discovered a breeding compatibility between Earthers and his race? More importantly, had he done anything else? She looked down at herself and placed a trembling hand on her stomach.

Did she already carry a child? A Kalquorian child?

She raced back to the vid. "Contact Rajhir's clan," she commanded in a screamy voice. Before the machine complied, she said, "Cancel!"

I've got to get hold of myself, she thought, running a trembling hand through her hair. *If they think something's wrong, they might do something...bad.*

"Be calm," she said, taking deep breaths. "Nothing's wrong, everything's great. All quiet on the front."

Once the shakes subsided, she ordered the vid to contact the clan again, arranging her expression to look disappointed but warm. She hoped.

Luck smiled on her. The vid tonelessly invited, "Leave a message." The Kalquorians had stepped out.

"Aw, you're not there," she said. "It's just as well; I have bad news. I'm really sorry, but something's come up, and I have to postpone our dinner." She realized she was talking too fast but couldn't stop herself. "Formal duties as a representative of Earth and all that nonsense. You know how it is. I'll call you back later to find out when we can get together. Bye."

The instant she disconnected, her apologetic smile fled. She rubbed her face clean of the perspiration mask that covered it and wiped her hands on her sweats.

Bullet dodged, she thought. Or had it been? Were they already on their way over? It was early yet, but that meant little, especially if they intended to accomplish more than dinner. If they were en route, she couldn't be home when they arrived. Certainly sharp-eyed Breft would see through any excuse she gave them if they met face to face.

Her heart pounding, Amelia fled her quarters.

Chapter Eight

Vrill's home was an ode to sensuality. The scentwood exuded a tropical fragrance. The fire banked around the base of a fountain, which splashed an accompaniment to the main room's waterfall basin. In the middle of the fountain, the stone figures of a Plasian man and woman shared an ecstatic embrace; the female figure rode the male, her arms and legs wrapped about his naked body. The fountain sprinkled water on her enraptured face.

Carved phalluses of different sizes and species decorated shelves and tables. Amelia had overcome enough of her embarrassment in the past to recognize the artistic talent that went into the statuettes. Some were made of stone, some were crystal, and some were carved from exotic woods and rubbed gleaming smooth by years of handling.

Silken fabric draped the walls and ceiling, creating a lush jeweled turquoise setting. The folds of material pulled back from the windows, allowing the suns to paint gold tones on the carpet's white plush.

Amelia stood pale and shivering just inside the closed door as Vrill stared at her. The Plasian took Amelia's sweating hand in her cool one. "What has happened dear friend?"

Amelia burst into tears. "I don't know. I don't know what to think."

Vrill slid an arm around her waist and eased her towards the overstuffed lounger. "Settle yourself here. You're shaking all over! I'll fix you a drink to soothe your nerves, and you'll tell me what's happened."

Amelia told her the entire story, starting from the night of the party. She sipped the drink Vrill prepared, and she did feel a little more relaxed. She told her friend everything, including the recent temptation to return to Kalquor with the clan. By the time she revealed her fear she might be pregnant, the drink had soothed her tears away.

Confusion and concern mixed freely on Vrill's face at the end of Amelia's story. She patted the human on the shoulder. "It's simple enough to discover if you carry a child. Wait here."

Vrill left her spot by Amelia. She returned carrying what looked like a glass tube with a syringe within it. "Hold out your arm," she said.

Amelia obeyed. Vrill pressed one end of the tube against the inside of Amelia's forearm. The needle inside moved quickly; it withdrew before she registered the prick of pain.

Vrill took the tube from Amelia's arm on which a single drop of blood appeared. The tube flashed orange.

"No baby," Vrill said. She smiled. "Not that being pregnant is such a concern. If you're not ready for a child, you can freeze the embryo until you want it."

Amelia felt more weight slip from her. "What a relief. I still don't know if Flencik tested me for compatibility though. What if he did? What do I do?"

Vrill's brows knitted together. "Don't be offended, but I find your behavior truly confusing, even rather insane. You admit Rajhir's clan gives you more sensual pleasure than any Earther has provided you. The Kalquorians can give you a life most of us only dream of -- a life of devotion, loyalty, and dedication to your happiness. Most importantly, Flencik can reverse your nerve damage. He can give you back your art, which is your whole life and a gift to the rest of the universe."

"What about the other women? For all I know, they've been taken against their will!"

"For all you know, they went gladly. Even if they didn't, how is it your concern? You didn't kidnap them."

Amelia struggled for the words to make Vrill understand. "I thought having fun with the Kalquorians wouldn't affect anyone else. Nobody else would know, and no one would get hurt. Now I realize this relationship might have opened the doors to innocent women being victimized."

Vrill pursed her lips. "Do you have any idea what the life of a Matara is like?"

"What does that have to do with anything?"

"Hear me out. The Matara wants for nothing. The rest of the clan would go hungry to feed her. They would go naked to clothe her. They would kill for her; they would die for her. Her smile is their sun; her tears, their hell. She is their goddess to worship and adore."

Vrill took a breath before continuing. "Let us theorize the Kalquorians have abducted these missing women. Kalquor is a rich planet in ores and natural resources. Everyone there has a share of the wealth. The Earther Mataras will live in fine homes. They will enjoy the best foods, clothes, jewels, and any material goods they wish for. Their clans will care for them, ensuring good health and long lives. You already know from experience that their medical care is centuries ahead of Earth's. Most of all, the clans will love these women unconditionally, for that is the Kalquorian way. Do your Earth men offer that? Only a few, sadly enough. Most of your men, by your own admission, see you as slaves to their lusts at the worst and slaves for breeding at best. Earther women are slaves already! So what if the Earther Mataras fight or beg for their freedom at first? As time passes, they will know their good fortune and cherish their new lives. You know your own life will only get better with Rajhir's clan."

Amelia shook her head. "We're not that simple a race, Vrill. We have a saying on Earth: 'a gilded cage is still a cage'. It has to be our free choice to live with them."

"They would give you your heart's desire," Vrill said. "How could you not choose that?"

Amelia knew then that their cultures were too different for Vrill to understand. Never had she felt so alone.

* * * *

Late that night, Amelia rushed into her quarters and locked the door behind her. She leaned against it, listening to her heart quiet. Getting the short distance from the shuttle to her door had been a terrifying five seconds that seemed to never end. Every shadow seemed a threat. Every pool of darkness menaced. Every sound was the snarl of an angry Kalquorian. She'd run as fast as possible to the safety of her quarters; if the Kalquorians were waiting outside, she'd escaped. She had gained the safety of her apartment. If they pounded on the door all night, their only reward would be sore knuckles.

Amelia's gasping breath quieted as she relaxed. She pressed the light button. Nothing happened. She tried again, but the apartment remained dark. None of the floating globes flared to life.

The triple moons, dim sisters to the twin suns, shone through the banks of windows, casting everything into silhouette. She groped her way to the com to call Maintenance. The silence bore down on her like a weight. Instead of the quiet of emptiness, she heard the silence of held breath, of watching eyes. Amelia looked at the unmoving shadows, her hand poised over the com.

Get hold of yourself. No one was waiting for you outside, and no one's in here. The clan doesn't have the security code to your apartment.

Despite her internal advice, creeping terror forced her to call out. "Hello? Is someone here?"

Her voice quavered in the still air. No one answered. Feeling foolish yet relieved, she shook her head at herself. "Come on, Amelia. You're too old to be scared of the dark."

"Call Maintenance," she commanded the com. As the oppressive silence spun on uninterrupted, Amelia's heart quickened. The com sat unresponsive. Dead, like the globes.

She backed away from the desk, her eyes searching the shadows. Every muscle screamed to run. She kept control by the slightest of margins.

I'll go back to Vrill's, she thought, trying to look everywhere at once as she backed towards the door. *I'll spend the night and call Maintenance from her place tomorrow morning.*

A part of her knew her own foolishness. Before she backed into Breft, she knew escape ceased to be an option. Massive arms wrapped around her, pinning her against the Nobek. Resignation deadened her

limbs. She accepted the capture. She protested only with a low moan behind the hand that covered her mouth.

Two hulking shadows stepped before her. Fingers stroked her hair as Rajhir's voice floated in the air.

"Don't be afraid, my little one. You know we would never hurt you. Our Matara comes to no harm."

He bent toward her. His breath was warm against her neck as he sank his fangs in. He bit, pumping the intoxicant into her blood until only Breft's grip kept her upright. Darkness blacker than the night shut down her vision. She was swept up into the cradle of strong arms. She heard the door open. The night breeze caressed her skin as she lost consciousness.

Chapter Nine

Something pressed against Amelia's lips; a mouth devoured hers. Her brain fuzzed by sleep, she responded, parting her lips to permit the warm tongue entry. A thrill of passion shot between her legs, jolting her awake as the kiss ended.

"Sweet Amelia," Rajhir's voice breathed. "Our Matara wakes."

She opened her eyes. Amber globes floated against the ceiling, casting hazy light over her surroundings. The dark tinted windows made it impossible to gauge whether a new day had dawned. Scentwood crackled in the pit, wafting sensual musk into the Kalquorian clan's quarters.

The three naked aliens bent over her as she lay embedded in cloudlike cushions of the lounger. They fondled her bare skin, making her wet, and the scent of their arousal filled her senses. She saw their readiness for pleasuring and felt desire tumble through her body despite a stab of fear.

"Why have you brought me here?" she said, shoving Flencik's hands from her breasts. He returned to massaging the soft mounds, brushing her resistance away as if shooing off a fly.

Rajhir's fingertips traced the contours of her face, his lips curled in a smile. "I think you already know why. Why else would you hide from us? I will tell you anyway; you are compatible with us for the purpose of childbearing. You will take your place in this clan. We claim our Matara."

Despite the smile, he delivered his statement with cold command. It told her he entertained no compromise, no debate. No argument could sway him. No mercy and no way out.

Panic fed her masochistic desire, but she struggled, slapping Rajhir and Flencik's hands and kicking Breft who stroked her sex. "You have no right to kidnap me! You can't force me to be your Matara!"

Flencik seemed not to feel her hands snapping against his flesh. His tone mild, he said, "We do not force. We will convince you to join us."

Her hands curled into tiny fists. "Let me go!"

She struck a glancing blow to Rajhir's chin. He blinked; his only reaction. Flencik caught her wrists and pinned them over her head against the lounger. Breft restrained her by the ankles and held her legs

apart for Rajhir. The Dramok positioned himself for the first thrust,
holding her hips and pressing his stiffness against her. Her passion
sparked once again, and she sobbed with helpless shame as her hips
bucked toward his maleness. He knew she wanted him. They knew
she wanted them all.

Rajhir entered her, ignoring her conflicting reactions. He slid in, their
combined wetness easing his path. His face softened with ecstasy.
"Your body betrays your desire. You will stay, little one. In time you
will understand you belong to us."

She cried, hating them and wanting them at the same time. Rajhir
licked her tears from her cheeks as he moved within her. Her body
welcomed his thrusts even as her mind fought against submission. The
friction of their sexes sparked a fire within her, then an inferno. "No,"
she said, shaking her head, trying to deny the climax that roared
through her body. "No!" she screamed as it had its way with her,
pulsing the flesh surrounding Rajhir's. The clan's leader continued his
rhythmic thrusts as she shuddered beneath him.

Her body, in full revolt to her wishes, betrayed her over and over. He
brought her to shuddering climax twice more before releasing his seed
into her womb. Then he traded places with Breft. Rajhir held her
ankles as the Nobek had despite her lacking the strength or will to resist
them anymore.

Amelia felt incapable of any more orgasms. Breft penetrated deep
into her, his thrusts strong. His predatory gaze drilled into her soul, and
he licked his lips while staring into her eyes. Again the heat built within
her and exploded, her ragged cries that of an animal. Breft came, his
own growls beast-like too.

"Please," she said as Flencik took Breft's place. Need worked the
Imdiko's face, his penises livid exclamation marks. Watching his
clanmates' pleasure drove him beyond conscience to achieve his own.
He ignored her weak pleas for mercy. Against his usual placid nature,
the Imdiko's taking of Amelia was rough, almost brutal. To her own
weary shame, she responded to his invasion, her hips bucking to meet
each pounding thrust. She wanted him to hurt her until she hated him.
She wanted him to drive away the longing that persisted despite
knowing she must escape the clan.

Instead, the pain of his forceful lovemaking intensified her desire.
Her entire body quaked with climax, the flame of orgasm reaching to
her fingers and toes. Then she lay limp beneath Flencik, all her strength
sapped as his penis pulsed and the ribbon of semen unfurled in her

belly.

He bit her, sending the intoxicant into her body once more to render her unconscious. She dove into the oblivion, eager to escape them, to escape herself. Her last thought before darkness overtook her was *I have to keep resisting. They'll understand how wrong it is to force me sooner or later.*

But how long to outlast them, to convince them she would never willingly join the clan?

* * * *

A sting on Amelia's inner thigh woke her from heavy sleep. She whimpered, but was too lethargic to open her eyes. The pain ended almost as soon as it began. Warmth flowed throughout her body from that spot on her leg, and after a few moments of languorous curiosity, she figured out a clan member was biting her there with his fangs.

The fangs retracted, and the mouth kissed and licked its way up her thigh. Amelia kept her eyes closed, all her concentration centered on the hot wet path climbing closer and closer to her female center.

The mouth reached the crease where her leg joined to her vulva and licked her there before pausing. She heard a deep intake of breath as the man crouched between her legs inhaled her scent. Fingers parted her sex, and she imagined what he saw: soft folds of flesh in varying shades of pink, glistening with wetness. The man exhaled with a low, drawn out growl, and Amelia felt her lower regions tighten with desire.

The fingers spread the lips of her sex wider, and she felt the warmth of his breath as he contemplated the view. Amelia lay quiet and open beneath his gaze, her body warming with anticipation of what he might do to her next.

Another deep inhale, another growl. She remained still, euphoria coursing through her body as the intoxicant did its work.

"Are you awake, little one?" Rajhir breathed, his voice deep but tentative as if afraid speech would break the spell he held on her.

Amelia didn't answer. What would he do to her if he thought her still asleep, completely pliable to his wishes? Would he continue his seemingly clandestine exploration? Or would he withdraw in disappointment from her, disinterested in her unresponsiveness?

I'd better say something, she thought. Leaden though her limbs felt, she was eager for pleasuring.

You're supposed to be resisting him, you whore. Remember what his race has done!

Amelia frowned inwardly at the shrill memory of her mother's voice. What was she warning Amelia about? She tried to get her sluggish mind to work, to remember exactly what had happened to her.

Before her thoughts could clear, the tip of Rajhir's tongue touched her sex, gently tracing the outlines of her secret folds. The melting warmth travelling through her belly quieted all concerns.

His fingers kept her open for his tasting, allowing him access deep inside her. The teasing, barely-there touch became a gentle lapping as he consumed the wetness flowing from her body. Amelia's breathing deepened with pleasure as his tongue laved her over and over.

A chuckle sounded from overhead. "She's unconscious, but she's still feeling it," Breft said.

"And liking it very much." Flencik's voice came from her right.

Knowing the other two were there watching Rajhir pleasure her seemingly helpless body made her sex spasm. A tiny whimper escaped her parted lips. Very male laughter answered the sound.

Rajhir's mouth closed over Amelia's sex. He fed on her quivering flesh, his growls vibrating the sensitive part of her until her back arched in response. She managed to pry her heavy eyelids open long enough to see Breft naked and leaning over her against the back of the lounger and Flencik, naked also, kneeling on the other side. Both watched her face with avid eyes as Rajhir continued to devour her from below.

Amelia's eyes slid shut again. Waves of pleasure rippled through her body. Her world centered on Rajhir's mouth on her, on his tongue probing her entrance, on his lips closing over her clitoris to gently suck on the bud.

"You're awake now, aren't you?" Flencik's fingers stroked her hair.

Amelia emitted a wordless singsong, unsure if she was trying to answer his question or simply vocalizing her pleasure. Another burst of masculine laughter rang out.

"Awake and senseless with lovemaking. You're a master, my Dramok," Breft chuckled.

Rajhir growled his own wordless response and returned to feasting on Amelia's sex. He licked and sucked and mouthed her as if starving. Her moans were almost constant now; one bled into the next until she was nearly humming. She lay completely still beneath him, unable to discern if she was weak from desire or his earlier bite. Either way, her limbs were leaden, unable to do more than twitch and tremble, and she was totally at his mercy.

He coaxed her to orgasm with his mouth alone. The waves of

pleasure built higher and higher until bright, sweet sensation rolled gently through her belly. She felt her womb melt and flow like a river overflowing its banks. She cried her pleasure with quiet breathless "oh's", sounding like a delighted child on Christmas morning.

Rajhir fed from her body until her spasms quieted. She slit her eyes open to see him boost himself to his knees. He kneeled between her legs, his arousal curved high against his abdomen.

"Feeling better?" he asked.

"That was nice." Her voice was still breathy. She knew she should be concerned about something, but looking into Rajhir's dark eyes, knowing he was about to seek his own release, her muddled mind refused to clear. *Must not be that important,* she decided.

"Good. Now I will let you be nice to me." He lowered himself over her, the length of his body pressed to hers. Her legs, already spread from his earlier attentions, finally found the strength to wrap around his waist. His penises lay heavily against her belly, pulsing and hot.

Rajhir's mouth found hers, and he kissed her much as he'd pleasured her lower regions. The kiss was eager, devouring. His tongue plunged into her mouth to twine around its twin. She tasted her own sea salt flavor on him.

He positioned himself to enter her without breaking the kiss. She moaned into his mouth as he pressed into her, burying his flesh in hers in one slippery smooth motion. She gripped his shoulders as he drove against her, hurting her in that deep, wonderful way that always translated into pleasure. He grabbed her hips, his fingers digging deeply into the flesh of her buttocks as he pulled her harder against his fierce rhythm. The change in angle meant he was rubbing against that sensitive spot inside her, making her cry out, making her claw at his shoulders and back, making her convulse with pleasure that threatened to turn her inside out.

Rajhir rode her harder, his growl becoming a roar. He lifted himself as if doing a pushup so they could watch him plunge in and out of her. Amelia shrieked again, the sight and sensation overloading her last vestiges of control. Her nails raked Rajhir's chest, and he bared his fangs at her in a snarl.

Suddenly his back bowed as his climax took over, and he screamed at the ceiling as his rhythm faltered. Amelia felt him spasm inside her, felt him surrendering to her body.

Rajhir collapsed on top of her, his breath sobbing in and out. She lay still beneath him, feeling the last of his convulsions inside her body. He felt so warm, so good, so right. Yet alarms were still going off in her subconscious, letting her know she was forgetting something very important.

If it's something that will ruin this moment, I don't want to remember. I just want to stay like this for as long as possible, happy, contented, possessed...

Imprisoned.

Amelia gasped as the memory of her conversation with Jack Frank and the clan's abduction returned. She pushed weakly against Rajhir. "You kidnapped me!"

He lifted his face from her hair to regard her, his face carefully neutral. "We claimed you for our Matara."

Amelia fought the languor that kept her pliable to her captors. "No, no, I can't. This is wrong."

"The choice is no longer yours, little one." He stroked her cheek lovingly despite the harshness of his words. "Not only is your joining the clan good for us, it is the best option for you. Earth is killing your spirit."

She tried to come up with an argument, but damn it, she couldn't *think*. "It's not fair," she sighed. "You bit me."

"Yes, sweet Amelia. It's keeping you from being unhappy with us for the moment." He kissed her with the lightest pressure on the lips.

He withdrew his body from hers. Flencik touched some of the claw marks on his chest. "Would you like me to treat these?"

Rajhir looked at the injuries with pride. "Of course not. I think she gave me more than you. Deeper too."

Flencik narrowed his eyes at his leader's smug grin. "Let me see what I can do about that."

He bent over Amelia, his hands finding her breasts. He pinched her nipples, and she cried out, arching against him as pleasure found her yet again. He lowered his face to hers, claiming her mouth with his own.

All thoughts of resistance fled Amelia's mind as desire fed the intoxicating effects of Rajhir's bite. She gave herself over to Flencik, allowing him to suck her tongue into his mouth as he filled his hands with her soft flesh.

One of his hands left her breasts to travel down to stroke her sex with gentle fingertips. She tossed her head as he found her pleasure bud, the touch electric. He recaptured her mouth with his and continued to tease her clitoris with feathery strokes. She cried out, her hips jerking involuntarily.

Flencik wrapped his other arm around her, clasping her chest to his. He climbed up on the lounger and tangled his legs in hers. She lay trapped in his grip.

He kept teasing her with light touches to her clitoris. She squirmed in an effort to rub the aching bud harder against his fingers, but he held her securely, not allowing her to find satisfaction.

"Please," she groaned, remembering how he'd enjoyed her begging Breft before.

"No. Not yet," he smiled, the light in his eyes cruel.

Rajhir and Breft watched while he played with her, grinning as she moaned and writhed in alternate efforts to realize pleasure or escape. He held her easily, refusing to bring her to climax, yet stoking her internal fire hotter and hotter.

"Please Flencik, please do me," she begged for what felt like the hundredth time.

"What do you want?" he murmured in her hair, running fingertips over her straining bud.

"I want you inside me."

"Is that what you want? Do you really, truly want me inside you?" He ran a finger, slick from her wetness, all around her clitoris, not quite touching her there.

"Yes!" she screamed, the voluptuous heat in her belly driving her mad.

"As you wish."

His tone was more threat than tenderness, but Amelia had no time to consider what that might mean. He released her, got up from the lounger, and picked her up. She swung through the air until suddenly she found herself landing on all fours on the floor, and Flencik was behind her with his hands locked on her hips.

"Oh God, thank you," she moaned as he pulled her backwards toward his eager flesh. She felt him against her sex, still aching from Rajhir's assault. He stabbed into her tender flesh, his front organ hot velvet steel.

Amelia's arms collapsed under her, and she wailed into the plush carpet as Flencik drove himself into her. He found the spot inside her instantly and the pain of taking in the well-endowed Kalquorian was sublimated in the incredible sensation of his strokes against that bundle of nerves.

Flencik pulled back until the tip of his penis barely remained inside her. With deliberate strength, he ran the length of himself back in, finding the end of her womb as his groin slapped against her buttocks.

Amelia sobbed into the carpet as he worked her mercilessly. It felt so good after all the teasing, and orgasm was rushing at her, rising through her, crashing against her. Pleasure crested within her, and she cried out in gratitude at the release.

She found little relief however; a higher peak waited beyond that the first climax, and yet a higher one after that. She screamed as fast as she could draw breath. One explosion after another burst through her until her world was nothing but desire and sensation.

Flencik abruptly pulled out of her, leaving her gasping. Before she could catch her breath properly however, he pressed himself against her anus, seeking entrance into that taboo orifice. She sobbed as he took her, still too caught up in pleasure to resist. His smaller penis found her vagina, and the double penetration brought her screaming again.

Flencik wasn't rough, but his size was enough to make her feel he might split her in half. Even as she sobbed, her body convulsed in orgasm. Amelia couldn't separate pleasure and pain; the two were one and the same for her. One moment she struggled to escape the Imdiko, the next she thrust backward against him to take him deeper. It was torture, it was ecstasy; it was heaven, it was hell.

She looked back at her lover, wanting to see his face as he took her. He loomed over and behind her, a terrible god of destructive lust. His pupils had nearly swallowed the purple irises; his eyes were black wells in his straining face. His fangs were bared as he watched himself work her writhing body. He flicked his gaze to her face, and he grinned to see her looking back at him. His thrusts became more powerful, and she shrieked as he drove her over the precipice again. His roar joined her cry, and he pulsed within her, filling her with his seed.

Utterly destroyed, Amelia lay motionless on the floor, her face in the carpet again. Flencik held her buttocks up to his groin as he convulsed within her, his vocalizations quieting from howls to soft grunts to sighs. Then he was quiet for a moment before giving her bottom a few light spanks and withdrawing.

"I can't stand yet," he gasped. "Breft, will you fetch my portable kit?"

"Of course."

Amelia heard the Nobek walk away to enter the room behind the copper door. She couldn't stand either; she couldn't move even a finger. She ached in all the right places, but some of the aches were deepening into real hurt. She wondered how much damage Flencik had inflicted on her.

"Amelia, are you conscious?" Rajhir sounded a little worried.

She managed a sighing whimper as she heard Breft return to the room. He snorted. "I notice you did not ask if she is all right."

"She is not, but she will be in a moment." Flencik moved slightly behind her. She heard movement she couldn't identify, a rustling as if objects were being pushed around. Then fingers, covered in a cool, moist substance, gently stroked her anus. The pain from rough use disappeared immediately, and the relief eased tension Amelia hadn't realized she'd been holding.

The fingers withdrew, then one covered in more of the salve he'd used on her gently penetrated her anus, relieving hurt which had become serious.

He treated her sex as well. Amelia still had no strength to move, but all the pain was now gone. "Better," she breathed.

"I am sorry I didn't have this on hand to relieve you right away," Flencik said. "Hold still. I took away your pain, and now I have to treat some injuries. They will heal quickly. None are serious," he added reassuringly.

She felt warmth against her buttocks, as if he'd turned a heat lamp on. The warmth increased, but not unpleasantly.

"Hand me the probe," Flencik said, presumably to Breft. More rustling, a metallic clink, and the heat focused stronger to her violated flesh. Something small and hard slid into her vagina, and the warmth was within her. It felt strangely nice. Amelia lay still, letting Flencik treat the delightful abuse he'd given her.

After several minutes, the medical instrument was withdrawn. The point of heat moved to her rectum, and Flencik sent the instrument into her. He kept it there longer, probably because he'd inflicted more injury to the less elastic flesh.

Amelia's head was beginning to clear from the effects of Rajhir's bite. She wondered how the hell she was supposed to resist the Kalquorians if they kept her intoxicated all the time.

There's got to be a way out of this, she thought. She had to find some means of escape. But how?

"It is done," Flencik announced, and he withdrew the instrument from her body. "All lacerations and bruising are healed."

"For now," Breft growled, and Amelia's heart skipped a beat. He couldn't possibly plan to make love after what Flencik had put her through.

"I'm tired," she whimpered as callused hands stroked her upturned buttocks. She began to crawl away.

Breft seized her ankles and dragged her backward towards himself with an evil laugh. Amelia looked back at Flencik for help, but he only smiled. He placed a small metallic rod into a case, snapped the case shut, and moved out of the way.

"You might want to bite her again. I do not think she will cooperate anymore."

"I do not mind if she fights me," Breft said. He flipped Amelia onto her back and lay on top of her, clasping her wrists over her head with one hand.

Amelia struggled despite knowing Breft's strength was too much for her. "I don't want to. You're all being too rough."

"You like it rough," Breft whispered, rubbing his rigid sexes against her legs. "You like pain. It makes the pleasure sweeter for you."

"No," she lied, tears of humiliation coming to her eyes. "I don't like pain. I don't like being kidnapped. And I don't like you." She clenched her legs together.

"You will soon like me very much," he promised, using his muscular thighs to easily pry apart her legs. He opened her wide. She cried out as his sexes touched hers.

"If you get tired of holding her, there are the restraints, if they will fit her." Rajhir said. He relaxed on the lounger, watching the show.

"Ooh, I forgot about those," Breft said. He grinned, and his fangs unhinged for a moment.

Flencik returned from his lab and flopped down next to Rajhir. "So did I. Since she is being difficult, now would be a good time to in break them."

"Break them in," Breft corrected absently.

Amelia yanked hard on her arms. She didn't want to be restrained, not when they were being so cruel. Breft's hand was like a vise, holding her easily.

He stood, pulling her up with him. "Where were they?"

Rajhir pointed to a curtained wall. "Behind that."

Breft half-pulled, half dragged Amelia to the wall the Dramok indicated. He swept the curtain aside to reveal metal cuffs attached to the wall: two slightly above Amelia's shoulder height, and two near the floor.

"Plasians know how to have fun," he remarked, looking the restraints over.

"Don't you dare!" Amelia shouted. She tried to kick Breft. He dodged the blow easily and used his own leg to sweep hers out from under her. He caught her about the waist to keep her from falling to the floor.

Quicker than she could think, he had her up against the wall. A cuff snapped around one wrist, and he stretched the other arm to manacle it as well. Amelia was bound helplessly.

"Such tiny wrists," Breft mused. "She is as small-boned as the Plasians." He crouched down to cuff her ankles, easily overpowering her desperate struggles. "These fit her perfectly."

Arms and legs spread, Amelia had no way to protect herself. She hung from the wall, completely at Breft's mercy. With nothing else left to do, she hung her head and sobbed.

"Why are you crying?" the Nobek asked softly. He ran his hands up and down the insides of her legs. "You know you will enjoy what I do to you."

"It's perverted. No one should like this," Amelia answered.

"But you do." Breft traced his finger through the fresh warm moisture wetting her pubic curls.

She squirmed at his touch and cried harder. *Nasty girl! Whore!* Her mother's voice had rarely been so loud.

"Why do you call it perverted?" Rajhir asked. "It hurts no one and makes you feel desire."

"There is nothing wrong with being bound," Breft added. He stroked her sex with a bold touch. "It adds excitement to lovemaking. You liked it the day of the picnic."

"You bit me and I was drunk. I couldn't help it that day." Her voice was hoarse with tears, but her insides were melting with his stimulation. "Don't make me do this. I don't want to be bad."

Breft stepped close to whisper in her ear. "But you are bad, my little Amelia. You are bad, and I will reward you for it."

Her heart quickened. Two of his fingers plunged inside her and she spasmed with a cry. Her arms strained against the cuffs, but the restraints held.

Breft worked his fingers in her, making her wetter, making her hotter. She twisted, trying to dislodge the digits, but she simply could not move far enough to escape the pleasuring. His fingers continued to stroke her core without missing a beat.

He bent his head to whisper in her ear. "There is nowhere to go. You cannot hide. You love me doing this to you."

Amelia turned her face as far away from his as she could, squeezing her eyes shut and willing her body to quiet.

"Amelia, I am going to enjoy having you trapped helpless while I make love to you," Breft breathed. She felt him draw close. His body pressed against hers, his sexes thick between them. Amelia couldn't repress the shiver that ran through her.

His hand moved from her sex to his own, positioning himself for the first thrust. "Wide open for my pleasure. You are mine, my sweet."

He entered her deliberately, as if to savor his command over her helpless body. Amelia groaned between her clenched teeth. Damn him, it felt so good for him to fill her slowly.

"You are so tight and yet soft and yielding. Warm," he whispered. His hands stroked up and down her ribs, hips, and thighs. "I love being inside you, feeling you all around me. I love how your stomach trembles when you get close to pleasure. Even now, while you refuse to look at me, I feel how wet you are. I feel your sex clutching mine, drawing me in deeper."

"Shut up," Amelia whimpered. His warm breath tickled her ear, making things below squeeze tight. The things he said and the low confident voice he said them with only intensified the sensations of his lovemaking. She trembled noticeably and hated herself for the weakness.

"Feel me taking you. Know I can do whatever I wish to your delicious little body, and you cannot stop me."

Amelia heard the predatory smile in his voice as he so very slowly pumped his penises in and out of her. Every stroke was delightful torture, making her hips roll forward to greet him despite her attempts to not respond. His tongue licked delicately at the curves of her ear. Amelia jerked at the unexpected sensual contact. Her hands and feet stopped short in their bonds, reminding her of Breft's complete control over her. The heat in her womb grew.

Where are you now, Mama? Why aren't you telling me how evil, how perverted I am? Tell me of the punishments in hell I'll suffer for sins of the flesh. Tell me of the eternity of flames for a few moments of pleasure. Make me not want this. Save me, damn you!

Mama's voice was silent, lost in the gentle thrusts of Breft's hot flesh, lost in his whispered temptations.

"I would like to set you free in the forest and let you run from me. I would like to hunt you like prey, to follow your scent, to sense your fear as I draw close. I will chase you down, throw you to the ground, tear your clothes from your body. I take you like an animal, biting and clawing and rutting while you struggle to escape, a struggle you cannot win. I take you hard, prying you open with my sexes, and you climax for me, screaming while I take all I wish."

Amelia moaned. His rhythm quickened, the friction making her hotter, wetter. Her teeth unclenched to allow her gasping breath to come faster. She moved up and down against the wall as Breft drove against her.

He continued to tease her with whispered fantasy. "I think I will leave you bound to the wall so I can take you when I please. So I can do this—" he cupped her breasts and pinched her nipples until she spasmed with a cry "—as I walk by. You will be my beautiful, pleasurable decoration. You will hang here for the enjoyment of my eyes and my body. You who once created art will be artwork yourself."

Amelia was sobbing now as his thrusts grew more powerful. She felt her helplessness keenly; she knew he could make good on his threats to leave her cuffed to the wall, to make her a toy to play with when he wished. The fear enhanced the heat in her loins, and she felt her body cycling up that wonderful peak once more.

Breft grabbed her chin and made her face him. His mouth smashed down on hers, forcing hers open to take his tongue. He held her head still while his free hand molded her breasts with rough care. Her moans under his assault were continuous as his hips quickened against her. He plunged into her, and he growled.

Amelia felt the hardness of his fangs against her lips, and she knew he was close. Her own peak was within reach, sweeping closer. Breft pounded her against the wall, his rhythm faltering even as his hips drove harder. He reared back, his fangs nicking her tongue as he pulled his face away to roar his climax. The cut stung for an instant, then Amelia's own orgasm flooded her body, leaving her clawing at the wall and thrashing in her bonds.

Breft stayed inside her until she quieted. Before he disengaged, he leaned close to whisper once more in her ear. "I would die for you, my little Earther."

Amelia started at the feeling in his voice. He looked away as he moved away from her, as if afraid to meet her eyes. He walked to the bathing basin and plunged in, splashing water to the floor. He sank down and sighed as water swirled around his muscled frame. His face relaxed into a contented smile.

Rajhir still sat on the lounger, his eyes taking in the view of Amelia cuffed to the wall. Flencik emerged from the cooking area with a tray of food. He brought it to Amelia.

"You must be starving." He waved a nellus berry beneath her nose. "Eat."

She longed to take the morsel he offered, but pride stiffened her spine. "Let me out of these manacles first."

"I will let you out when you eat." He ran the berry across her lips, teasing her.

Anything to be released, she thought, parting her lips for the first bite. Then she thought better of it and jerked her head away. "No," she said between clenched teeth.

"Amelia." The one word held soft reproach.

"Let me go."

He sighed heavily. "If I let you out of the cuffs, you will eat?"

"Not just the cuffs. *Let me go.*"

The lounger creaked, letting Amelia know Rajhir had risen from his seat. She heard his heavy tread approach. Fear threaded through her belly.

"Amelia, you will eat the food Flencik gives you."

"No."

A splash signaled Breft's exit from the basin. They were about to gang up on her. She lifted her chin and looked at the three grim faces surrounding her, hopefully appearing more resolute than she felt.

"What do you think you will accomplish by refusing your meal?" Rajhir asked. His voice was quiet and controlled, but Amelia saw the darkness in his eyes. "What do you get out of making yourself miserable?"

"It's called a hunger strike. I won't eat in protest of you kidnapping me and holding me against my will. If you care anything about me, you'll let me go. If not, I starve to death." Amelia felt a stab of pride at how steady her words sounded.

Breft made a sound of exasperation. "I will bite her, and she will eat. Argument over." He moved toward her.

Rajhir's arm shot out, barring the Nobek from sinking his fangs in Amelia's neck. "No. Put the food away, Flencik."

Flencik stared at the clan's leader. "She needs to eat. It has been almost a day since she last—"

"Let her feel hunger." Rajhir stared into Amelia's eyes. He spoke to her, his voice steel under the outward softness. "We could have done this gently, but you have made your decision. I tell you now I will not be coerced into releasing you from my clan. Until you eat you will be punished. No more bites, no more intoxication to ease your conscience when we bring your body to pleasure." His grin appeared, frightening in its savagery. "And we will be enjoying your body with great frequency. We will enjoy your body in ways that you fear; with bondage, with pain, and with domination. We will do this because you respond to those ways best. You will be humiliated because you cannot avoid the desire your body feels."

Amelia swallowed past her fear. "I'm not bluffing, Rajhir."

"I know. It will hurt us to see you suffer, but you must accept you are our Matara."

"I can't. What you're doing is wrong."

"Then you leave me no choice. Those who adore you must torment you until you agree to eat." The savage anticipation on his face had been replaced by sadness. He turned away.

Breft also turned his back on Amelia, returning to the basin. He sat in the water heavily. He looked at her, and his expression was also sad. He and Rajhir looked as if she'd crushed their feelings.

Flencik stood before her with the tray of food, indecision stamped on his broad face. He looked at Rajhir.

"Put it away, Imdiko." Rajhir's tone was gentle.

Flencik turned back to Amelia. "Please, Amelia," he implored. "I know you are hungry."

She was starving. Her stomach growled, trying to convince her of her foolishness. She stiffened her spine and looked into his beseeching eyes. "Let me go."

Flencik's shoulders drooped. He walked away from her, carrying the tray of delicious food into the kitchen. His head hung down. As he passed Rajhir, Amelia heard him murmur, "I hate this."

Rajhir didn't respond. He simply stood in the middle of the room, staring into space. No one said anything else for a long time.

Chapter Ten

Amelia squeezed her eyes shut, as if doing so would also shut out the sensations of the vibrating instrument Flencik pressed to her sex. The soft, fleshlike pad thrummed against her exposed clitoris, making her arch in her bonds. She cried out.

Breft had left on a mysterious errand earlier, but she'd gotten no relief from the desires of the other two clan members. Rajhir and Flencik had placed her in the restraints facing the wall after she'd wakened from restless sleep. Now the Dramok focused his mouth and fingers on her anus as Flencik teased her sensitive womanhood with his new toy. He'd concocted it from his medical supplies, informing Amelia with a devilish grin of what it would do to her. Amelia had never heard of the vibrating sex toys her less repressed ancestors had enjoyed; the thought of such a thing would have horrified her. Watching Flencik manufacture his instrument from nonorganic skin grafting material, a vaginal examination probe, and the small motor of a muscle-stimulating device, she'd been convinced she'd never respond to the bizarre contraption. It would be too perverted for even her freakish sexual hungers.

She was wrong.

The probe, made almost Kalquorian penis-thick by the covering of fake skin, operated like a piston. It extended into her vagina then retracted, pushing in and out at varying speeds which Flencik controlled with a switch. A lip of the skin grafting material covered her clitoris. The muscle stimulation motor was wired into the pad, sending vibrations of varying strength, again controlled by a switch.

Amelia's hips bucked uncontrollably as the device delivered pleasure. She heard Flencik chuckle through her groans. "I say the test is a success."

Rajhir rubbed a callused thumb over her anus. "I agree. It will be good to use on her while we sleep or are unable to pleasure her because of other duties. Will the harness work?"

"I hope so. It will be useless if someone must to hold it in place all the time."

Flencik kept the device pressed against Amelia's quivering flesh as he threaded its straps around her waist and thighs. While he worked to attach it to her body, Rajhir pressed his thumb into her nether orifice, sending fresh pleasure through her body. Quiet sobs punctuated her louder moans as Amelia inwardly berated herself for enjoying such vile activities.

The clan had made good on Rajhir's threat to pleasure Amelia with sex that included bondage and rough play. Flencik's machine was only the latest indignation she'd been forced to endure. The more helpless they made her, the more depraved the sex, the hungrier her body responded. She had no ability to stop the orgasms that left her hanging exhausted in the manacles.

"Let us see if it will hold," Flencik murmured, securing the last strap in place. He turned the vibrator to its highest setting and the probe to its fastest pace before taking his hand off the device.

The intensity of the stimulation sent Amelia writhing violently. She felt the probe jackhammering her womb, rubbing that most sensitive spot with unrelenting pressure. Flencik had molded the fleshy lip to her clitoris; the vibration seemed to thrum through her very soul. Her head fell back, and her legs went out from under her as all strength drained from her body. With wordless sobs she tried to beg the men to make it stop, but speech proved impossible. Orgasm attacked her with incredible swiftness. The pleasure spiked within her womb, almost painful in its excruciating ecstasy. As the climax crested she lost ability to draw breath. She hung suspended on its point for an eternity, caught between the instant of anticipation and realization. Then she tipped over, and climax steamrolled through her. She found her voice, shrieking to shake the very heavens. She fought the restraints, desperate to escape before the pleasure killed her. Already it built again, threatening to burst her wide open.

"Hold her still," Flencik said, reaching between her legs. Rajhir wrapped his arms around her thighs, halting her struggles long enough for the Imdiko to turn the device off.

Amelia sagged against the wall, gasping and shuddering. Rajhir released her legs and patted her buttocks with affection. "The straps held, but I am not certain you should use that at full strength too often."

Flencik laughed as he removed the device from her still-spasming sex. "No higher than medium setting. At least we know she cannot thrash it loose."

"You bastards," Amelia whispered. She felt weak as a newborn.

"Poor little Matara," Rajhir said, kissing her flushed cheek. "Was it too much?"

She turned away from him, resting her forehead against the wall. She should hate them. She wanted to hate them. Why couldn't she?

Rajhir's fingertips brushed the still trembling lips of her sex. Sensitive from Flencik's demonic vibrator, her hips jerked as her breath caught. Damn it...would she never be able to curb her responses to the Kalquorians?

"Are you ready to eat like a good girl?" he asked. His fingers brushed her again, a clear warning he would subject her to more carnal activity should she refuse.

Tears prickled her eyes, but she stiffened her resolve. "I will not."

"Then we will begin again." He gripped her hips and pressed up against her backside, his penises going to orifices as if drawn by magnets. Amelia braced herself for the delicious pain of his larger organ invading her tightest entrance. She was already moist in anticipation.

Rajhir was just pressing himself into her when the door to the outside swung open, admitting Breft. He strode into the room, hefting a large gray box in his arms.

"You may wish to wait on her punishment until you see this." His dark eyes sparkled with mischief as he grinned at them all.

Rajhir moved back, and Amelia allowed herself to relax a little. God only knew what Breft was up to, but she welcomed the momentary reprieve. It couldn't be any worse than Flencik's device, she reasoned.

"I have looked for new ways to enjoy our Matara, and this appeals to me." He lifted the top of the box and waved the other two men over to view the contents.

Amelia peered over her shoulder to see what new horror awaited her, but her view was blocked by the Kalquorians clustered around Breft's acquisition. The Nobek murmured something, and the other two burst into uproarious laughter.

Not good, Amelia thought. Her stomach executed a slow flip. She pulled against the cuffs holding her to the wall, knowing the futility of the attempt but helpless not to try anyway.

"It too easy goes together," Flencik commented behind her.

"It is sturdy," Breft reassured. "It will take her weight and ours, along with strenuous activity."

That earned another round of raucous laughter, and Amelia jerked against her restraints again. Panic made her heart flutter.

"How did your toy perform?" Breft asked. "Did she respond?"

Rajhir and Flencik snickered. Rajhir said something in Kalquorian, to which Breft laughed harder than ever.

"You should make more and sell them to the Plasians," he managed after the hilarity subsided. "They will make a god of you, Flencik."

"I will take it into consideration. Is this right?"

"You will strain your back at that level. Adjust the height. Now it looks good." Breft's voice raised in a singsong. "A-meee-lia? Look what I brought you."

She cringed at the teasing voice. Slowly she looked over her shoulder towards the grinning clan and the contraption they'd assembled.

At first glance, it looked like a tall table with a padded top. It reached just below groin level on Breft. There was a cushioned hole at one end of its three-foot length, much like the head rest on the massage table Amelia had taken therapy on after her accident. It was too short for a massage table however. Her legs would hang down, and her ass would be in the air.

Her gaze traveled down the metal legs of the table. When she saw the soft restraints attached, she finally understood what she was looking at.

She turned her face back to the wall, afraid her expression would give her away. Her breath quickened, her sex tightened, and moisture seeped down her thighs.

Misinterpreting her hiding her face for dread, Rajhir reminded her, "We do not have to do this. Agree to eat."

Amelia licked her lips but refused to answer. She knew her voice would betray her, would tell them how much she wanted them to strap her to the table, to do all the things they delighted in doing to her. Her body trembled in eager anticipation of the coming punishment.

"Very well," Rajhir said.

She heard the excitement in his voice, the expectant joy that he would be able to lay her on the table, tie her down, and enjoy her body to their mutual pleasure.

She resisted them only because pride demanded it. If the Kalquorians noticed her struggles seemed half-hearted, she hoped they attributed it to the weakness of hunger. They easily secured her to the table.

It was much more comfortable than being manacled to the wall. Amelia's face rested in the cushioned opening. The cloth cuffs gently held her wrists and ankles to the cool metal legs. The end of the soft tabletop ended just above her groin, leaving her sex open and easily accessible to her lovers.

They wasted no time in taking advantage of her vulnerability. Mouths, tongues and teeth attacked her buttocks and thighs. She jerked in response to the erotic sensations of being kissed, licked, and nipped all around her secret flesh. When a set of teeth sank into one buttock hard enough to leave marks, she groaned with heightened desire. The mixture of bondage and pain had the effect on her it always did: it made her want more.

Another bite on the opposite buttock elicited a second soft moan from Amelia's throat. She lifted her hips as far as the restraints allowed, inviting further attention.

"You are having too much fun, little girl," Breft chuckled. "Whatever would your government say?"

"Naughty Amelia likes naughty pleasures," Flencik said, flicking his tongue over her anus.

Amelia's cheeks burned. Tears dropped from her eyes to the floor below. Why did her body insist on responding to such filthy acts? Even as shame washed over her, her legs strained against the restraints in an effort to open herself more to Flencik's wickedly teasing tongue.

More biting mixed pain with Flencik's pleasuring. A tongue ran up her inner thigh, stopping just short of her moist sex. It disappeared to reappear on the opposite thigh to trace an identical path. She writhed, aching for them to touch her secret flesh. Instead they teased her for what felt like forever.

Fingers tugged gently at her pubic hair, giving her sensation so very close to where she wanted it. A tongue traced the crease between thigh and pubis. Rough hands massaged her buttocks, stopping occasionally to pinch. One thick finger penetrated her rectum, moving in and out of her like a small penis.

She endured the delightful torment with whimpers and moans, wriggling as much as her bonds allowed. At long last a tongue touched her vaginal orifice, delicately tracing her trembling core. Pleasure tumbled through her belly at the tentative pressure. She groaned and lifted her hips for more.

The man offering his tongue obliged her invitation, but instead of relieving her need, it only intensified the ache. The tip of his tongue continued its barely-there touch, inflaming her desire.

Meanwhile the biter had moved to her inner thighs, and the finger invading her nether orifice quickened its pace. Amelia's breath came in sobs, but she no longer cried in shame. She cried because they made her feel so good, and she felt gratitude to be the recipient of their attentions.

Face it, you're glad they're holding you captive. It gives you an excuse to keep having sex with them. In many ways, being imprisoned has freed you.

But it wasn't just the sex, even the not-so-depraved acts that didn't trigger shame. It was the affection in Rajhir's voice and the warmth in his eyes when he spoke to her. It was Flencik's gentle smiles and concern for her wellbeing. It was Breft's admission he'd give his life for her. It was so many things, big and small. They were adding up, and Amelia found herself wanting to give in to their demands.

The tongue teasing her sex suddenly forced its way in, catching her by surprise. She cried out at the marvelous invasion, bucking against the face of the man behind her. He chuckled against her sensitive flesh, sending sweet vibrations to melt her. The tongue whipped in and out, pausing to flick her straining pleasure bud before each plunge into her wet warmth.

A second finger pressed its way into the cleft of her buttocks, widening her tightest aperture to take two thick digits. The pressure felt delightful.

The fingers, the tongue, and the teeth were setting her on fire. Her moans came continuously. Her hands clutched at the table legs while the men worked her eager flesh. She began chanting a breathless plea of "Please...please...please...please..."

"Do you want us to fuck you?" Breft's voice was hot in her ear.

"Yes." She was too far gone to care about the profanity.

"Say it."

"Fuck me."

"Make me believe it."

"Fuck me!" she screamed.

The tongue and fingers disappeared. They were immediately replaced with the turgid sexes of an enthusiastic Kalquorian. Amelia knew the clan by feel alone now, and she moaned as Rajhir moved slowly, sweetly inside her. The dual penetration filled her to perfection.

He rocked his hips against her, taking his time to love her with thoroughness. He shifted until he found the sweet spot inside her, making her weep with delight. As he moved within her welcoming warmth, his fingertips traced her shoulderblades, her ribs, her spine, the roundness of her buttocks. The tenderness of his touch brought a lump to her throat. She felt genuine affection in the contact.

As if reading her mind, Rajhir murmured, "I love you, Amelia."

"We all do," Flencik added.

That undid her completely. She sobbed at the unexpected admission. She felt the truth of their simple declaration and felt something inside herself shatter. All the pain of her mother's judgments and society's disapproval fell upon her with their full weight. Her own people, even her mother, would revile her for her desires; they would see her condemned in both this life and the next for her sins. The aliens not only accepted her, but actually loved her as she was. It was a dream come true. But her dream was other Earther females' nightmare.

I have to remember that. No matter how much I want this, no matter how I feel about this clan, I must deny myself.

The thought made her cry harder. To have to reject her heart's desire seemed the cruelest blow she could imagine. Death may well have been kinder.

The clan let her cry without speaking; Rajhir continued to make tender love to her. He was liquid silk, slipping through her with practiced ease. How could their joining be wrong when they fit so perfectly?

As he moved against the bundle of nerves within her that felt best, her tears gradually receded. The continuous pressure rubbing that sensitive spot overrode the ache in her heart. The weaker her sobs, the stronger his lovemaking became. God, he felt so good. She swallowed the last of her weeping, desperate for the brief comfort of physical release.

She gasped for breath as his thrusts grew in power, intensifying the sensations warming her womb. His hands closed over her shoulders, pulling her as close to his driving sex as her bonds allowed.

All thought ceased for Amelia; all she knew was the agonizing pleasure building in her belly. She urged Rajhir on with inarticulate cries, encouraging him to work her body faster and harder. He pounded her insides, his grunts of effort making her wetter, hotter, hungrier for more. She felt her climax beginning, that wonderful raw sensation consuming her nether regions, growing fierce and savage like a primitive animal. It expanded until it devoured every cell of her being, and she disintegrated in its violent bliss.

She heard Rajhir's roar of completion and added her voice to the savage cries. He pulsed within her as if he might explode, and her sex spasmed anew, sucking at him in an attempt to consume him entirely.

As soon as Rajhir quieted, Breft took his place. The Nobek bent to cover her body with his warmth as he too began his lovemaking with tender care. She felt the planes of his chest against her shoulders, the tightness of his abdominals in the small of her back and buttocks. His breath was hot in her ear. His movements within her sex and anus were languorous, but Amelia was still roused from Rajhir's vigorous lovemaking. The juxtaposition of Breft's gentleness made her tremble. She fought the growing heat of desire.

"Close," she warned her lover, feeling the impending orgasm moving nearer.

"Go ahead, my sweet. Let it happen." The encouraging rumble of his voice tickled her ear.

Permission granted, she succumbed. The climax rolled through her, making her tight around Breft's slowly moving penises. He sighed as she shuddered beneath him, growing thicker in response to her passion.

He kept the same quiet pace however, allowing her to prolong her gratification.

After the orgasm spent itself and before the next one could claim her, Breft slipped out. He shifted to place his larger organ into her sex, letting the smaller one stroke her clitoris as he resumed slow lovemaking. Amelia groaned to feel him fill her womanhood so well. She clutched at him with inner muscles to make him groan in return.

He began to tease her with gentle cruelty, quickening his pace until she again gasped with imminent completion. Before she tipped over into ecstacy, he slowed to deny her satisfaction. On the slow strokes, he pulled back until he left her body but for the tip of his penis. He paused, letting the sensation of near-exodus torment her until she strained against her bonds to take him back in. Slowly, so very slowly, he crept back inside her, letting her feel the sensation of her body yielding to his penetration. Her sheath closed in to absorb the length of him as if she would make him a part of herself.

When he buried himself within her, when his groin met hers, the walls of her vaginal walls grasped to keep him in place. He growled with the effort of extracting himself from her clinging sleeve.

After a few minutes of this delightful play, Breft increased the speed of his lovemaking. His hips swung back and forth like a pendulum, moving easily in their combined wetness. He rocked in and out, increasing his momentum until his body met hers with sharp slaps. His strokes shortened as he kept himself deep within her, battering her womb, making her cry out as she climbed toward the pinnacle of pleasure. Then, the moment just before sensation could completely claim her, he stopped. He held her still, refusing her glorious dissolution even as he groaned from his own denial. He kept Amelia like this until her breathing quieted enough to reassure him she would not come too easily.

When Breft moved again, it was to grind slow circles within her. Then he withdrew gradually to start all over again to her agonized delight.

When at last neither could take any further torment, Breft found a quick rhythm that drove them steadily toward shared satisfaction. He shifted every few moments to apply pressure to a different point of her sheath. She shuddered to feel him exploring her so thoroughly with his sex. Her moans from climax seemed to emanate from her very womb.

Breft spent himself with a long, drawn-out groan. He lay over her for a few moments, his chest heaving against her back. She loved the feel of his weight crushing her to the tabletop.

Amelia hadn't regained her strength when Breft lifted himself from her body. She blinked when she saw Flencik peering up at her from beneath the table.

"Hello," he murmured. He freed her wrists from the restraints and disappeared.

Amelia blinked in confusion. She felt the tug of the ankle cuffs being removed too. Was Flencik letting her up without taking his own pleasure?

Arms bigger round than her thighs slid under her body to scoop her up and turn her over. Too weak from lovemaking to resist, she allowed Flencik to bind her to the table legs again, but now she was face up. He loomed over her with a wicked grin.

"Let us see the strength Breft's table truly is," he said.

He climbed up to straddle her torso, his knees on either side of her ribcage. The table creaked under his massive weight but held without further complaint.

Flencik's penis was swollen and flushed with color before her eyes. He gripped the table corner with one hand and caressed her cheek with the other. Then he gently pinched her nose shut between his thumb and forefinger.

Amelia opened her mouth for air. "What the—"

He quickly cut off her words by pressing his larger sex to her lips. When she obediently parted them to allow him entrance, he released her nose.

"Good girl," he sighed, sliding to the back of her throat, his gradual movement giving her time to relax and resist the gag reflex. His cinnamon flavor saturated her senses.

Flencik pumped his hips, taking her mouth with deliberate, measured thrusts. He was hot against her tongue, the vein on the underside of his organ throbbing. She looked up the chiseled length of his torso, at his arm muscles bunching to take the majority of his weight, at his dark eyes half-lidded with pleasure as he watched himself disappear between her lips.

Despite the earlier attentions of Rajhir and Breft, her sex ached with desire. She wished one of the other men would fill her there while Flencik used her mouth. Moisture soaked her inner thighs.

Flencik's own lubrication flowed freely, and each time he drew back from the warmth of her mouth, she sucked his juices greedily. She had always delighted in his flavor, but hunger made him more delicious than ever. She rubbed her tongue against him, hoping he would climax in her mouth so she might fill her empty stomach with his seed.

Instead he withdrew, his eyes narrowed as if guessing what she wanted. He dismounted and stepped to the end of the table where her greedy sex beckoned. He dropped to his knees. The table height put her right at the level of his face. He inhaled deeply and smiled at the mingled scent of her and his clanmates.

He cupped her buttocks in both hands, his thumbs spreading the mounds apart. He ran his tongue up the cleft, ending at her engorged clitoris. Amelia writhed.

He lapped her juices with his rough, wet tongue, and her eager sex kept him well supplied. She squirmed as sensation transmitted from his fervent mouth to her belly, making her perspire and shiver with mingled heat and chills.

Flencik gorged himself on her flesh until he brought her over the edge. He sucked hard on her quivering sex as if he'd turn her inside out by the force of his mouth alone. Amelia's voice turned hoarse from the strength of her cries. Her head whipped from side to side.

Before she'd quite recovered, Flencik got to his feet and touched her between the legs with his organs. He rubbed the tips against her trembling body, letting her feel him at her threshold. He ran the dual penises up and down her crevice, making her sigh with pleasure.

How she loved the sensation of Flencik hard and ready for her! Knowing he desired her body was the greatest aphrodisiac of all. No matter how many times he and the others made her climax, seeing them burning for her yet again always renewed her senses.

While Flencik rubbed himself lightly against Amelia, he caressed her body with reverence. It was as if he worshipped her body with his hands. First he stroked her long hair from her face, lifting tresses to his nose to inhale the fragrance. He traced the arches of her eyebrows with his thumbs. A forefinger ran the length of her slender nose. He leaned close to trace her lips with the tip of his tongue. He cupped her head and tilted it back to expose the long line of her throat so he could kiss the delicate line of her jaw. His mouth tasted the column of her throat, ending in the hollow of her collarbone.

He ran his fingertips down her arms, tickling the crease of her elbows. Then his fingers traveled back up to curve around her breasts.

He traced the areolas with a delicate touch. Her erect nipples throbbed.

Flencik ran his palms down her ribcage, curving in at her waist and flaring back out over her hips. He wet one fingertip in his mouth to swirl it around her navel.

The entire time he spent stroking the upper regions of her body, he continued to caress her sex with his own. The heat of his need radiated, increasing her own craving.

Flencik's hands tightened on her hips, warning Amelia of the impending penetration. He pierced her with a smooth motion, moving gently to fuse them together. She looked down the length of her body and her breath caught at the sight of him disappearing into her. She watched the huge Kalquorian emerge again, slick and shining.

Their gasps melded with the soft, wet sounds of their coupling. Flencik slid in and out of her easily. Amelia continued to watch him take her, mesmerized by the motion, the musky cinnamon aroma, the sounds, and the sensations. She felt hypnotized.

Then Flencik shifted, making him rub hard against the bundle of nerves at the front of her sheath. Amelia cried out, arching against the table at the stab of pleasure. Flencik grunted and drove himself against the spot again. She clutched her sex around him in spontaneous reaction. He groaned as his pleasure mounted. He held her tight, his fingertips digging into her hips as he concentrated his attack on her sweet spot. She screamed as her vagina clutched him, milking him even as he thrust harder.

He bellowed when he exploded within her. Their sexes throbbed in tandem, synced with each other. *So perfect. So perfect,* Amelia thought, her wordless moans urging on the straining man between her thighs. Even as his own pleasure descended from its glorious peak, Flencik labored over her until she shuddered anew.

His head hung down as he panted, his long jet-black curls spiraling to her belly. For her part, Amelia's eyes closed in satisfied fatigue, her body finally relaxing as Flencik gradually softened inside her.

Soft chuckles brought her eyes open. Flencik lifted his head. They both looked toward the lounger where Rajhir and Breft kneeled, leaning over the back cushions to watch.

"My dear little Amelia," Breft grinned. "You enjoyed the table, yes?"

Rajhir's grin was even bigger. "She enjoyed being tied to the table. She takes pleasure in many things her people claim are taboo."

"Including us."

Flencik slipped from inside her but remained standing between her legs. Despite having just climaxed, he stared at her tied, helpless body with such heat she turned her face away. She couldn't look at him, at any of them.

She'd lost control again, damn it! It was hard to know what burned brightest within her: the anger or the humiliation. Had she no pride? No conscience? No shame? She was nothing but a debauched animal, less than human!

When the dreaded question passed Rajhir's lips, her furious resolve was once again firmly in place.

"Will you eat now, little one?"

"No."

"Then Flencik will let you enjoy his device while we sleep."

Amelia's anger dissolved into miserable dismay. They'd made perfect love to her, had confessed the depth of their emotions, and now the sweet glow of it was to be ruined by the uncaring stimulation of the vibrator.

She squeezed her eyes shut as the Imdiko strapped the profane object to her. Her sex was still damp from lovemaking, and when he switched the probe on, it plunged in and out effortlessly. Then the vibrations started, and she bit down on her lips to keep from begging them to let her eat, to let her be their Matara, to anything they demanded just so she wouldn't have to endure being pleasured by a machine.

They watched her in silence for awhile; watched as she writhed and moaned. She knew they hoped she would succumb to the embarrassment of perverted sexual ecstasy.

She wanted to. She wanted to be released from the delicious torture of being bound while an untiring device gave her orgasm after orgasm. She wanted her empty, groaning belly to be filled with nellus from Flencik's fingers. She wanted to acquiesce to their demands in everything, to obey any and all commands they put to her.

Most of all, she wanted to again hear them say they loved her.

They finally left the room to rest, leaving her to strain against her bonds in vain while the terrible, wonderful toy between her legs plunged and throbbed.

Chapter Eleven

Amelia's heart fluttered as the clan gathered around where she crouched naked against the wall. Despite the tickle of fear and desire, she maintained her sulky expression. She must make them believe she despised them, though doing so hurt her heart. Calling them names, screaming terrible things, it all pained her as if she'd been on the receiving end of her abuse.

She'd lost track of time since the abduction. The windows of the clan's apartment remained tinted dark. Only the burning scentwood and glowing globes lent the room its dim light. It seemed she slept bare minutes at a time before the Kalquorians woke her for another round of entreating her to eat and accept her role as their Matara. They continued to torment her with lovemaking. Sometimes their attention was tender, sometimes rough. She secretly welcomed it all, basking in the love behind their demands. Always they bound her and often they hurt her, but they always finished with her pleasure reaching climax. No matter how she treated them, she was never denied the shattering orgasms that made her cry out with unrestrained delight.

Fatigue and hunger wore her down. Worst of all, her resolve crumbled minute by minute. The longer they held her prisoner, the more she questioned why she fought them. She had to admit, privately at least, that all she wanted was to surrender to them. To utterly abandon what God, Earth, her mother, and she expected of herself.

She searched for anger on their faces and found none; they looked at her with expressions knotted in worry. Their concern, so naked for her to see, made her want to capitulate more than ever. She entertained no doubt they cared for her, that they loved her as no one ever had. It was in every touch, every word, every glance they gifted her with.

Flencik's voice wavered in torment. "She fights eating. She fights everything."

Rajhir's fists clenched. He asked Amelia, "Why do you not accept our love?"

Even as tears threatened, Amelia glared at him. "It's not love when you force me to stay here against my will."

"We give you everything. As Matara, you are the center of the clan."

His refusal to understand sparked her anger, giving her strength to dispute him. "I'm not your Matara!"

Flencik crouched down to plead with her. "You must eat. You grow weak."

She looked down, unable to withstand the emotion in his features. "I want nothing from you except to be let go." She felt the lie stain her very soul.

The fury in Breft's voice made her look up again. "If she will not eat voluntarily, we must force her. Enough of playing her games already!"

Rajhir's voice betrayed nothing. "We will not bite her. We will give her no excuses to hide behind."

"The pleasure we give her, as distasteful as she finds it, is not changing her mind. Her behavior warrants real penalty. She must be punished."

The Imdiko straightened, his attitude towards Breft turning threatening. "What do you suggest? Would you beat her like a child to behave as we wish?"

The Nobek's jaw unclenched. A smile teased the corners of his mouth despite Flencik towering over him. "Not beat, but a little discipline may teach her. Real discipline." He looked down at Amelia, and his smile grew. A chill wormed its way into her belly at his calculating expression.

Rajhir asked in a hopeful voice, "What do you mean?"

Breft's stare pinned her motionless to the floor. "A moderate amount of pain will not scar her."

"We already administer pain with the sex. She loves it."

Breft laughed as Amelia's face grew hot. "Indeed she does. The difference is that we will not be pleasuring her this time. She may respond to such a lesson." He turned his gaze to Flencik. "You say she is like a naughty child. We must punish her as such."

Rajhir nodded. "The Earthers call it...*dulma*?"

"Spanking." Breft spoke the word with the air of a man relishing a particularly fine wine.

Amelia breath froze in her lungs. Breft was an animal, she thought. Surely the others saw the savagery of his suggestion!

Instead of rejecting the proposal as her heart insisted he must, Rajhir asked Flencik, "What do you think?"

The Imdiko thought a moment before speaking. "The discomfort of *dulma* is temporary. Even if real damage is inflicted, I can treat it. If spanking will make Amelia eat, I agree."

Amelia's heart seemed to stutter to a halt in her chest. She emitted a strangled gurgle. If the clan heard her distress, they ignored it.

"I will administer the punishment," Rajhir said. He looked from Breft to Flencik. "As the protector and the nurturer of this clan, you will oversee to avoid injury to your Matara." At their nods he held a hand out to Amelia. "Come to me, little one."

Something besides terror filled her. Amelia's sex tickled a warning, and her horror grew. Being roughly dominated by the clan always excited her, but the threat of real physical punishment without sex should not! Yet desire spiked through her, leaving her trembling. How could she want this? What was wrong with her?

She shrank away, pressing her back against the wall. "Don't you dare touch me!"

Rajhir moved in a blur. Before she knew it, he grabbed her and slung her over his shoulder. She battered his back to no avail as he carried her to the lounger. In one motion he sat down and draped her struggling body over his thighs.

Her hair swept the floor by his foot. His hand pressed against the middle of her back, holding her torso still despite her flailing arms and legs.

"Let me go, damn you!" she shrieked. She tried to ignore the ache of arousal.

Rajhir's voice, drifting from overhead, sounded kind. "The pain is only for a little while. It ends when you agree to eat. When you tell me you comply, I will stop."

He won't go through with it, Amelia thought frantically. *He wouldn't dare.*

The first *crack* of his palm descending on her buttocks exploded in the air like a gunshot. The stinging strike surprised Amelia from her struggles. Warmth replaced the pain, radiating from her hindquarters.

He hit me. She lay frozen on his thighs, feeling tingling heat spread over her flesh.

The hand descended on her rear again. Rajhir really meant to spank Amelia like an unruly child. Humiliation warmed her face even as his heavy palm warmed her buttocks.

"Stop!" she cried, but again the report of flesh striking flesh echoed through the room. She doubled her struggles to escape his discipline.

He held her like a vise. Rajhir rained slaps on her stinging rear over and over as she lay defenseless on his lap. She felt the eyes of Flencik and Breft watching the punishment. Her embarrassment grew, and she sobbed. How could her situation get worse?

To her horror, it did. The heat of her spanked flesh spread to her sex. As always her helplessness against her tormentors heightened her sexual hunger. Wetness trickled from her core even as Rajhir continued to administer the punishment.

She cried in harsh sobs, shamed by her body's response. Rajhir ceased spanking her.

"She cries so," he said. "Her skin reddens. Is she damaged, Flencik?"

Amelia's wails lessened to whimpers. She willed her throbbing sex to quiet, to end its betrayal. She watched Flencik's approach through the web of her hair. A shiver passed over her as she saw his and Breft's aroused state. Only then did she feel Rajhir's erection pressing against her ribs. If they discovered she was just as excited, what else might they do to her? A stab of pleasure greeted that thought, and fresh tears slid down her cheeks. What a deviant she was to feel arousal at such thoughts!

At least Rajhir had ended the spanking, and she could gain control over her traitorous body. She let herself lie limp across Rajhir's thighs as Flencik swept cool hands over her buttocks. She felt his breath waft over her smarting skin.

"No damage beyond a little bruising. It is nothing I cannot heal," he said. He shoved his hand between her thighs and cupped her sex. Amelia cried out in mingled surprise and desire. "Wet," he grunted, withdrawing. Amelia sobbed at both the discovery of her debasement and being deprived of his touch.

"Then we reward rather than punish her," Rajhir said. "It is no different from the usual discipline."

"I think this is different. There is no sexual play, yet she responds anyway. Such humiliation punishes her well. If pain does not convince her, perhaps shame will." Flencik stepped back.

"You support continuing this?"

The Imdiko's tone hardened. "I do. In fact, we will spank her until she obeys us. If you tire, I will take over. We will all take turns. If she is injured, I will heal her, and we will begin again."

Breft's voice sounded surprised. "I did not think you would approve of such extremes."

"Her hunger strike has gone on too long. I cannot allow her to continue endangering her health."

Rajhir delivered a stinging slap to Amelia's burning rear. "You have heard the words of your Imdiko, little one. The punishment continues until you agree to eat, no matter how long it takes."

Amelia felt faint at his words. She couldn't face anymore of this! "Please stop," Amelia wailed.

"That is up to you."

Again his hand peppered her backside, sending fresh waves of heat pulsing from her smarting flesh. She felt Rajhir's thigh supporting her lower torso turn slick as her demanding sex betrayed her. Her sobs mingled with moans. Her buttocks felt raw from the blows. Rajhir showed no sign of tiring; instead his frustration seemed to feed his strength as his hand descended harder than ever.

Defeated, she cried, "I'll eat! Please Rajhir! Please, no more."

Rajhir gave her bottom one last reproving slap before turning her over and cuddling her in his arms. Flencik hurried to the kitchen area. Breft sat next to Rajhir and smoothed Amelia's hair from her streaming eyes. Wanting to hide from them, she burrowed her face against Rajhir's chest.

"Why are you embarrassed?" he asked. "Such sexual responsiveness is a gift, sweet Amelia. It should be a source of pride. You are fortunate." He tilted her chin to expose her tearstained face. "Flencik has brought you food. You will eat now."

The three men fed her nellus and desrel with their fingers. She accepted the nourishment, keeping her eyes downcast to avoid seeing the Kalquorians' faces.

"Good Matara," Rajhir said. "Eat well and I will not have to spank you again."

"Until you wish it," Breft added with a smirk.

All through the meal, her buttocks stung. Worse, her sex pulsed with longing, hungry for attention. Like it or not, the spanking had awakened her desire for her captors once again. Amelia hated herself for the weakness.

After she'd eaten enough to satisfy Flencik, Rajhir flipped her on her belly again. His hard thighs felt like tree trunks beneath her. She cried out, anticipating the sting of his hand.

"Hush, little one," Rajhir said, trailing his fingers through her hair. "Flencik will put salve on. Now that you have done as we wish, you will suffer no more discomfort."

Flencik's touch lulled her as he smoothed a cool cream over her buttocks. It soothed the sting instantly, and her flesh stopped feeling as though it glowed red hot.

If only her desire could be cooled! Her clitoris throbbed still, aching for Flencik's expert fingers to brush against it.

Be strong, her inner voice advised. *You've only lost the battle, not the war. Give them nothing voluntarily.*

When his fingers closed on that nub of flesh, she jerked away. Rajhir growled, "Amelia," and gave her buttocks a light slap. She wept but submitted to their fondling. She found it impossible to endure another spanking.

They had her in turn, two watching as each clanmate took his pleasure with her. They whispered love words as they enjoyed her always fervent body. She fought none of them, allowing each man to do as he pleased. She submitted every command put to her, and they possessed her in all possible ways. She obeyed so they wouldn't spank her again. She didn't fear the discipline itself; she feared how much she wanted it. Over and over, she cried out her pleasure as they took her and she relived the spanking in her mind.

The punishment should have solidified her resolve to not give in to their demands. On the contrary, she wanted to be their Matara more than ever. They'd tricked her, kidnapped her, bound her, and spanked her. Any sane being would hate the Kalquorians for their despicable actions.

How was it possible Amelia had fallen so desperately in love with them?

* * * *

Amelia woke, sunken deep into the lounger's softness and surrounded by the permanent twilight of the clan's quarters.

Rajhir, godlike in his nudity, appeared at her side. His hands brushed her cheeks. "You are awake?"

Amelia strained to see through the gloom. "Where are the others?"

"I made them go. Flencik forgets his own needs in his devotion to you. He is at a meditation retreat. As for Breft, a Nobek cannot be closed up for long. He hunts in the northern forest to satisfy his need for action. They will both return at sundown."

So it's day, Amelia mused. *But what day? How long have I been here? Has anyone noticed I'm missing yet?*

Rajhir continued to stroke her face. "I promised Flencik I would bathe you. Would you like that?"

She pushed at his hands. "Does it matter? You don't give me any choices."

The Dramok's lips tightened. He gathered her in his arms and carried her to the basin. She lay wooden against his chest, knowing she'd soften beneath his touch and despising herself for her weakness.

He lowered her into the warm water and began to wash her. He massaged her muscles as he bathed her. She stared down at the water lapping against her belly, wishing she had the freedom to enjoy his attentions.

After a long silence broken only by the trickle of the waterfall, Rajhir spoke. "I know this is difficult for you. If I had the choice, I would -- romantic? I would romantic you."

Tears stung her eyes and sprinkled into the basin. "You're in command of this clan. How could you not have a choice?"

His voice grated with emotion. "There is no time. Our people are becoming few. We must reproduce quickly to continue our culture."

The grief in his voice squelched her anger. She looked up to see his eyes shining. Tears? From this hard Kalquorian?

In a wondering tone she asked, "Why can't you? What's wrong with the women of your planet?"

He looked deep into her eyes as if seeking understanding. "The first difficulty is Kalquorian females ovulate only once your Earth year. Still, we had increased our population steadily through the generations. Then, two centuries ago, a virus spread among our people that damaged the — I don't have the word for it — the part that makes a fetus female?"

"The X chromosome?" At the look of confusion on Rajhir's face, Amelia attempted to explain. "In Earthers, two X chromosomes make a female, and one X and a Y make a male."

"Chromosome," Rajhir repeated slowly. "Perhaps that is it. Flencik would know. The problem is most female fetuses do not survive to birth because of defects. Ninety percent of the children born alive are male. The majority of our few females are infertile. With time, Kalquor has fewer females, fewer births. We have not been able to manipulate the embryos through medical means because Kalquorian physiology is too strong." Tears trekked down his cheeks. "Our people are dying. We have searched many years for females of other species to mate with, to continue our culture. You are our final chance. If our mating with Earthers does not produce living children free of the defects, in 300 years Kalquorians will be gone."

Amelia's heart thudded painfully. "Wait. Let me make sure I understand. Your people will be totally extinct in 300 years?"

Rajhir nodded. He pulled her close so that her wet breasts pressed against his chest. "We are a desperate people, but we know love. We would not hurt you by forcing you to be our Matara if we could help it. If I knew another way so you do not suffer, so you feel we do not force you, I would use that way. You are precious to me, Amelia. I love you."

She cried at the despair and longing on his face. His obvious pain softened her. She kissed the tears wetting his cheeks. Her arms wrapped around his neck. His lips sank down to cover hers, and she opened to his kiss. He lifted her from the basin and laid her down on the deep pile of the floor.

Despite the strong body settling over hers, Amelia felt Rajhir's vulnerability. She wanted to see more of that side of him. She pushed against his chest. "Let me."

His dark cat eyes searched her face, but when she shoved again he rolled over onto his back. Amelia bent over him and explored the length of his body. She traced the fine line running from his hairline to the bridge of his nose with her fingertips. From there, she continued down to the curve of his lips. He laid still, his eyes drinking in her face.

Amelia lowered her mouth to his, flicking her tongue over his teeth. She tasted the silk of his tongue and his mouth's soft inner flesh. She laid full length against him, letting him feel her breasts pressing against his chest and the wetness trickling from between her thighs to moisten his belly. He moaned but remained motionless.

She moved down, her palms flattened against the broad chest. She lowered her cheek to his breast and listened to his heart's bass drumbeat. She wandered further down to his tapered waist knotted with muscle. What did bodybuilders call the double line of bumps on their abs? A six pack. Kalquorian physiology allowed Rajhir to sport a supersized eight pack.

Amelia paused over his upright penises and inhaled his cinnamon scent. Then she moved on to his thighs, letting her hair's gossamer strands trail his sex, the only touch she gave him there. She heard his breath catch, and she smiled, delighted with her own teasing.

His legs corded with tension. Amelia ran her hands over the marble flesh, appreciating the lines with an artist's eye. Not even a Michaelangelo sculpture compared to the perfection of Rajhir's body. She stroked a living, breathing work of art.

"Amelia." His strained voice broke into her reverie. She looked up to meet his eyes. The desire, the wanting in them shook her. Rajhir looked like a desperately thirsty man eyeing a pitcher of water. She didn't have to be a mind reader to know soon he'd turn that frantic need against her.

"Lie still," she said, drawing her body over his, her wet sex hovering over his swollen members. "Let me take care of everything. I'll give you what you need."

"Need *you*," he gasped, his struggle apparent. "I need you right now."

"I know. Lie still for me, Rajhir. Don't move." Their sexes touched, drawn together. Tendons stood out in his neck as he fought against invading her warmth.

She lowered herself onto him, moaning as his turgid penises parted the lips of her sex and nether orifice. Down she went, filling herself with him, taking him within her warmth.

She took him slowly at first, savoring his gasped pleas for release. She reveled in the illusion he was hers to command, to torture, to reward as her whims dictated.

"You want to throw me down and take your pleasure now, don't you?" she said, laughing at his working face. She raised her hips until only his penis tips remained inside her.

"Amelia..."

"I'm the one in control here." She impaled herself on him again, taking her time. His chest heaved with the effort of his restraint. His torment delighted her.

"...please..."

"The tables are turned. You have to do as I wish." She lifted, almost releasing him once more.

"...Matara..."

"Submit to my will." Her own need became excruciating. She wanted to ride him, to fill herself with him until she burst.

"...mercy..."

Her body begged for release in tandem with Rajhir. She pistoned herself on the iron of his sexes, demanding he soothe her need; taking him, forcing him for her own pleasure.

Rajhir's hips bucked, all conscious control ripped from him. His iron hands locked onto her waist, driving her down as his loins slammed upward, shoving himself deep inside her womb and anus. The snarling Dramok thrust beneath her, all savagery now. Amelia sobbed laughter as orgasm crested in a tidal wave. She loosed a scream of triumph as her guts shuddered. Rajhir's howl answered her.

When the last tremor passed, she wilted on top of her Kalquorian lover like a flower battered by the wind. His arms wrapped around her, and she felt his strength. Had she really had the nerve to pretend to control this man?

He rolled over so that they lay on their sides facing each other. The intensity in his voice when he spoke stunned her. "I will always love you. Choose the clan, Amelia. Be our Matara."

His plea tore her heart in two. Her soul battled with her loyalty to her own race. "I want to," she said, agony bringing tears to her eyes. "I don't know that I can. It's so hard to decide, Rajhir. Either way I go, it hurts me somehow." She buried her face against his neck, burrowing into his warmth. "Hold me. Make me feel safe for a little while."

"I will keep you safe forever," he murmured in her ear. For a few moments in his arms she allowed herself to contemplate her heart's desire.

Chapter Twelve

The next day dawned with the insistent beeping of the vid rousing the group. Breft extricated himself from the knot of limbs on the lounger to answer its summons.

"Recorded message," he informed them as he sat at the desk and switched on the monitor. Flencik stroked Amelia's hair and Rajhir stretched the drowsiness from his muscles as the Nobek scanned the monitor.

Breft barked something in Kalquorian. His clanmates rose from Amelia's side. They yanked on their clothes.

Amelia propped herself up on her elbows. "Where are you going? What's happening?"

Rajhir sat down to pull on his boots. "We slept late. Flencik and I are due at meetings."

Flencik got his tunic arranged and sat beside Amelia to put on his own boots as Rajhir stood and paced by the door. "I forgot complete of meetings."

Breft absently corrected him. "You meant to say, 'I completely forgot about the meetings.'"

Flencik ignored the lesson. "Stop glaring at me, Rajhir. I hurry."

Amelia flicked her gaze towards Breft who remained engrossed by the message on vid. "You're leaving me alone with him?" she whispered to Flencik.

He finished strapping on his boots. He favored her with a smile. "Breft will not harm you. Breft is fierce and demands obedience, but he protects his Matara." He patted her shoulder. "We will not be gone long."

He rose, and Rajhir opened the door to the outside. Daylight splashed into the twilight gloom of the clan's quarters. Rajhir walked out. Before following him, Flencik nodded goodbye to Amelia. "I will bring back nellus."

The door slammed shut behind him, leaving her imprisoned with Breft.

The Nobek regarded her with curiosity. He stepped around the desk so nothing stood between them. He sat on its edge and crossed his arms over his chest.

"I heard what you said to Flencik. Do I frighten you so much, little

Amelia?"

She swallowed. Her heart thumped hard. "I think you're dangerous to anyone who crosses you," she said, her voice a strengthless whisper.

He nodded. "I am. Not just on my own behalf but also for my clan." He smiled a little, and she felt relief that no fury appeared on his face. He said, "You have no more to fear from me than you do from Flencik."

The softness of his voice permitted her anger to burst forth. "The spanking was your idea, Breft. It hurt me."

He chuckled as if indulging a cranky child. "You were hurting yourself even more by not eating. You enjoy being punished. If you were truthful, you'd admit you suffer more from humiliation than pain."

Amelia jumped to her feet, her fists knotted at her sides. "You're heartless! You know nothing of kindness."

Sadness touched his smile. "To coddle is the Imdiko's way. A Nobek must be ever alert and ready to protect his clan at all times. Still, I know compassion."

"You don't show it."

"It is not easy for me." He looked down at his hands as if they possessed the answers to diffuse Amelia's anger. "To fight, to kill, to die for Rajhir, Flencik and you are simple things. I can do them without conscience or thought."

"How can you be like that?"

"I was taken from my mother and trained for battle at a very young age with other boys. There were no lullabies, no hugs, no soft bosom to hide away in. There were only lessons in fighting and subterfuge. We hunted dangerous animals with no weapons. We fought each other in bloody tournaments until only one was left standing. Before we reached puberty we were cunning warriors."

Amelia shuddered. "That's terrible."

"No, it was necessary. The universe is full of danger, and the Nobeks are Kalquor's defense. Most of all, we are charged with keeping our clans safe. I was taught to be loyal to my clan before I even became a part of one." His smile turned bitter, and Amelia again saw the predator in him. "My heart beat with rage at the thought of anyone threatening the members of my clan, whoever they might turn out to be. I eagerly learned hand-to-hand combat, of weapons, of ambushing my enemies."

Breft fell silent. After several moments Amelia gathered her courage to speak. "What of love?"

"Nothing. That was left to Rajhir and Flencik once they took me into the clan."

"A tall order, given what you went through."

"Flencik's gentleness was difficult for me to understand. I was hard like a stone wall, and he was yielding. I had never met anyone like him."

His softened expression sparked Amelia's suspicions. "Are the males in clans lovers?"

He shrugged. "Our need for sexual release is great. There are too few Kalquorian women for us to enjoy traditional lovemaking among our own kind. We are not always among compatible females of other species either. We give each other pleasure when there is no other means to satisfy the flesh with."

He spoke of it so offhandedly that Amelia assumed same-sex relations were normal Kalquorian behavior not worthy of discussion. She rolled the knowledge around, wanting to see if her puritanical upbringing gave her issues with the situation. Homosexuality was a death penalty offense on Earth. More than anything, same-sex relationships were abhorred and those caught performing such acts were the most brutally punished.

To her knowledge, Amelia had never met anyone who preferred his own sex to females. She expected to be repulsed, but thinking about the men of Rajhir's clan being intimate with each other, imagining their magnificent bodies twined together in the act of love actually sounded rather titillating. Finding herself curious, not dismayed or disgusted, she waited for Breft to resume his story.

His eyes grew dark with memory, and a frown creased his face. "I hurt Flencik one of our first times together. I am much younger than he and Rajhir. When I came to them, my urges were greater and more frequent than theirs. Being the nurturer, Flencik did his best to ease the demands of my young body, but even he grew fatigued trying to keep up with me."

As he told his story, Amelia imagined a younger Breft, the hunger in his lean face more pronounced. The tale unfolded before her mind's eye.

Breft, already naked in preparation for love, eyed Flencik with a desperate desire. The Imdiko emerged from his bath, and the glistening skin made his magnificent body more chiseled. Seeing him that way intensified Breft's hunger to feel the other's wet flesh against his own.

"I need," he said.

Flencik smiled, his eyes warming at the sight of his new clanmate. "Poor Breft. Youth is a brute to our people." He stepped close and patted the bunched muscle of the Nobek's shoulder. His hand slipped down and tugged once at Breft's larger penis. He released the turgid organ and stepped away. "I'm not in the mood. You have to provide your own release this time."

The brief contact made Breft's body thrum with tension. He reached toward Flencik in supplication. The Imdiko shook his head with a smile as he backed away another step. "I'm tired, Breft. I'm worn out from keeping up with you."

Breft understood days of attending youthful hungers might be wearing on Flencik. As the top doctor on the entire planet of Kalquor, his schedule was packed, with little time to catch his breath. In the search for a medical solution to the imminent extinction of their people, he often forgot to eat and sleep. Concerned with Flencik's wellbeing, Rajhir had insisted he take the week off.

Breft hadn't allowed the Imdiko much rest. Sympathy for Flencik's exhaustion did nothing to quiet the ache in the young Nobek's loins. Pleasuring himself only offered hollow satisfaction. Having never touched a female, he knew nothing like the joy of touching Flencik's solidity, of tasting and feeling his warmth.

"You are the Imdiko." Breft heard the tremor in his own voice, and it added anger to his frustration. "You must care for me. That is your duty."

He drew close and pulled at Flencik, pressing himself against the larger Kalquorian. The Imdiko grabbed Breft by the shoulders and thrust him away. "I've given you satisfaction twice today already. You'll have to take care of it yourself."

He turned away. A moan that originated from Breft's aching groin spilled from his lips. He lunged for Flencik in a haze of desperation. He brought the bigger man crashing to the floor.

Flencik thrashed beneath him, but Breft had been well-schooled in subduing enemies larger than himself. The Imdiko's bulk offered little defense, and Breft gave him no avenue for escape. Once Breft got him face down on the floor, Flencik was at his mercy. Breft rode the writhing body beneath him, enjoying his mastery. Every effort Flencik made to evade his clanmate's need only increased Breft's desire.

Breft's hunger for his clanmate allowed for no mercy. He straddled Flencik's buttocks, pushing his manhood at the cleft between them. He barely heard Flencik's shout, "Breft, stop!" He guided himself to the muscular flesh and pressed into the enfolding heat. Breft closed his eyes and pistoned his hips. He felt the tightness of the Imdiko close over his iron flesh. Thought ceased in the sweetness of Flencik's warmth. All Breft knew was the throbbing ache that must be obeyed. He thrust over and over, driving for the rescue of release. His body strained towards the lightening flash of climax. At last the dam burst, releasing the unmerciful pressure that drove him. His gasps lengthened into moans as his semen rushed in a ribbon of wet heat to coat Flencik's inner flesh.

Breft came back to himself in degrees. He felt himself rising and falling on Flencik's broad back as the Imdiko breathed. Otherwise, his clanmate lay still beneath him. Breft pushed himself up.

A wave of coldness overtook his body. Bruises peppered Flencik's back. The marks Breft had inflicted in his attack glared at him in accusation. With a cry of horror, he threw himself from his violated clanmate.

Flencik lumbered to his feet and stared at Breft. His eyes were unreadable, his face emotionless.

A scream welled within Breft's gut, but it stuck there, shredding his insides. All he managed was a hoarse whisper. "Flencik...no...my Imdiko...Flencik..."

"Breft." Flencik reached for the Nobek.

The scream inside Breft tore loose. "No!" He flung himself across the room to the closet where he stored his personal belongings. He shoved past clothing until his hands found his blade, handed down to him from his worshipped mentor, a hard but wise Nobek. He gripped it to thrust it into his own betraying body.

Flencik crashed into him, knocking him face down to the ground. Air whooped from Breft's lungs, but his fist held the blade like iron. No Nobek in his first year of training loosened his grip on his weapon during a fight. Flencik's hand clamped on his wrist, struggling to keep Breft from stabbing himself. He used his weight to keep the howling Nobek flat on the floor.

"Breft! Stop it!" Flencik bellowed in his ear.

"Release me!" Breft said. "I've hurt my Imdiko! I've betrayed my clan! I must die!"

He heard the home's door open, and Flencik cried, "Rajhir, help me!"

Heavy steps thudded the floor. Fingers tangled into the black waves of Breft's hair and yanked his head back. Breft looked into Rajhir's stern glare.

"Stop fighting and drop your blade," the Dramok commanded.

Obeying his leader was instinct, and the only way he would ever be disarmed. Breft's hand opened, and the blade clattered to the floor. Rajhir kicked it away and helped Flencik haul Breft to his feet.

The Nobek bowed his head before them, waiting for the blows that must surely fall. His crime deserved the sentence of death. Why had they stopped him?

"Breft, look at me."

Again, Rajhir's voice commanded immediate obedience. Breft's head snapped up and faced his clanmates who stood before him, shoulder to shoulder.

They smiled at him.

Stunned, Breft gaped. "What--"

"Sit down." Rajhir motioned him to the conversation area. "We will talk of what has happened."

Feeling unreal, Breft sat on a cushion. Rajhir and Flencik settled on either side of him, their larger bodies sandwiching his. Rajhir cupped Breft's chin in his hand and tilted his head so their eyes met. "Are you all right?"

Breft blinked. "Am I...but Flencik...I hurt...he's the one who's..."

Rajhir interrupted. "Look at Flencik. He's not badly injured. He's not even angry with you."

"Why would I be?" Breft jerked at the good-natured tone of the Imdiko. His confusion mounted when he saw Flencik looking at him with the same compassion he'd always shown. "I can't very well fault you for doing exactly what we wanted you to do."

"You're insane." The words fell from the Nobek's lips before he realized he'd spoken.

"Not at all," Flencik answered. He sounded amused. "I bathed in front of you. I touched you even as I said no. I was baiting you, Breft."

The Nobek gaped at him. "Why would you do such a thing? You know how my needs torture me!"

Rajhir patted his knee. "Your training as a Nobek has made you a fine fighter, an unmatched protector for us, for all of Kalquor. However, it hasn't prepared you to be a part of the clan. To take your place with us you must learn gentleness." He caressed Breft's cheek. "Fierceness is fine for those who threaten, but you cannot turn your savagery against us. You have to learn to touch us softly." He inclined his head to brush his lips against Breft's. Breft shivered at the touch. "To not force your passion at our expense."

Flencik touched him too, his hands gentle. Despite his disgust with himself, Breft's body responded to their petting, and desire tormented him anew. He feared his hunger now, feared how it made him into a mindless animal. "I don't know how to be gentle," he said.

"We understand that," Flencik whispered. His breath warmed Breft's ear. "We've been waiting for you to lose that iron control over yourself."

"You held out beyond our expectations," Rajhir added.

Wonder drove back some of the fog of arousal. "You wanted me to force myself on you!"

Flencik shifted and grimaced. "I wouldn't say 'want', but we realized it was necessary. Your entire self-worth is wrapped up in protecting us from all harm. To have you hurt us yourself will teach you the lesson better than anything else can."

Rajhir's expression was kind. "You are now open to learning compassion and to be tender. You'll do anything to not harm Flencik again, won't you, young Nobek?"

Fresh agony overcame Breft. "I shouldn't be allowed to live. I'm a traitor."

"Don't be ridiculous. I pushed you to lose control." Flencik pressed against him, his hand sliding up the inside of the Nobek's thigh. Breft's savage hunger came roaring back, and he reached for him.

Rajhir restrained him and forced him to sit still for Flencik's attention. "The lesson begins. We will now teach you the gentleness your future Matara requires of you."

* * * *

Breft told Amelia, "It took long for me to learn to be gentle, but I never lost control against a member of my clan again. It was a good lesson they taught me. The only pain I inflict on my clanmates now is the kind that brings pleasure."

She hugged herself and wished his arms surrounded her. "You have to fight your own nature to not be a brute?"

He shook his head. "There is no struggle anymore. I like to be caring. I feel a warmth inside where once there was only emptiness." He smiled, and his sharp features became handsome to Amelia. "As I said, training for a Nobek begins in childhood. I wasn't allowed to be caring from an early age. I am glad Flencik and Rajhir let me be that way now."

He came to her. When he took her in his arms, she settled against him with a sigh. He gazed at her with a tender expression. "I want to show you I can be kind, and you will not be afraid of me any longer."

"Yes," she whispered.

His kisses lit on her skin like the flutter of butterfly wings, tickling and delicious. The brush of his fingertips made her shiver. He took his time, his mouth tender as he tasted every inch of her flesh. His hands traced her curves, taking her form in without demand. For the first time since encountering the Kalquorians, Amelia felt safe with Breft. She knew he would never truly harm her and wanted him to realize her understanding. She opened herself to him.

Breft eased into her. He held her against himself so that they moved as one sinuous creature. She couldn't tell where she began and he ended, so complete was their joining. Breft wasn't just inside Amelia; he was part of her.

Their rhythm was a slow, steady pulse, and Amelia's orgasm stretched for a sensuous eternity. Breft watched her face register the thrill of release with a smile. He continued to rock slowly, gently within her until he brought her to another climax before finally allowing his own ecstasy.

He kissed her deeply afterward. She lay against him and realized with a start that it wasn't simply that she felt safe with Breft. She felt truly safe for the first time in her life.

I guess there's nothing left to do but accept conquest.

As Breft continued to kiss her she blinked back sudden tears. She savored her defeat at the hands of her abductors even as she savored the feel of the Nobek's lips against hers. Her will had been conquered; she could now accept it with grace. It wasn't hard; in losing, she'd won everything.

"You win," she sighed when his mouth finally left hers.

"Win?" He smiled his puzzlement.

If this is a sin, forgive me God. And may the women whose lives I've damned to slavery forgive me as well, because I cannot deny my love for Breft, Flencik and Rajhir any longer. She took a deep breath. "I accept being your Matara. I agree to join your clan."

Chapter Thirteen

The next week passed in a happy haze for Amelia. Each day the clan accompanied her to her former quarters so she could work on her painting. Flencik treated her hands when needed to allow her to paint for hours on end.

The Imdiko took great delight in reminding her, "Soon we will go to Kalquor. I will you cure permanently."

"I can't wait," she said. She meant it.

While Amelia painted, the rest of the clan kept busy. Flencik directed the packing of her belongings. He and Rajhir transferred them to the clan's quarters. Breft, to Amelia's amusement, stayed close to her at all times. She understood his continued suspicion of her motives; after all, the Nobek's nature demanded it.

"You are not offended I do not trust you yet?" he asked. He looked worried.

She smiled. "You'll figure out soon enough that I don't want to run away. If babysitting makes you feel better, do it."

Amelia knew she'd made the right choice. Her happiness with the clan was complete, no longer marred by doubts. She begged for details of how her life on their planet would unfold. Even Breft wore an expression of cautious joy.

Amelia wanted nothing of her earlier life to impinge on her newfound destiny. Her first act upon returning to her former quarters was to turn off the vid, silencing its beeped demands that she review dozens of messages.

Once Flencik finished overseeing the transfer of Amelia's belongings, he dove into planning the formal ceremony making her a recognized member of the clan.

"Why can't we do it here on Plasius? The sooner, the better," Amelia said. She frowned at the lake outside and added highlights to the waves in her painting. Only tiny details remained for the canvas; otherwise, she called the work complete. Indeed, she'd created a work beyond her own hopes. Without the threat of pain rushing her, the extra attention to this painting made her earlier art look like a child's scribblings.

"The ceremony must be conducted by the clan's—" Flencik paused and looked to Breft for help.

"Priest," the Nobek supplied.

"You are already our Matara," Rajhir said. "The ceremony celebrates our union and tells others we are a unit. Ours will be of great importance to Kalquor. You are the first Earther Matara and the revival of hope for our world."

"You need a gown for the ceremony," Flencik said.

Breft's eyes gleamed. "I liked what you wore the first time we met."

Amelia chimed laughter. "You did a good job of showing that, you fiend!"

"You should wear another like it."

"Only if you promise not to rip it off me this time."

Flencik chuckled and said, "No promise. When you wear clothes, I want to uncover you fast."

That earned laughter all around. When the hilarity subsided, Rajir said, "Plasian clothes are prettier than Kalquor's. More flattering for one shaped such as you. It would be good for you to get a gown here for the ceremony."

"All right, I will. I'm not very good at choosing formal attire though. Maybe Vrill will help me."

"Vrill chooses good clothes?"

"She chose the gown you saw me in that first night."

Rajhir grinned. "Vrill chooses very good!"

The looks the men exchanged woke Amelia's desire. It seemed a good opportunity to ask her most important question. She put her paintbrush down. "How long after the ceremony do I have to wait before I can get pregnant?"

"There is no need to wait," Rajhir said. "If you were pregnant now, there would be even more reason to celebrate with the ceremony. Of course we are all right with you waiting a little while. We do not need to hurry the childbearing."

"But your people are dying out. Earther women only have so many fertile years."

Flencik patted her head as if she was a child herself. "You are young with much time. I have means to extend your fertility in later years. It is a matter of managing your cycle."

"Managing my cycle? You mean you can control my ovulation?"

He nodded. "I can delay it to save the eggs until we are ready for them. When you wish to start a child, I can give you medicine to make you ready for fertilization."

Amelia stood. "Can you do it today? Now?"

They stared at her. She wondered if she'd said something wrong until Rajhir came to her with tears streaming down his cheeks and enveloped her in his arms. "You would do this for us so soon? Are you truly ready?"

She reached up to brush his face dry even as she herself cried at his emotion. Breft and Flencik crowded close to them. "It's what Kalquor needs. More importantly, it's what my clan wants."

"Do *you* want this, Amelia?"

She felt so good inside she felt she must burst. "I want us to be together and happy forever. I want to be the mother of your children. Take me back to our quarters now and give me this medicine. Let me give you a child."

Chapter Fourteen

The marketplace near the clan's quarters buzzed with activity. Every Plasian seemed to be out shopping despite the blazing suns' glare. Amelia sat at a table beneath a tree's shade outside an eatery. She nibbled nellus and sipped cool shel with quiet satisfaction. Despite her overall contentment, it felt odd to be alone after so many days and nights with the Kalquorians. Without them, she had a sense of nakedness.

At a table nearby, a Plasian couple forgot their lunch in their ardor for each other. The male slipped the strap of his companion's top off one silky shoulder to expose her breast. He massaged the flushed mound, teasing its stiffening tip with his thumb. The woman reached out of sight beneath the table. The rhythmic flexing of her arm told Amelia all she needed to know. The pair moaned into each others' mouths.

Watching their sex play, Amelia felt her own wetness. Why wasn't she with her Kalquorian mates, touching and being touched? She needed a dress for the uniting ceremony, but right now she ached for the clan's attentions.

"Here's the troublemaker at last." Vrill folded herself into the chair next to Amelia's.

The Earther threw her arms around her friend. "Vrill! How have you been?"

Vrill returned the embrace. "Fine, but I want to hear about you. I'm glad to see you looking more gorgeous than ever."

"I've joined the clan."

"Wonderful!" Vrill looked relieved.

"That's not all." Amelia felt her face flush. A smile spread over her face. "I'm pregnant with their child."

Vrill squealed and hugged her again. "I'm so happy for you!" She sat back and regarded Amelia with the brightest of smiles. "I'm glad you came to your senses and stopped letting rigid Earther values dictate your life. Where are those yummy Kalquorians of yours?"

Amelia sipped more shel and glanced towards the amorous Plasian couple. The female now bent over her partner's lap. The back of her dark furred head bobbed in and out of view as she suckled his flesh. Her skirt rumpled at her waist, exposing her bronze buttocks which thrust up at the sky. The male's hand cupped one globe, and he dipped a long finger in and out of her anus. His eyes were closed as he shut out the world to revel in sensation.

Amelia dragged her eyes away from the delightful scene and answered Vrill. "They let me come here alone. Rajhir said it's to show their trust in me, but if Breft isn't somewhere near, I'll kiss a Tragoom."

Vrill grimaced at the mention of the squat, warty race that had a bad habit of eating enemies and occasionally their few allies. Not even the most sympathetic could find anything pleasant in a Tragoom's appearance. "Ugh. There's being uninhibited, and then there's insanity. I'm surprised your clan's let you out at all given the uproar around here lately."

Vrill had Amelia's undivided attention. "What do you mean? What's going on?"

"You haven't heard?" Vrill chuckled. "Innocent Amelia, the center of conflict between Plasius and Earth, and you don't even know it!"

A chill trickled down Amelia's spine. "What are you talking about?"

Vrill plucked a nellus from Amelia's plate. "Earth demands Saucin Israla send police to rescue you from the Kalquorians. I guess they don't realize we require no police here." She popped the fruit in her mouth and chewed with obvious delight before continuing. "Earth says you've been kidnapped. This is an unspeakable crime against all Earthers, and if Plasius doesn't help recover you, we're guilty of abetting this injustice."

Amelia's stomach churned. "What is the Saucin doing about it?"

"She's mediating between Dramok Rajhir and Earth. The clan claims you've joined them of your own free will. As their Matara, your welfare is no longer Earth's concern."

"Why hasn't Rajhir told me about this?" Amelia said.

Vrill patted her shoulder without concern. "If I remember Kalquorian custom, the Matara is not to be troubled by any conflict outside the clan. More importantly, a Matara expecting birth is never exposed to stress."

"But I could tell Earth myself that I've willingly joined the Kalquorian clan. There's no need for problems between our planets."

Vrill nodded. "If you can convince your clan to let you speak to Earth, perhaps hostilities might be avoided."

"I'll see what I can do." Amelia set her jaw. "Rajhir *must* allow me to speak."

Vrill stood. "Good. First we have to take care of a more important matter."

"What?" Amelia steeled herself for more bad news.

"Your gown for the ceremony, of course! You can't wear those lumpy clothes you brought from Earth. In fact, you need a whole new wardrobe." Vrill tugged Amelia to her feet. "Let's go."

Amelia groaned but allowed her friend to drag her along. "Only a Plasian would be more concerned about fashion than the possibility of war."

Vrill laughed. "We all must die sometime, but we can look good doing it!"

* * * *

"Why won't you let me talk to Earth?" Amelia heard the frustration in her own voice.

The clan had been waiting in their quarters when she returned from her shopping trip. They exhibited visible relief when she walked in the door. That canceled Amelia's suspicions that Breft had followed her. Fortunately, no Tragooms lurked in the vicinity to kiss.

She insisted on calling Earth. Rajhir responded by thundering, "No!"

Breft's tone was quieter but still tense. "This is not your problem, little one. Earth's claims on you are our concern alone. We will handle it."

"How can it not be my problem? Earth is threatening Kalquor and Plasius because of me!"

Rajhir's eyes sparked purple fire. "We take care of you. You are not to be troubled by events outside your clan. Vrill should not have spoken."

He paced the floor, his hands clenching and opening, clenching and opening. The tendons stood out in his neck. Flencik hovered near Amelia as if to protect her from their leader's wrath. Even Breft thrummed with tension, his dark eyes following Rajhir.

Amelia walked into the Dramok's path, forcing him to halt. He stood over her, glaring down. She fought off a stab of fear along with a sudden rush of desire.

"I *am* troubled, Rajhir. I don't want hostilities between our races because of me." She ran her hands over the planes of his torso, up his corded neck, and to his face. She pressed her palms to his cheeks. "I can put a stop to this nonsense. All it would take is telling them I am with you by my own free will."

She pressed herself against him. Did he relax just a little? Did she dare to hope this colossus might yield to her? "Please, my love. Let me ease their worries, and therefore mine."

He pulled away. "I will not allow you to be bothered with Earth's nonsense."

Amelia's eyes pricked with tears. "Then Earth is right. I'm no more than your prisoner, a slave for your sexual appetites."

Rajhir's eyes widened, and his face darkened with renewed fury. She heard Breft hiss and Flencik's warning, "Amelia!" She acknowledged neither, keeping her gaze locked on Rajhir's face.

The Dramok's hands clasped her shoulders. He squeezed, stopping the pressure just short of pain. "We kept you against your will in the beginning, but you chose to join this clan. You are here by choice now."

"Then prove it by giving me this chance to speak to my home world. Otherwise you're taking away my freedom and proving them right."

For a moment his grip tightened to where she did feel pain. She verged on crying out when he relaxed his hold.

"Call." He nodded toward the vid.

His sudden acquiescence surprised her so much that she looked at him for a few moments. *Go!* her mind shouted. *Before he changes his mind.*

Moving in slow motion, she approached the vid. "Earth Liaison Jack Frank," she said. The vid beeped acknowledgment. A series of clicks announced its compliance.

A shadow fell over her. Rajhir stood at her shoulder, frowning. Breft and Flencik joined them.

Frank's face appeared on the vid screen. Amelia watched his eyes widen in shock.

"Amelia! Where are you?"

"With my clan."

Frank's mouth opened and closed like a gasping fish. His pink face deepened to red, alarming Amelia. She thought he might have a heart attack right in front of her.

"Jack! Are you all right?"

"Am I -- am I--" His eyes bulged. "Are *you* all right? We heard you'd been taken prisoner."

"I've chosen to join the Kalquorian clan."

His face edged towards purple. "You chose...impossible! Mixing with another species is blasphemy against God!"

Amelia sighed. She'd be glad to have this interview over and done with. "I've become their Matara, and I'm going to Kalquor to live with them."

"It's all right, Amelia. We know they're forcing you to say that, but an Earth transport is on its way to rescue you. It'll be there by tomorrow."

"I don't need rescuing. Listen to what I'm saying. I'm with the clan of my own free will."

"That's what two other women said before they escaped the

Kalquorians who kidnapped them."

Amelia's heart plunged to her stomach. "What are you talking about?"

For once, Frank's pomposity was nowhere to be found. He looked terrified. "All of our women who have been abducted and taken to Kalquor contacted Earth and said it's what they want. However, two of the women changed their minds. When they told the clans they'd joined they wanted out, the clans refused to let them leave. Those two women managed to escape, and now the truth is out. Who knows how many other females decided to leave the clans and were prevented from doing so? And how many were forced to send messages saying they wanted to go to Kalquor when in fact they didn't?" He leaned forward so that his anxious face filled the vid screen. "Amelia, whether you think you've chosen the Kalquorians or not, you are nothing but a sex slave to them! This situation is an affront to God! You must escape and renounce your sins!"

Amelia swallowed. Behind her, the clan stayed silent. She felt their eyes on her, waiting for her reaction.

Why had she insisted on making this call? She didn't want to know others had been forced to Kalquor. She didn't want to know her happiness was hell to others. She didn't want to acknowledge that her own clan kept her a prisoner until she finally admitted she wanted to be with them.

"Amelia?" Frank's voice trembled.

"I have to go to Kalquor. I love these men, and I -- I'm pregnant with their child." By the end of her statement, her voice tapered to a whisper.

He heard her anyway. "You don't have to have that monster, Amelia!" His voice rose to an earsplitting scream. "For your eternal soul, get away from them! We'll get you out of there, we'll tear that thing out of you, we'll--"

Rajhir roared. Flencik swung Amelia out of the way as the Dramok lunged at the vid. "You will not threaten our Matara or her child!" he shouted at the gaping liaison. "She chooses us! She goes to Kalquor!" He smashed his fist on the vid controls, breaking the connection. Jack Frank's face disappeared.

Rajhir twisted around to face Amelia. "Our child is not a monster," he said. "You know this!"

"I know, Rajhir." She hugged herself, crossing protective arms over her belly. "Please don't be angry. I'd never let anyone take our baby from me."

His face softened, and he gathered her in his arms. "Matara, Matara," he breathed, kissing her face. "You made the right choice to go with us. We will love you always."

Flencik stroked her hair. "The two women your Liaison Frank mentioned were released by the clans that took them. They were lesbians and could not be happy with the men."

Breft added, "Even for the sake of having children for Kalquor, we could not force such an unnatural state on these women."

"And they claimed they escaped?" Amelia asked.

"It is not known what they told Earth," Breft growled. "We only know what your government officials say. No one has heard from the women since they returned to Earth."

"If Earth learned they were lesbians, then their lives are better over." Amelia's voice caught. "Homosexuality is a capital crime. They could be dead now — or worse."

"Perhaps they lied to keep themselves safe. It is understandable given the circumstances."

"They're still in for a bad time, especially if they've had sex. If the clans that took them drugged them or bit them—"

"They most assuredly did." Rajhir chuckled. "They would take every advantage to seduce Earther women as we did with you."

"Then they'll wish they died. They still might." Amelia felt tears roll down her cheeks. "But not before suffering horribly. Unmarried, nonvirginal women are intolerable."

"Even if taken against their will?" Flencik was shocked.

"They must have done something to entice the men. That's Earth gov's thinking anyway." Amelia sniffled.

Rajhir's voice was soft. "That is the fear you faced on Earth, was it not? You did not come to us a virgin, Amelia. I admit it surprised me. You were too inhibited, too frightened of the consequences to have given yourself willingly."

"Was your first lover like with us?" Breft asked. He sat at her feet so he could look up into her eyes. His steady gaze comforted her.

She rubbed the tears from her eyes. "How do you mean?"

"Without our bite or drugs or alcohol, you try to hold back your desire. Still, you enjoy the sex. Did you enjoy the man who took your virtue as you do with us? Hesitant, frightened, but wanting it just the same?"

Amelia remembered Mr. Perkins, his filthy rental, the brutal use he made of her once a week for six months. She swallowed. "I enjoyed it. Not like with you because we all care for one another. For him, it was just sexual satisfaction. He used me, he hurt me, he could have ruined my life, but I still liked it."

She broke down, harsh sobs exploding from her chest. Her legs gave out beneath her, and the men moved as one to stop her fall. The clan carried her to the lounger and draped her across their laps while old grief and terror released itself.

"Why?" she cried out between sobs. "Why would I like it? What is wrong with me?"

"Nothing, nothing, little one," Rajhir murmured in her ear. "You have come through your ordeal remarkably well."

"How can you say that?" Amelia wailed. "I like it when I'm dominated, when I feel powerless. I like it when the men I've been with take advantage of me. I like being too helpless to resist. I even liked being spanked like an unruly five year old. How can I possibly be normal when pain and helplessness makes me feel so good?"

"Because you still feel something," Flencik said. "The reports from Kalquor tell us most Earther women have no sexual urges at all, even with drugs or the bite to enhance pleasure." He stroked her cheek, his cat eyes sad. "Your leaders have made it almost impossible for Eather females to enjoy sex as it should be. Be glad you can have the pleasure you do."

"But if you knew what I let them do, you'd be disgusted with me! Maybe not the first man, but the second one —— you'd know what a freak, what an abomination I am ——"

"Amelia! Amelia!" Rajhir clasped her face between his hands. "Never call yourself these terrible things. I will not hear this."

His mouth covered hers, as if to devour the ugly words. His kiss was forceful, almost violent. She let him punish her with the embrace. Her lips felt swollen and bruised when he finished, but emotionally she felt better, cleansed even.

"You could never be anything except our beloved," Rajhir said, his thumb tracing the tender flesh of her mouth. "To prove this, you will tell us of this second man and what he did to you."

"Oh no, please, I can't ——" Amelia started, but Breft's face darted forward. His fangs sank into her neck as Rajhir and Flencik held her still. Her resistance faded almost immediately as euphoria crept in. She relaxed, melting in the center of the warm embrace of the three bodies surrounding hers. She sighed, closed her eyes, and floated on a sea of bliss.

The mouth under her jaw withdrew. From some distance, she heard Rajhir's voice. "Amelia?"

Funny how he sounded far away, yet his deep baritone rumbled through her body. She smiled at how it vibrated through her.

"Amelia?"

"Hmmm?"

"Open your eyes."

Her lids parted so she could look into the three faces peering down at her. "Hi guys," she purred.

Flencik darted a glance at Breft. "You injected too much."

"Perhaps, but she will not mind telling us what we want to know."

"She is Matara now, not a prisoner."

"Not our prisoner, but Earth still binds her."

"Indeed it does," Rajhir agreed. "It is time we break the hold her old life yet maintains."

He smiled at her, and Amelia felt her whole body smile back. He was so handsome, so sexy! Another thrill went through her body at the sound of his deep voice. "You will not mind telling us of this second man now?"

Amelia licked her lips. "Talking isn't at the top of my list right this moment."

That drew three deep-throated chuckles. "I am sure it is not, little one. I will hear your story first, however." As she started to protest, he kissed the tip of her nose. "Be a good girl, and you will be well rewarded."

Heat grew in her belly at the look in his eyes. "Promise?"

"You have my word on it."

"All right." Languid in their arms, the potency of Breft's bite streaming through her body, she no longer felt the anguish of only moments ago. Nothing could penetrate her euphoric mood; she lounged safe from all the pain of her life.

Even remembering the face of the man who'd brought her the greatest pain, the most terrible shame, and the blood-freezing fear failed to conquer the security she now enjoyed.

"His name was Keith Garroway. He was my boss, and he was the chief of police."

* * * *

"How bad do you want to keep your job?" Chief Garroway asked as he locked his office door.

Twenty-one year old Amelia felt something inside her shrivel at his words. "Have I done something wrong?" she asked, casting about in her memory for the mistake she must have made to precipitate this sudden threat to her secretarial position. She and her now bedridden mother depended on her tiny paycheck.

"I didn't say you'd done anything wrong," the police chief said. "I asked if you want to keep your job."

Amelia felt tiny in the chair across from his desk as he came to loom over her. Garroway wasn't Kalquorian big, but he was tall for an Earther. Tall, muscled, and resting one hand on the gun in his belt.

"I really need this job sir," she answered, fighting to keep the urge to sob out of her voice. "My mother is ill, she's dying, and the doctors' bills —"

"I don't want to hear your sad story, princess." He looked from her face to the locked door back to her face. "I know all that shit already. You just keep your mouth shut, and you'll keep your job. Stay quiet and nothing bad happens." He patted his gun as if for emphasis.

"What —" she started, then his hands were clutching her breasts. She gasped and tried to jerk away.

He paused groping long enough to lightly slap her cheek. "Hold still and shut the fuck up. Don't fuck with me," he warned as he yanked on the buttons of her blouse. "You know what happens to sluts. And if I get the slightest inkling you'll turn me in, I'll blow your brains out."

Amelia heard the lack of emotion in his voice and knew he wasn't bluffing. She held herself very still and bit her lips to keep from crying. Tears slid down her cheeks, but Chief Garroway paid those no mind as he exposed her breasts. He grunted appreciation as he spilled the heavy globes from her bra. He got on his knees and bent towards her, his mouth open. He latched onto her breast and sucked hard. His teeth closed over her flesh as he clutched the other with an iron grip. She squeezed her eyes shut so she didn't have to watch him bite, slap, and pinch the tender mounds, leaving angry red marks on her golden skin. Shame filled her as her body responded to Garroway's brutal play. She clenched her thighs together, trying to keep warm moisture from trickling from her suddenly avid sex.

While eagerly sucking one throbbing nipple, he thrust his hands under her skirt. He grasped the soft white cotton of her thin panties and yanked them down to her ankles.

Amelia gasped but offered no resistance. Garroway clamped his fist above her elbow and yanked her to her feet as he rose. "Kneel on the seat," he whispered hoarsely.

She obeyed, knowing what would come next and trying not to think about it. She gripped the back of the chair hard. He flipped her skirt up to expose her buttocks. His meaty palm cracked against one cheek, making her jump. She gasped, but withheld a cry of pain. He slapped the other side, and she jumped again. Her buttocks burned, and Amelia felt sure he'd left handprints.

The sound of his zipper opening was like a demon's shriek. Then his rigid member was there, bludgeoning its merciless way into her tender flesh. It had been years since her affair with Mr. Perkins. She was tight, and despite the betraying wetness and her best efforts to relax, Garroway's thick penis hurt as he ground it into her. His hands gripped her hips, and he shoved her back, impaling her cruelly on himself.

He forced himself into her taut aperture, not waiting for her body to adjust to his. She couldn't help the little bird cries of pain as he stabbed into her womb over and over. His brutal thrusts threatened to knock the chair over. Occasionally he slapped her buttocks as he drove her. She whimpered with each explosive crack against her flesh. In contrast, Garroway was quiet as he took his violent pleasure with her body.

How long he drove her, she didn't know. She was no longer wet. He abraded her inner flesh with his tireless pounding; the burning pain became agony. Tears rained from her eyes. Her knuckles turned white as she gripped the back of the chair, fighting desperately to hang on and not scream. Still he thrust into her as if he'd never stop.

Amelia had never known such pain. She thought she might die, that Chief Garroway might actually fuck her to death. Surely the castration and scarification suffered by those convicted of sex crimes could not feel worse!

After an eternity of torture, Garroway's rhythm finally faltered. He thrust even deeper, hitting something inside Amelia's core that radiated shrieking pain throughout her belly. She couldn't hold back the cry that escaped between her gritted teeth. Garroway's breath caught, and he emitted a low groan as he spent himself into her raw, screaming sex.

He withdrew. Amelia waited for the pain to ease back; she couldn't possibly move now. She shuddered in shock's aftermath as her tormented womb pulsed waves of anguish. Her sobbing gasps filled the room.

At last she gingerly climbed off the chair. Her legs shook violently as she bent to pull her panties up. Only when she'd adjusted her clothing did she turn to face the silent chief of police.

He pointed his gun at her face.

Amelia's knees gave way, and she fell into the chair behind her. Garroway's aim never wavered; the barrel followed her descent with ease. She stared into the black hole before her, too terrified to remember how to pray. She couldn't look anywhere else. She couldn't even look into the chief's face when he spoke.

"Every day at this time, you're gonna come in here, close the door, and lock it behind you. We'll have our fun, then we'll act like nothing's happened. I'm fixed, so don't think you've got a license to whore around. You get pregnant and my name comes up, I'll kill you. You talk about our little agreement, I'll kill you. You quit your job here, I'll come to your house, rape your bag of bones mama, kill her, then rape and kill you." He grabbed a handful of Amelia's hair and yanked her head back so she stared into his face. "Have we got an understanding?"

She tried to swallow, but her throat was dry. "Yes sir," she croaked.

"Then get the hell out and go back to work." He released her and holstered his gun. He sat down behind his desk and shuffled through a stack of papers as if Amelia had already left.

Amelia struggled to her feet and left the office. She made her way to the women's restroom to check her appearance. Her reflection in the cracked mirror shocked her; except for tear tracks in her makeup, she looked normal. Somehow she'd expected terror and guilt to be stamped on her visage, a clear accusation for all to see. But no; once she'd re-applied powder and brushed her hair, she was the same Amelia who'd walked into the police station this morning, poured herself a cup of coffee, and plunged into the neverending round of filing, typing, and answering the telephone.

She'd even traded the fear for numbness now that the rape was over. *For today* her mind reminded her. Because Chief Garroway intended to repeat the assault tomorrow and every day she came to work.

She'd have to let him. If it was only her life at stake, she might dare to run. But he'd said he'd kill Mama. Worse, he'd rape Mama.

Don't think about it her inner voice advised. *I have to get through the rest of the day yet. Then I have to take care of Mama for the night. She's not stupid; if you let down your guard for a second, she'll know something has happened. So don't think about it for now. It didn't happen. It won't happen tomorrow or ever again. Just go on that, and I'll wait to think about it when I'm alone. Maybe.*

Amelia collected herself and returned to work. She went home that night and tended to her mother, who in her haze of pain noticed nothing amiss.

Amelia went to work the next day, drank her morning cup of coffee, and went about her usual tasks. At the noon break, she entered the chief's office, closed the door, locked it, and submitted to his sadistic use of her body.

For over two years, she managed to keep her mind a careful blank when it came to those hellish minutes Garroway possessed her. He liked to hurt her, making her shudder with the pain she dared not voice. He called her vile names. He threatened her with beatings from his baton, with shocking her with his taser, with blowing her face off with his gun. Sometimes he'd take her mouth, one hand fisted painfully in her hair, one hand holding his service revolver so the barrel rested between her eyes, his finger on the trigger. Once he fucked her with it as she lay naked and prone on his desk. He showed her it was loaded before he did it. His face registered cold satisfaction when hers dissolved in tears. She bled when he jerked the cold metal out to shove his sex inside. He came very hard that day.

Most days she bore the pain and fear and then cast the latest episode from her mind as she left his office. If she tried to remember those lost moments, which she almost never did, it was like recalling a long-ago nightmare. Most of the details were missing, leaving only hazy images and a sense of doom barely averted.

But there were a few times when Garroway took his pleasure with little abuse. He was always rough and never tender, but once in awhile he got on top of her and fucked her without threats or slaps. When that happened, Amelia would feel the horror of her sex warming, of her juices flowing, of pleasure filling her until her body quaked with unwanted orgasm. Those days were worse than when he did hurt her badly. She found such episodes were more difficult to erase from her memory. When her body defied her hatred and fear of Garroway, when it climaxed in spite of her revulsion, Amelia thought she might lose her sanity.

She painted on her days off in a feverish haze, frantic to exorcise demons she dared not consciously acknowledge. The images emerging from Amelia's canvases were black and red, angry and jagged. The subject matter didn't matter. Even flowered meadows were visions of anguished madness when painted by Amelia's brush. She never bothered to explain the hectic chaos of her artwork to those who viewed it.

Rabid evangelicals who exalted in the delightful nightmare of God's Final Judgment on sinners bought her work by the dozens. It was the greatest success she enjoyed on her home planet. With the added income, Amelia was able to keep her mother supplied with all the painkillers she needed until the cancer finally devoured the wasted creature.

* * * *

"Mama never found out, thank God," Amelia told the surrounding Kalquorians.

"Poor Amelia," Flencik sighed. "It is indeed a wonder any remnant of sexual interest remains."

"Oh, it's alive and well," Amelia said, reaching for him. Rajhir caught her wrist. "You promised," she pouted.

"In a moment. First we must make facts clear."

"What facts?"

"First: you are not to blame for what those men did to you. You were given no choice. You did what was needed for survival."

"If you say so." Amelia tried to twist her arm out of his grip. She couldn't budge.

Flencik glared at Breft. "She is too intoxicated to care."

"She will remember and consider it properly later." Rajhir continued his lecture. "Fact two: there is nothing you have done or allowed done to make us despise you."

Amelia stopped squirming as his words penetrated the fog of lust consuming her. "Really? Even though I liked some of it?"

Flencik picked up for Rajhir. "Even if you received pleasure from *all* of it. Which brings us to fact three: you like a little pain and humiliation because these things make it safe for you to enjoy sex."

She gaped at him. "Run that by me again."

He nodded. "Think, Amelia. You have been taught that sex for pleasure, even within marriage, is sinful and deserving of punishment severe enough to be fatal. When you are forced or hurt or shamed, a part of you recognizes you are already enduring punishment. Your body is free to enjoy sexual intercourse."

"That's twisted," she said.

"It is normal considering what you have been through." He stroked her hair. "You are now completely safe from men like your Perkins or Garroway. We have given and will continue to give you the pleasure you respond to without true harm being done."

The euphoric warmth overtook her again. She wiggled the fingers of the hand Rajhir held trapped. "And since you promised, it's time you get me to respond again."

Rajhir rumbled laughter as he kissed her fingertips. "Absolutely."

The three men tumbled her onto the lounger, pulling clothes off her and themselves. She found herself in the midst of a forest of muscled arms, in a sea of grasping hands that stroked, rubbed, pinched, caressed. Mouths kissed, licked, nipped, tasted.

She closed her eyes with a sigh, surrendering herself entirely to sensation. They filled her with their passion, opening moist channels to spend their pleasure. She rode each orgasm in blissful intoxication, receiving one man in her mouth, one in her womb, and one in her anus. She served them with uncontained joy. The air hung heavy with sighs, grunts, and cries of ecstasy accomplished.

The rest of the day was lost to pleasure, as if to bid goodbye to Plasius in the sensual manner of its indigenous populace. *Vrill would approve*, Amelia thought proudly. She knelt before Rajhir, who clutched his hands around her head as he pumped into her mouth. She rubbed the underside of his penis with her tongue, giving him delicious friction. He sighed as he withdrew his slick penis to the tip then slid inside to the back of her throat. He held her hair back so he could watch himself take her.

Flencik rode her from behind, his larger penis pressing deeply into her tight-rimmed anus while the smaller dipped into her vulva. Pain and pleasure combined to keep her desire at its peak. She trembled from the frequent and intense climaxes his hard use gave her.

Beneath her crouched body, Breft suckled her breasts, gently sucking, then biting just to the point of pain, suctioning a tender mound as far into his mouth as possible, licking the tips with a delicate tongue. His fingers teased her clitoris, the dainty tickle a counterpoint to Flencik's force. She poured honey over his hand.

With every explosive contraction of her womb she enslaved herself more completely to them in her heart. She could not serve them enough, could not offer her body to them in enough ways. When they poured their love into her, her one thought was of how much she loved all three, and how life would be hell without them.

Chapter Fifteen

Amelia woke the next morning to the sunlight of another golden Plasian morning streaming into the quarters. It took her a few moments to miss the comfortable bulk of the Kalquorians. She lay alone on the plush lounger.

She blinked. The three Kalquorians were all fully dressed. Rajhir sat at the vid with his back to her, muttering commands to the machine. Breft stood behind his shoulder, watching the screen with interest.

Flencik bustled in the kitchen area. He lifted a tray and turned towards Amelia. He started to see her sit up.

"Good morning," he said, smiling at her as he carried her breakfast to the lounger. "I am glad you woke yourself. Now you will not be mad I wake you."

"As if I could ever get mad at you," she answered. He sat behind her, balancing the tray on his knees. She snuggled back against him, enjoying the warmth of his arm circling around her.

"Good morning, Amelia." Breft left the vid to lean down and kiss her on the tip of her nose. He stepped back to allow Rajhir to do the same.

"You grow more beautiful each day," the Dramok told her. "You are well?"

"Yes." Amelia loved the ritual of their greetings when she woke. She didn't think she'd ever tire of it.

Flencik pressed a morsel of desrel to her lips. She ate it delicately from his fingers. Rajhir returned to the vid, and Breft followed him.

"What are you doing?" she asked between bites. Flencik's attention made speaking difficult. As soon as she swallowed one mouthful, he pressed more food in.

"Arranging for the soonest possible transport to Kalquor," Rajhir replied without looking around. "We must leave Plasius quickly. An Earth military transport arrived early while we still slept."

Breft shot her a glance. "They may try to take you back by force."

Amelia's stomach churned with new anxiety. "You think they're here because of me?"

Breft and Rajhir exchanged a look. After a long moment of silence, Rajhir answered. "They have already demanded Israla hand you over to them."

Amelia gasped. "What did she say?"

Breft's face twisted into an unpleasant smile. "She told them, in their own language, to 'go fuck themselves'. If I understand the meaning right, it was a very appropriate, if impossible, suggestion."

Amelia pushed Flencik's hovering hand away from her mouth. "How soon will we leave for Kalquor?" she asked.

"Tonight. I am arranging passage now. I will visit Saucin Israla this morning and finish my official duties." Rajhir stood and addressed Breft. "You check the transport and map our route from here so we avoid all contact with hostile Earthers."

"There will not be any threat to the Matara," Breft affirmed. He smiled his most predatory smile at her before striding out to obey Rajhir's orders.

"Flencik, prepare our belongings. Arrange for them to be loaded on the transport."

Flencik nodded. "When Amelia finishes her meal, I will begin."

Amelia eased herself free of the Imdiko. "I think I've had enough to eat."

He frowned at her plate, still half full. "Done?"

"The excitement's killed my appetite." She tried on a reassuring smile.

He rose, satisfied. "I will pack right away."

Rajhir added, "I will see the Saucin now." He came to Amelia, who perched bolt upright on the lounger. "Do not fear, Matara. Earth will not have you." His purple eyes burned. He bent down to kiss her lingeringly before sweeping out of the quarters, leaving her alone with Flencik.

And confusion. And fear. The arrival of Earth's military terrified her. She'd seen the looks on her clan's faces. They were concerned too.

Only last night she'd thought of how life without the trio of Kalquorians would be hell. Now, as if summoned by her fears, Earthers had arrived to take her away.

No! No! her racing mind screamed. She wanted a place to run and hide. Surely the soldiers would arrive at their door any moment now, and though Flencik's size and strength was formidable, he'd be no match for a platoon of armed men.

Flencik's voice sounded from the other room. "I almost forgot — Vrill called and left a message for you to call back as soon as possible."

"Thanks." Amelia found a robe to wrap herself in and approached the vid. Maybe saying goodbye to her dearest Plasian friend would keep her calm until the escape. Hearing Vrill banter about Amelia's rich sex life would be a welcome distraction.

"Call Ambassador Vrill." Amelia heard the tremor in her own

command and cleared her throat. She forced a bright smile and waited for Vrill to answer.

It took so long that Amelia almost cancelled the call, but the vid finally beeped and the Plasian appeared on the screen.

Vrill's hair was mussed, and she adjusted an askew shoulder strap of whatever scanty thing she was wearing today. *Looks like I interrupted something*, Amelia thought with amusement. Seeing Vrill fresh from an apparent liaison helped chase away some of her trepidation.

"Should I call at a better time?" Amelia smiled, arching an eyebrow.

Vrill licked her lips. Her chest heaved as if from some great exertion. "Now is fine. Can you come over right away?"

"What's the rush? Aren't you, uh, entertaining a guest?"

"No, not at all. Can you come?"

Amelia frowned. "I'm afraid not. Earthers have shown up to take me away, so we're leaving for Kalquor tonight. Are you all right?"

Vrill bit her lip. She *was* upset; Amelia felt sure of it. "I know about your military coming here." She took a deep breath and looked away from the screen. "I was sure you'd be leaving. I have something I want to give you, but you have to come here."

"I don't see how I can. The clan is very worried."

"As they should be." Vrill now looked angry. She faced the screen again. "Perhaps we should just say our goodbyes now."

"I'm sorry, Vrill. I didn't mean to leave on such short notice—"

"That's fine. Have a wonderful life. You deserve it." Vrill broke the connection.

Amelia stared open mouthed at the empty vid screen. "What-the-hell?" she said, enunciating with slow disbelief. Why had Vrill been so angry? Amelia had confided some of the worst punishments Earth meted out to sexual heretics; surely Vrill understood the threat to Amelia and her unborn child!

She left the vid and joined Flencik in the other room. For a few moments she contented herself by watching him pack the clan's belongings. He moved like a bulky cyclone. A contented smile sat on his face as he bustled about.

She swallowed the lump in her throat and forced a cheerful tone. "You work fast."

Flencik looked at her. His smile grew to one of genuine pleasure at her company as he continued his hurried but careful packing. "I am making sure we can leave when the transport is ready to depart. Did you speak to Vrill?"

She took a deep breath. "She's really upset with me for leaving so abruptly. She wanted me to visit her one last time."

"Too dangerous." Flencik tossed a full case of packed belongings on the pile he'd already completed. Amelia was impressed with his organizational skills. She watched him open an empty case and begin to fill it as well.

"I suppose." She tried to keep hurt out of her voice, but Flencik, always on the alert for her distress whether physical or emotional, detected the pain. He immediately stopped packing and came to her.

"My poor Matara," he soothed, kissing her cheeks. His tenderness undid Amelia, and she clung to him, crying softly.

He continued to kiss her face, stroking her hair with soothing hands. She wrapped her arms around his neck, hanging onto him as if for dear life. Earth wanted to tear her away from her clan; she could almost feel her enemies clutching at her.

Flencik picked her up, holding her tight to his torso. She wrapped her legs around his waist, her robe falling away so her naked sex pressed against him. The Imdiko's hands shifted so that they cupped her bared buttocks. Amelia became wet instantly.

His comforting kisses turned passionate. His tongue swept into her mouth to taste, to devour. She moaned and ground her aching female flesh against the granite muscle of his abdomen. Her movements made his tunic ride up so that she felt the warmth of his flesh.

Flencik growled into her mouth as he gripped her buttocks hard. He pushed her up against the wall. She moaned to feel herself trapped between the hard surface and the equally hard Kalquorian. She moved her wet sex against his belly, sliding up and down to delight her secret flesh.

He growled again, a bestial sound that aroused Amelia all the more. She gripped him even harder, trying to fuse her torso to his. One of his hands left its bruising grip on her backside and fumbled at his pants closure. He freed himself, and his thickness was suddenly underneath her, pushing to invade her warmth. His hips thrust upward, and Amelia screamed her pleasure at the sudden impaling.

Flencik heaved against her as if he'd drive her right through the wall at her back. She cried with each delicious plunge he made into her flesh. His angle was wrong for his smaller penis to enter her nether orifice, so he pressed a thick finger into the tight aperture.

She groaned to be filled completely.

His mouth worked hers hungrily. He pressed hard against her, his hips pumping furiously, his finger plunging in and out. He shifted, applying pressure on various parts of her clinging sheath until he found that sweet spot. Amelia shrieked into his mouth, which he answered with a roaring growl.

Over and over his sex rubbed the bundle of nerves she liked best. The pleasure was almost too much to bear; Amelia writhed and fought to escape the delicious torture, to catch her breath. Flencik kept her positioned so the friction remained where he wanted.

He drove against her mercilessly, and her desire built beyond endurance. She screamed nonstop now; the heat in her womb consumed her. It built higher until she must burst, and still release would not come.

She kicked and clawed at the growling man holding her prisoner against the wall. Her struggles were that of a mouse against a lion; Flencik seemed to not notice the nails leaving trails of blood down his neck and back. Her hands tangled in his coal black curls and pulled desperately. She couldn't budge him.

Suddenly the dam within her belly broke; orgasm exploded throughout her body. She flailed helplessly in the Kalquorian's iron grip, her body beyond conscious control. Her lover's rhythm faltered, but she barely registered it in the haze of pulsing ecstacy. His bellow of completion was a dim background noise to the pounding roar of her ears.

She slid down the wall as Flencik's legs buckled beneath them. His knees hit the floor hard, driving his pulsing sex deeper into hers; Amelia clenched around him in renewed climax. She bit into his shoulder as pleasure tore through her body. She tasted his blood, a coppery sweet flavor filling her mouth.

He panted and she sobbed as desire slowly ebbed to leave their bodies limp with exhaustion. Amelia sagged within the protective curl of the Imdiko. As the last touch of pleasure twinged, she fainted.

When she came to moments later, Flencik was just beginning to stir. He slowly rolled them onto the floor to lie belly to belly. His chest was still heaving as he gasped, "Are you all right?"

"I thought I was going to die. It was wonderful," Amelia whispered, her strength too sapped to provide even a voice.

He rasped a sound that, had he the breath, would have been laughter. He caressed her cheek with trembling fingers.

Flencik recovered his strength first. He propped himself on one elbow to look down at Amelia with adoration. "You are amazing."

"Oh no, look what I did." She traced the still-bleeding oval of teeth marks on his shoulder. "You'd better treat this right away."

He grinned. "You know how I am about my marks of honor."

Amelia shook her head at him. "Don't be macho. This is a mess."

"If it concerns you so much, I should not let you see my back."

At her groan he kissed the tip of her nose. "I like I made you as an animal. I like you wild."

Her face went hot. "Stop teasing me. It's embarrassing to lose control like that."

He thumped his chest, an alien Tarzan. "I am a great lover to do this. I will show the others what I made you do."

Amelia couldn't help but giggle. "Have you learned the word incorrigible yet?"

"Does it mean great lover?"

She laughed out loud. "At least you made me forget the Earth military and Vrill for a little while."

He kissed her tenderly. "I really am sorry you cannot visit your friend."

"Damn the Earth military." Her bitterness quickly eclipsed the afterglow of their coupling.

Flencik frowned his own displeasure. "I hope Breft and Rajhir will return soon. I do not like you being without the protection of all of your clan."

A thought made her sit up. "The Earthers would never think to look for me at Vrill's."

"You cannot go to Vrill's. It is too dangerous."

"It's even more dangerous for me to be here. They no doubt know the location of the clan's quarters. They may come for me."

Flencik snorted. "They would be fools to do so. Breft would demolish half the troops before they could react, and Rajhir is himself a force to be feared."

"They're not here right now, and you could be hurt because of me," Amelia fretted. "I would rather die than—"

"Do not say such things!" Flencik wrapped his massive arms around her in a fierce protective gesture. "I am no fighter, but I will let nothing happen to you. Losing you would be worse than any physical injury I would endure."

He kissed her hard, as if to reassure himself she was still safe and sound. She clung to him, pretending the muscled alien could indeed protect her from her own people.

It was only an illusion, and she knew it. As soon as Flencik's mouth left hers she gasped, "Let me hide at Vrill's. You can come for me as soon as the others return or even wait until the transport's ready."

He shook his head. "The Earthers could take you on your way there."

"Not if the shuttle goes straight from here to her home. I won't stop for any reason, and if I think I'm being followed, I'll re-route right back here."

He frowned hard. "I do not like letting you out of my sight."

She raised herself on tip toe to give him a gentle kiss. "I don't either. But I really believe it's safer for all of us if they don't find me with you...if they don't find me at all."

"Your idea does make sense." Flencik blew out an exasperated growl. "Why did those *gurlucks* have to come? Why cannot they accept your happiness and let you go?"

Amelia rested her cheek against his chest. "I don't know. What's a *gurluck?*"

Flencik managed a rueful chuckle. "Did I say that? It is not a word meant for my Matara's pretty ears." He kissed the top of her head.

"Shall I go then?"

He sighed.   "Yes, but I am putting you in the shuttle and programming your route myself." He tilted her head back to look in her eyes. "You keep watch for any Earthers. Any sign of them, you will call me and come straight back."

"If that happens, you contact Rajhir and Breft right away."

"Agreed. If you are not followed, call as soon as you are safely locked inside Vrill's home. If I do not hear from you in——" he calculated silently for a moment before giving her a Plasian timeframe that roughly corresponded to fifteen Earth minutes "——then I am coming after you."

"Okay. Thanks Flencik. I really would have hated leaving Vrill so upset." She hugged him hard.

"I am more worried about Breft than Earthers now. He will most likely beat me for this."

"He'll see the sense of our plan. He'll probably be mad because he didn't think of it himself."

Flencik snorted his disbelief and held her tight, as if he'd never let her go. But he finally released her, saying, "I will send you to Vrill now."

Chapter Sixteen

Amelia's trip to Vrill's home had been uneventful with no sign of Earther pursuit. She had a sick feeling in her stomach nonetheless that had nothing to do with the embryo she carried. If she hadn't been so certain her presence put Flencik in danger, she'd have stayed put in the clan's quarters.

Now she stood on Vrill's doorstep, feeling exposed. She banged on the door, looking over her shoulder for grim soldiers bent on hauling her before Earth justice. Nothing stirred in the shimmering glare of the Plasian morning.

Amelia pressed the visitor announcing microphone next to the door. "Are you there Vrill? It's Amelia. Please let me in."

To her immeasurable relief, the door snicked open a crack. Amelia pushed in, not bothering to even look at her hostess before shoving the door shut behind herself and locking it. "Sorry to be so abrupt, but I don't want anyone to see me here, especially Earthers—"

Her voice died as she turned around to face a dozen Earther soldiers aiming guns at her.

A grizzled middle-aged man, nowhere near the size of a Kalquorian but imposing nonetheless, stepped forward. His greasy, lined face wore hectic red splotches. He looked Amelia over with the expression of someone eyeing particularly disgusting roadkill.

"Secure this whore!" he barked, his voice grating like he gargled gravel every morning. Two youthful soldiers slung their rifles and lunged at Amelia. They roughly pulled her to the floor, knocking the wind out of her. She grunted as one planted a knee in her back. She cried out as her arms were twisted cruelly back, bringing the nerve damage to life. Metal snapped around her wrists and her hands clamored pain.

"She's secured, General Croft sir!" The young man pinning Amelia to the floor squeaked like a mouse in his excitement.

"Get her on her feet." Amelia was hauled upright with rough, sweating hands. She gaped at her surroundings.

They'd trashed Vrill's home, or at least the room they stood in now. Furniture was overturned. Vrill's precious collection of crystal phalluses, some worth more than Amelia's lifetime income, were smashed into tiny glittering shards. The wood ones, formerly polished to a high gleam from generations of use, were so many splintered toothpicks. Others made of stone and marble were ground into pebbles and dust.

Worst of all, Vrill lay motionless on the floor, purple-black blood pooling under her furred head.

"Vrill!" Amelia screamed, finally regaining her senses to struggle. "You monstrous bastards! You killed her!"

General Croft's fist smashed into her jaw, and Amelia's world went gray. Her knees buckled, and the soldiers supporting her let her fall to the floor.

"Shut up, slut! She got what all the residents of this Sodom and Gomorrah deserved."

Amelia barely heard him over the ringing in her ears and her own sobs. Poor Vrill. Amelia now understood the strangeness of their earlier conversation. No doubt the soldiers had been present when Amelia returned her friend's call. The Plasian must have been forced to invite Amelia over. Vrill's anger had come from sudden defiance, a refusal to deliver the clan's Matara to the cruel General Croft. Trying to save Amelia had cost Vrill her life.

"Stand her up again," the general growled. The soldiers jerked her up, pain making her grit her teeth. Her jaw throbbed, and the ground beneath seemed to tilt.

I will not faint. I will not cry out. I will not give the son of a bitch the satisfaction.

She glared at the hulking general with hatred, unmindful of the tears she shed for Vrill.

His lip curled at her defiance. "You are in custody for lewd and lascivious behavior, adultery, willfully committing crimes under the Earth Purity and Morality Act, and treason. In your absence, you have been found guilty of these crimes and sentenced to surgical barreness without the benefit of anesthesia, female castration without the benefit of anesthesia, scarification of your sinful flesh without the benefit of anesthesia, and hard labor until death, all to be carried out immediately after you give birth to the Kalquorian abomination."

"I've had no trial," Amelia protested.

"You confessed your crimes in a recorded transmission to Earth Liaison Jack Frank. Sentence was summarily passed when viewed by the judge assigned your crime."

Croft suddenly spat in her face. Amelia gasped. Many of the avidly watching soldiers laughed in high, screamy voices. The general's saliva, warm and thick like bile, traced a slow path down her cheek. She wanted to throw up.

"Damn filthy whore," Croft snarled. "How dare you! You're a nasty Jezebel, rutting with degenerate aliens like a bitch in heat."

"It wasn't like that!" Amelia screamed. "If you'd just listen——"

He slapped her hard, cutting her off. "Shut up, slut! I see what's under those wide eyes and that pretty face. I see what you really are. You disgust me. What you've done disgusts me. If it were left up to me, I'd rip out the monstrosity they impregnated you with." He flexed his fingers in front of her face. "I'd reach up inside you and tear it out with my bare hands."

More than righteous fury filled Croft's eyes. Whites showed all around the murky irises. His breath came in bursts. His mouth trembled with emotion. Amelia realized she looked into the face of insanity. He wasn't threatening her with empty words. He really did want to rip the clan's baby from her guts. She sucked in her still-flat belly to shield the embryo from the madman. Her voice was a strengthless whisper. "Don't you dare hurt my child."

He punched her in the face again, and this time she did lose consciousness. When she woke again, she was on the floor with Croft leaning over her, slapping her throbbing face. She wailed as his meaty paw cracked against her cheek.

"You awake, whore? Good." He pulled her upright with a handful of hair. She noticed through the haze of pain that none of the soldiers were laughing now. They all looked terrified.

Before Croft's irrational hatred, she managed to moan, "Please. Please."

"Shut up," he said. "Your begging and everything else about you sickens me."

"Plea--"

"Shut up!" He grabbed the collar of her blouse and shook her. Her head rocked back and snapped forward. Her neck creaked a warning. "Shut up or I'll shut you up for good! I'll kill you, you disgusting cunt!"

He threw her on the floor and kicked her buttocks and back with heavy boots. She screamed, curling into herself to defend her belly. Croft reached down and wrapped thick fingers around her throat. He squeezed.

Amelia's windpipe closed from the pressure. She pulled desperately, uselessly, to free her hands locked in the cuffs. Croft's face filled her vision as he throttled her. His bloodshot eyes were wider than ever, his mouth open and drooling. He breathed heavily into her face.

"Die, nasty bitch," he whispered with a lover's tone as he dug his fingers deeper into her throat. "Die for me now. Off to hell with you. That's right."

Dark spots were blotting out his horrible, ecstatic face. He squeezed and squeezed, cutting her life off. Behind the slow throb of her pulse in her ears, Amelia heard a beep, then another. More insistent beeps. From far away, a frightened voice asked, "Sir, should we answer that?"

Amelia's eyes slid closed. For an instant the pressure on her throat increased, then it was gone. Her lungs heaved, and air seared her raw throat. Her breath screamed in and out. The vid continued to beep. There was no other sound for several seconds.

"Throw her ass in the shuttle," Croft said. He sounded breathless himself. "And don't answer that damned thing. It's probably whoever the Plasian whore spreads her legs open for." Amelia opened her eyes in time to see him throw open the door and stomp outside into the blare of sunlight. The vid quieted in mid-beep.

Flencik, Amelia thought. Could he be the one calling? Was he on his way already, having not heard verification of her safe arrival?

Please don't let him get here before we leave. They've already killed Vrill. Not Flencik too!

"Holy shit, man," she heard a young man say. "He was gonna kill her, and she couldn't even defend herself. At least the Plasian got a chance to fight back."

"Shut the hell up," someone answered. The second voice was pitched high in panic. "If he hears you, we're all screwed."

The silent soldiers were almost gentle as they pulled Amelia from the floor. When her limp legs wouldn't support her, one young man stooped down to drape her over his shoulder and carried her outside.

Amelia tried to raise her head to look for a shuttle racing towards Vrill's home. Her aching neck refused to comply. She listened hard, praying not to hear the whistling sound of Flencik's arrival. Nothing stirred in the searing glare of the twin suns.

The soldier lowered Amelia into a seat within a cage inside the military shuttle. She watched helplessly as her ankles were shackled to the floor. The young soldier stepped out of the cage, and he looked at her with pity. He clanged the metal door shut, and he locked her inside. *Like I'm a savage animal*, she thought, fresh tears rolling down her bruised face. Her eyes cut to Croft, who sat across from her cage, watching her and fingering the handgun on his hip. He licked his lips. She noticed his erection with no surprise.

The real maniac runs loose killing innocents, and I'm imprisoned for the crime of falling in love.

The shuttle's engine rumbled to life. Amelia groaned, knowing it would take her to her death. Still, her main fear remained that Flencik would meet his as well if he got here now.

Hurry, damn you! Get us out of here now!

Even as she thought it, the shuttle's driver called, "Plasian shuttle approaching at high speed, sir."

Amelia's heart dropped to her shoes. She couldn't breathe.

"It's either her pet dicks or the other slut's friends. Get us to the transport now and radio ahead for them to prepare for takeoff." He glared at Amelia, stroked his gun, and licked his lips again.

Amelia closed her eyes in gratitude as the shuttle bore her away, taking from her beloved Imdiko, sparing his precious life.

Goodbye, my clan, my loves. I'm sorry for any pain I caused.

Chapter Eighteen

Rajhir signed off the vid and turned to his clanmates. "A squadron of our battle cruisers is en route from a nearby system."

"How far away is 'nearby'?" Breft asked.

"They'll be here before nightfall."

Flencik halted his frantic pacing of their quarters, his face working. "That will be too late!"

Rajhir felt the Imdiko's rage, the blame he battered himself with. Soon his guilt would overwhelm him, rendering him unable to contribute anything constructive.

As for Breft, the Nobek stood still, his arms crossed over his chest. His demeanor exhibited watchful patience. His confidence in Rajhir's ability to sort out this mess kept him quiet as he waited for his leader's order.

Could the Dramok reclaim Amelia? Her absence, only minutes old, gnawed at his insides, making it hard to think. Despite the room's austere appearance in the wake of Flencik's meticulous packing, the ghostly scent of her musk from making love to the Imdiko remained in the air. The aroma added to his grief.

My beautiful Matara, so innocent and confused. How those Earthers must have frightened you when they took you away!

Hopefully, fright was the only pain she suffered. If the Earthers succeeded in taking her back to their planet, she would face death, perhaps worse. Flencik's report of how he'd found Vrill and the horrific injuries she'd suffered threatened Rajhir's remarkable control.

What if getting Amelia back proved impossible? How could he face a lifetime without her? To think he'd never touch that silky auburn hair, never trace the line of her spine with his fingertips, never suckle the rose tips of her round breasts, never slip into the sweet warmth of her sex again -- inconceivable! Existence without Amelia would be a living death.

Then get hold of yourself, Dramok Rajhir. Collect your thoughts and act.

"Flencik, calm yourself," he said. Flencik jerked to attention at the commanding tone. "You had good reason to go along with Amelia's idea. It made sense the Earthers would come here to claim her."

"I should have known they had more sense than to challenge us directly," the Imdiko muttered.

"Even so, you could not have known they waited for her at Vrill's. Had you not allowed Amelia to go, you never would have found the ambassador in time to save her." Rajhir smiled grimly. "Israla's gratitude for Vrill's life is allowing us to bring our own military into Plasian space. We can force a confrontation if need be."

"What good is gratitude when those monsters have Amelia and can take her away at any moment?" Flencik's voice rose with anguished panic.

Rajhir stepped to the Imdiko and clamped his hands on Flencik's broad shoulders. "I need your mind to be clear. You cannot let fear overcome you, or we cannot rescue our Matara."

Flencik took a slow, deep breath and straightened. "I'll remain calm for Amelia's sake. I'm under control now."

"Good." Rajhir managed an encouraging smile. "We will meet with Israla in her office immediately. According to her, the Earthers took Amelia straight to their transport. We'll go with the Saucin to the docking area to voice our grievance with the Earthers. Plasius will not give clearance for the Earth transport to leave until this matter and that of their unprovoked attack on Vrill is settled to everyone's satisfaction."

"The Earthers won't wait for clearance to leave," Breft growled.

Rajhir's smile, more a snarl, returned. "The Earther transport is trapped in a stasis field. Plasius may not have military might, but these people have other ways to ensure cooperation."

"Still, the Earthers have no intention of releasing Amelia to us. Negotiations with those barbarians are a waste of time!" Breft's fangs appeared as he spoke, a clear indication his patience was spent.

"Indeed. That's why you're not going with us to debate the matter." Rajhir's gaze captured that of his Nobek. "Flencik and I will be quite agitated when we confront the Earthers. In fact, we'll cause a large distraction that will require everyone's full and undivided attention."

Breft's face lit up with predatory pleasure. "I see." He licked his lips in anticipation.

Rajhir allowed himself a chilling laugh. "The Earthers will not take our Matara without a fight. Our own transport to Kalquor is ready and cleared for take-off. Let's see to it that our entire clan is on it."

Chapter Nineteen

Amelia sat in the Earth transport's grim holding cell, her head hanging with defeated exhaustion. Twenty minutes ago Croft and the other soldiers had forced her to disembark the shuttle then brought her into this spartan cell, leaving her alone. The room echoed with her sobs.

Actually the room was beyond spartan. It was empty. The room lacked even a chair upon which to sit. Despite being metallic, the dull gray of the room's surfaces reflected nothing. Amelia huddled in one corner of the featureless cube, feeling beyond all hope.

She never should have left the clan's quarters. She should have listened to Flencik. Now her world was shattered, a beautiful world in which she'd finally discovered unequivocal love and understanding. Rajhir, Flencik and Breft had poured selfless devotion on her. She repaid it by abandoning them and taking their desperately needed offspring with her. She'd made her own unborn a hostage to the whims of Earth's bigoted government.

She expected no rescue. The Plasians, interested only in sensual pleasures, kept no military force. Not even a police force was needed for the peaceful culture. Poor Vrill's murder would receive no justice, only mourning. While the clan would no doubt try to negotiate a means to free Amelia, Earth would turn a deaf ear to their arguments. Three Kalquorians would be no match for an entire platoon of armed soldiers, so force was out of the question.

Amelia was lost.

The transport's engines had been running when they arrived, but she'd heard no hint that they'd taken off yet. Why were they still here? Croft had said they'd take off immediately. It wasn't fair that the transport should remain on Plasius so long; it gave her a taste of hope, a hope she knew was false. She and her child were doomed. Her chest hitched, but no tears remained to flow. She'd sapped herself of all tears along with her strength.

A click sounded from the metal door across the room. Amelia wearily raised her head as it swung open.

Two soldiers, as old and hard looking as Croft, their rifles unslung and trained on her, swept into the room. General Croft and an older, stoop-shouldered man followed them.

"This is what you came to see, Dr. Joyner," the general said, sweeping his arm toward Amelia.

The older man peered at her through thick spectacles, a surprise to Amelia since few wore corrective lenses in this day and age. He looked her up and down. "Did you use her as a punching bag, General?"

"She resisted capture," Croft lied effortlessly. "It was necessary to use force on the degenerate slut."

"And strangling her? Look at those fingerprints. Is that an approved method for subduing prisoners?"

"One of the men became zealous with his need to punish her for her heinous crimes. It did both him and her good. She's been quiet as a lamb since." A malicious smile appeared on Croft's face.

Amelia didn't bother to protest the falsehoods pouring from the general's mouth. She knew it would be a waste of breath, and she feared he would kill her in truth if she spoke against him. The man was too unstable to be pushed.

The doctor grunted. "She appears in good health otherwise. My examination will confirm that. Do you have any idea of when she conceived?"

"It must have been within the last six weeks. That's when the Kalquorian clan arrived on Plasius." Croft turned his frigid gaze to the doctor. "I don't agree with Earth's decision to allow the alien bastard to be born. It's an abomination of all that's decent."

Amelia's heart stuttered with a brief ray of joy that she'd be allowed to bear the clan's offspring.

Dr. Joyner humphed. "It will provide us with valuable research. Such a specimen has never been studied."

"What if it's dangerous?" Croft fumed. "We don't know what such an unholy beast will be capable of."

"The research lab is in a military facility," Joyner responded. He seemed to view the general with disdain. "All necessary precautions will be taken. Surely you have faith in the might of your own military?"

"Even the best security has a hole in it somewhere."

"There'd better not be." His eyes glazed as icy as Croft's. "We plan to clone the specimen for more test subjects if possible. We can't dissect the creature if there's only one."

Amelia's momentary hope shattered. Despite her fear of Croft, her voice croaked through her bruised throat in her attempt to scream at them. "What do you mean 'dissect'? You're talking about an innocent life! My child's life!"

Neither man reacted to her outburst. "I don't like the thought of that abomination getting loose," Croft said. "I think I'll make it a point to look over the security of your facility myself."

Joyner's porta-com buzzed for attention. He unclipped the black box, no bigger than a deck of cards, from his belt and held it to his mouth. "Go ahead."

A disembodied female voice crackled from the com.   "The examination room is ready, Doctor."

"On our way," Joyner said and re-attached his com to his belt. He nodded at Croft.

"Bring her," the general said. He followed the doctor out of the room.

"Come with us," one of the soldiers barked at Amelia.

"Please," she said, her voice little more than a hiss of breath. She knew begging was futile, but she couldn't stop herself. "You can't go along with this. It isn't right. I'm an Earth citi—"

The sight of the soldiers raising their guns and taking careful aim at her froze her voice. She saw no pity, no compassion on either face.

Amelia was at the mercy of those who had none.

Chapter Twenty

A female aide wearing a flowing transparent dress ushered Rajhir's clan into the Saucin's office. Apparently even the aide appreciated the gravity of the situation, because she didn't bother to flirt with the men. Her pretty face was grim as she left the room, closing the door behind her.

Rajhir wondered how many intergalactic treaties had been signed on the lounge cushions that lined every wall of the room. He himself had been on the receiving end of Israla's artful 'negotiation' skills during trade talks over the years. He'd signed many an official agreement with her coiled around him, doing those delightful things she did so well.

Most of those agreements happened on the wall-hugging lounger, but a few finished on the fur-covered floor. The most memorable treaty, a ten-year contract that traded Kalquorian ore for Plasian produce, reached its final compromise with Rajhir strapped down on Israla's blackwood desk. She watched as two of her aides pleasured him, directing their efforts with sharp commands. She deigned to touch him only once that day, when her mouth accepted his groaning release. How Flencik and Breft enjoyed hearing that story over and over!

Still, the joy of gaining a Matara, a single woman to devote all his love to, outweighed the loss of other women...even a woman of Israla's many skills. And the sweetness of Amelia's body and soul eclipsed all others completely.

Israla entered the room from the door opposite the one they'd come in. She glided across the sumptuous room to greet them. Under less dire circumstances, the Plasian's dress today -- or lack of it -- might still have given Rajhir pause. Israla wore sellil, a fabric that clung to the skin wherever draped. The Saucin's sellil was bronze to match her skin, giving her the illusion of nakedness. She might as well have been; the fabric was three inches wide at best, a strip of cloth winding about her lithe form. One end started at her right breast, covering the nipple without disguising the shape of her areola. It crossed over to her left breast, wound around her back to reappear at her tapered waist. From there, it draped between her legs, hiding the cleft of her smooth sex.

Israla's skin glistened pale bronze. The fur that topped her head was the natural olive of the Plasian. It snapped back and forth in agitation, like blades of grass in a hurricane. As she drew close, Rajhir detected a musky aroma, much like the perfume of Amelia's sex. His heart lurched, remembering that mysterious scent surrounding him when he'd knelt between his Earther Matara's thighs to bury his face in the honeyed sweetness of her.

That memory instead of Israla's appearance made him ache. He hungered for Amelia's flesh only. His bow to the Saucin consisted of complete respect.

"Saucin, I thank you for your help in recovering my clan's Matara."

Grimness lined Israla's otherwise perfect features. "This taking of Amelia Ryan is a great tragedy for Plasius as well as Kalquor. The honor she bestowed my world with her incomparable art is beyond measure. I will not see her so brutally treated."

Flencik's face paled. "Has she been hurt?"

Israla's frown grew deeper. "You do not need to worry over a few bruises that do not threaten her life. That is all the description I will give you. To tell you more will invite mindless anger when all your concentration for her safe release is so desperately needed." She took a deep breath as if to steady herself.

"Then her injuries are not life threatening," Rajhir said.

"Despite being badly treated, she did walk on her own from the shuttle to the Earthers' ship. They drove her under the threat of weapons. She wept. To face such intimidation must have damaged her glorious spirit. This concerns me more than superficial physical injury. You must find a way to free her."

Breft growled low in his throat. "I'll free her and destroy anyone who gets in the way."

Rajhir gripped his tensed shoulder in warning. "Our mission is to reclaim Amelia, not to exact revenge on her captors." He turned his attention back to Israla. "We must distract the Earthers so that the Nobek can rescue her."

Israla's eyes flicked toward the youngest member of the clan. "Will it be difficult to move around their transport?"

Breft said, "Your scanners gave me an excellent view of their ship's weaknesses. I've studied the vessel thoroughly. I'm confident that once I am inside the transport, I can move about the venting system undetected."

A smile eased Israla's face. "The trick is to keep the Earthers busy enough to allow you onto their transport and escape with Amelia. Keeping them here is not a problem. Their General Croft learned upon their return that a stasis field holds their ship in place."

"I'm sure he's less than happy about that," Rajhir said.

"He demanded a meeting, but I am delaying it until we are ready. My most pressing concern is his lack of patience. If you fail to recover Amelia, we must try to wait until your battle cruisers arrive."

"Do you think your stasis field will hold?" Breft asked.

"Not even a Nobek of your skills could find a way to break out of our stasis field." Israla allowed herself a confident smirk, which faded quickly. "But it only impedes the transport, not people. The Earthers can move about our city at will. They are heavily armed, and we are not. I fear more Plasians will be endangered."

Rajhir drew a heavy breath. "Our need is placing your people in jeopardy."

"No." A hard light filled her black marble eyes. "The Earthers' violent tyranny places my people in danger. I will not be swayed by threats."

"No matter how this turns out, we can never repay your kindness and bravery," Flencik said.

Israla suddenly smiled, her look filled with deviltry. "We will all do what we must to regain your Matara. I trust you can be threatening enough to hold the soldiers' attention?"

Rajhir snarled, displaying his fangs. Flencik followed suit, flexing his sizeable muscles so they stood out corded.

The Saucin caught her breath. Her eyes widened. She'd only seen Rajhir as a diplomat or in the throes of passion. He felt her shock at realizing how dangerous an angry Kalquorian could be.

She recovered quickly. "Very frightening, Dramok and Imdiko. They would be fools not to take such a demonstration seriously. However, if some are so stupid as to not pay attention to you, perhaps they will look at me." She ran her palm over her exposed left side, the temptress in her very much evident.

A bitter smile creased Rajhir's lips. "We may well be invisible to the Earthers when their eyes can feast upon you."

She chuckled with a born flirt's delight. "Whoever does not possess the sense to be tamed by fear may still be tamed with desire."

Chapter Twenty One

Amelia froze at the doorway of Doctor Joyner's 'examination room'.

A metal table dominated the middle of the space. It was equipped with the stirrups she'd seen dozens of times in her own gynecologist's office. Unfortunately, the benign references to a normal medical facility ended there.

Heavy black leather straps hung from the sides of the table. They wavered inches from the floor. They looked like a spider's trembling legs anticipating wrapping themselves around their victim. Straps attached on the stirrups too. Even a smaller set at the other end of the table, apparently to restrain the patient's head, lay in wait for her.

On the far side of the table stood an array of computers, monitors, and machines as forbidding as a panel of judges. Even worse, a table held surgical instruments lined up with military precision. Steel gleamed in the bald glare of the light. The blinding light sapped the room of all color, bleaching everything gray.

Amelia stood at the threshold of a torture chamber.

One of the soldiers behind Amelia shoved her into the room. She wheeled around to see the guards close and lock the door and flank each side of it. They pointed their guns at her.

"Remove your clothing," Dr. Joyner said.

She looked at him, at the people around her. A female nurse, still in the grip of youth's beauty, stood in a corner. Amelia had missed noticing her when she first entered. The white-garbed woman stepped forward to address Joyner. "Doctor, shouldn't these gentlemen leave the room?"

"This woman is dangerous," Croft said. "We're not going anywhere until I know she's properly restrained."

"That girl doesn't look very dangerous," the nurse murmured. She frowned.

"Attend to your duties," Joyner snapped, his face a thundercloud of sudden anger. The nurse bowed her head and fell quiet. Brief hope for a sympathetic attitude flared in Amelia's breast.

To Amelia the doctor said, "Remove your clothing, or I'll have the soldiers remove it for you."

Terror's paralysis left Amelia as rage swept through her. They condemned her as a criminal, treated her like a disease, and now they wanted to rob her of her dignity. And why? Because she'd fallen in love with members of a race her government feared and hated. Because

she carried a life that, despite its innocence of any wrongdoing, they despised and reviled. Instead of relying on facts, they'd judged her on the basis of stupidity and bigotry.

She was done with marching to the guillotine quietly.

Amelia, whose posture had been that of a cowering dog, straightened. "I will not submit to this. I have my rights, rights you can't take away on a whim!" She looked back and forth between Croft and Joyner. "I refuse to cooperate any further until I have legal representation."

Croft's face turned eggplant purple. He roared one word that made the nurse yelp in terror. "Strip!"

"NO!" Amelia shrieked back. Her hands bunched into fists. "I am not the enemy, and I'm not a traitor! Stop treating me like a criminal!"

Croft glanced at his soldiers. A snarl twisted his face. "If she doesn't take her clothes off by the time I count to five, shoot her. One...two..."

"Don't be a ridiculous ass, you fool," Joyner said, cutting Croft off. The general, not used to being ordered around, gaped at him. He seemed too stunned to move.

"The embryo she carries is too valuable to destroy, so put your indignation aside. This is research, not an anti-alien crusade," Joyner continued. He addressed the soldiers. "Since she won't remove her clothes herself, do it for her."

The soldiers looked to their commanding officer. Croft glared at the doctor. His fists opened and closed. Amelia wondered if he readied to snap Joyner's neck.

Joyner returned the stare. "General, do we need to contact Earth Command to settle who is in charge of Amelia Ryan?"

After a measure of silence, Croft spoke. His voice shook with rage. "Hand me your guns and strip her."

The soldiers moved immediately. After surrendering their rifles to Croft, they approached Amelia. The gleam in their eyes told her how much they relished the prospect of baring her flesh.

She hooked her hands into claws and hissed like a cat. Startled, they paused for a moment then came on.

The struggle was brief but violent. Amelia battled them like a cornered animal, punching, scratching, biting, kicking and kneeing any opening they gave her. She scored one soldier's cheek with her nails, leaving bloody channels in the close-shaved flesh. She compounded the insult by spitting in his face.

The men panted and cursed as they ripped her blouse from her body.

They manhandled her to the floor, pinning her to the cold surface as they wrestled her trousers off. One tore her bra away, and with a snarl twisting his face, pinched her nipples in turn with brutal fingers. "How do you like that?" he muttered. His erection pressed against her thigh. He disgusted her.

His partner ripped her panties into rags, exposing her secret flesh. Croft averted his eyes from her nakedness, his lip curling in an expression of disgust. For one crazed moment, Amelia thought of her mother.

Joyner said, "Get her on the table and secure the straps."

They lifted her, their sweating hands slippery on her wrists and ankles. She twisted, trying to slide loose, but they managed to keep their grip and haul her onto the table. Croft and Joyner stepped in to help. The four men strapped Amelia to the table. They forced her legs into the stirrups and bound them, leaving her sex open to the soldiers' avid scrutiny. Both sported obvious erections now. She felt the violation of their gazes crawling over her vulnerable skin.

"What's the drill?" the general asked Joyner. "You'll verify her pregnancy and then what?"

The doctor rearranged his instruments and rolled the table next to Amelia's thigh. "A thorough examination of her and the fetus. Then I'll induce a coma that won't affect the embryo but will keep her incapacitated for the duration of the pregnancy."

Amelia was too horrified at his words to scream.

"Once the child is born and it's isolated, she will be revived so that she can receive her sentence of sterilization, castration, and scarring. After which she'll be sent to the labor camp."

"Excellent. I'll inform–" Croft's com beeped, cutting him off. He grunted and answered it. "Croft here."

A disembodied voice pitched with excitement issued from the com. "Sir, Kalquorians are approaching the transport! Saucin Israla appears to be trying to reason with them, but they look angry. Sir, they're huge! What are your orders?"

Amelia found her voice to cry out. Rajhir, Flencik, and Breft had come for her! Tears of relief and terror for them flowed down her cheeks.

Croft spared a moment to glare at her. His attention returned to the com. "I'm on my way. Don't provoke the bastards, but under no circumstances allow them entrance onto the transport."

He snapped the com off and turned to his soldiers. "The prisoner is secure. Come with me, and be ready for anything."

Croft swept out of the room, and the soldiers followed in his wake.

Chapter Twenty Two

Private Juan Ramon's eyes drank in the loveliest vision of womanhood he'd ever seen.

Despite the two gargantuan Kalquorians who flanked her, Saucin Israla took center stage of his attention. Her skin had a sheen that made her look as if she'd just emerged from the ocean, or perhaps her bath. Her breasts, exposed but for the tiny strip of fabric, were bronze mounds that demanded kisses. He wanted to curl himself in her lap and suckle like a baby from her. She looked youthful, the resoluteness in her expression the only betrayal of her age. He saw the sternness in her eyes, and his heart leapt. This lush Plasian looked fragile, but he knew a strong, powerful woman when he saw one. He drew a shuddering sigh.

Ramon barely acknowledged other ships' crews gathering around the Earth transport. The busy space dock had come to a halt to watch the excitement. A buzz of conversation rose and fell, but the dazzled Ramon fell deaf to the chatter.

Ramon had entered the military right out of high school still an untried virgin. However innocent his body remained, his imagination made up for it. His boyhood friends' mothers were the stars of his fantasies. They had wisdom and experience, qualities that excited him. The girls his own age invited no interest; their innocence equaled his own, so they had no knowledge to offer. When he factored in the strict laws making extramarital relations deadly undertakings, seducing young girls became even less tittilating.

As he looked at the Saucin, he imagined that lissome body hovering over his, her sex's delicate lips parting to admit the exclamation point of his shaft, happily ending his purity forevermore.

His imaginings were based on the illegal pictures and illustrations his fellow soldiers bought on Earth's prolific black market. The pictures were known as 'secret sweeties' among the men. Ramon had committed those pictures of lush breasts, rounded buttocks, and secretive sexual folds to memory.

Israla was more slender than any of the secret sweeties, her curves less pronounced. Still, Ramon found all the seduction he needed in her intelligent eyes, in the knowledgeable expression on her face. He knew her guiding hand, along with other delightful body parts, could easily lead him from childhood into the exciting but fearsome life of a man.

The thump of boots on the transport's entrance ramp where Ramon stood guard woke him from his trance. At the sound of General Croft's voice, he snapped to attention.

"Saucin, I demand you remove the Kalquorians from this area and release my ship immediately!" Croft raged, his face crimson as he stormed past Ramon.

Two well-worn soldiers, one whose face bled rivers from deep cuts, scurried behind the general. Both sported obvious erections. It was nice to know the advanced age of the two men didn't inhibit the joys of the flesh. They had to be what, 45 or 50 years old? That made them ancient geezers in the naïve private's eyes.

They must have noticed the Saucin to be so excited, Ramon surmised. He wondered what had happened to the guy who was bleeding. It looked like he'd lost a fight with a tiger.

The Plasian leader's voice tickled Ramon's ears like the ringing of sweet bells. "One of my people has been injured while in your custody, General. Reparations must be made. In addition, the Kalquorians have lodged a formal abduction charge against you. You have taken a member of their clan by force."

"Abduction!" Croft's roar, louder than usual, made Ramon blink before his thoughts immersed themselves again in contemplation of Israla's beauty. The remainder of the general's comments distracted him only slightly. "Amelia Ryan is bound by the laws of Earth and is in violation of those laws. I'm taking her back where she belongs to face serious charges. You have no business harboring this fugitive."

The deep voice of one of the Kalquorians intruded. "Amelia is Matara of my clan, our most important member. She carries our child, the future of Kalquor."

"We do not recognize any claims of Kalquorians on Earthers!"

To Ramon's joy Israla spoke again, her chiming voice a heady aphrodisiac. "Plasius does recognize clan bonds. I also recognize the Kalquorian citizenship of the unborn child. I must consider all arguments in regard to Amelia Ryan's disposition."

In his fantasy, the Saucin spoke to Ramon in the same firm tone. She taught him, chastising him with stinging slaps on his naked buttocks when he failed to perform to her dictates. He licked his lips. He wondered how it felt to be spanked by Saucin Israla.

Croft's bellow again disrupted the fantasy. "We're taking her back to Earth! End of discussion!"

"You take her nowhere, Earther," the lead Kalquorian said, his voice low but full of threat. Animal instinct for danger kicked in, and Ramon finally took a good look at the aliens.

The Kalquorian speaker and his bigger companion stepped forward, closing in on Croft, their faces brutal with anger. Ramon gasped to see long fangs protruding from their upper jaws. The dark-skinned Kalquorians bulged corded muscle beyond any Earther body builder he'd ever seen. Those bastards were huge.

Ramon's hand went nervously to his sidearm, but its cold presence gave him no comfort. He wasn't sure his tiny gun with its grenade bullets would stop the behemoths. It would probably just piss them off if he shot them. Then they might tear his throat out with those nasty rattlesnake fangs.

Fuck this. I'm not giving them any reason to come after me. If they start fighting with Croft, I'm getting the hell out of here, he thought.

The Kalquorian's voice was an animal's growl, making Ramon's hair stand on end. "We will fight to the death for our Matara and child."

"Death is exactly what you'll get, you sick freaks." The general also stepped forward. He craned his neck back to stare into the lead Kalquorian's eyes. "You're outnumbered and unarmed. You wanna dance? Let's dance."

Both Kalquorians started forward. Croft reached for his sidearm. Ramon got ready to run for cover. Israla whipped around to face the massive aliens, pressing her palms against their chests. The sight of the Plasian leader's naked backside stopped Ramon's breath. Her rounded buttocks gleamed like polished marble, making him momentarily forget the escalating situation. Ramon barely resisted an urge to run to the Saucin and cup her perfect fleshy mounds.

"You will not fight!" Despite the lovelier tones, her voice held as much command as the general's and the lead Kalquorian's. The Kalquorians glowered at Croft but advanced no further.

Croft, for his part, was just as surprised as Ramon by Israla's nudity. His eyes bulged. His mouth worked. He left his gun on his hip, his hands going up as if to ward off Israla's nakedness. He backed up, bumping into the two staring soldiers who'd stormed off the transport with him. He nearly knocked the bleeding one over in his haste to get away from the trio of aliens.

"Is the entire universe corrupt?" he shouted. "Do you godless aliens have morals? Any grasp of decency?"

Private Copeland, the other guard posted on the ramp, snickered. The sound diverted Ramon enough for him to see Copeland motion him over. Ramon glanced around to make sure no one saw him abandon his post. Worry proved unjustified; everyone's attention focused on the drama involving the Kalquorians. He sidled across the transport's entrance ramp to Copeland's side.

"Look at that idiot challenging the aliens," Copeland whispered. "No way in hell I'd get in their faces. He should give up the girl before they squash him."

Copeland's words gave Ramon the courage to voice his own opinion. "If he starts a fight with them, I'm hiding until it's over. No way I'm crossing those two monsters."

"Not only is he stupid where the Kalquorians are concerned, but listen to him preaching to the hot Plasian chick! I always thought Croft preferred the boys," Copeland confided. "Now I'm sure of it. How else could he look at a gorgeous ass like that and spout morals and decency?"

"I sure hope he doesn't ruin our relations with the Plasians." Ramon felt little surprise at the tremble in his own voice. "I'd sell my soul to the devil to be stationed here where I could look at her every day. She's magnificent."

"She's an older one." Copeland leered. "To be so hot at her age, can you imagine what the girls our age are like?"

Ramon dismissed the thought of young Plasian girls. He wished for the wisdom of the Saucin.

He forgot to resume his position on the other side of the ramp. Copeland forgot to remind him. No one noticed the Kalquorian who slipped behind them onto the Earth transport.

Chapter Twenty Three

The doctor began his examination. Amelia bit her lip to keep from crying out as his gloved finger shoved its implacable way inside. The thick digit felt like a violation. Joyner's exam succeeded in doing what the clan's most demanding lovemaking never managed; Amelia felt as if he raped her.

The finger jerked out of her sex. This time a whimper escaped her throat. The doctor, his eyes never leaving the view between Amelia's legs, snapped, "Nurse, give me--"

The ceiling vent cover exploded into the room, smashing into the back of the doctor's head. He fell to the floor with a grunt as Breft burst from the ventilation shaft.

The nurse inhaled, ready to scream. Breft sprang at her, faster than Amelia's wide eyes could follow. One moment he was below the vent, the next he was halfway across the room, grabbing the nurse by the throat.

"No sound," he said, tightening his grip in warning. She trembled in his grasp and kept quiet.

The gasping doctor managed to get up on all fours. The Nobek kicked him in the side of the head while holding onto the nurse. The doctor slid into a boneless lump on the floor.

Breft sank his fangs into the nurse's neck. She whimpered, then her body relaxed in his grip. She sighed and smiled a little as the intoxicant took hold.

Breft withdrew and propped her in a corner where she watched him with half-closed eyes.

"Good female," Breft said with his trademark predator's smile. "You will stay here and keep quiet."

"Take me with you," she said. "I'll do whatever you wish."

Breft shook his head and stroked her cheek. "Kalquor would welcome you, but I cannot help you now. I must rescue my Matara. After we leave, get off this ship if you can and look to the Plasians for aid."

Through it all, Amelia watched, disbelieving that Breft had really come to rescue her. As he approached the table to which she was tied, her eyes filled with tears.

"Breft...oh Breft, I'm so glad to see you."

His hands cradled her head. "Who hurt you, little one? Was it this one?" He snarled at the unconscious doctor.

"Not him. I'll be all right, and they didn't harm the baby, thank goodness. Let's just get out of here."

He moved down to her ankles bound to the stirrups. As his hands grasped the straps on one foot he looked at her open sex. His breath caught.

"Amelia...Matara."

The heavy Kalquorian cinnamon smell permeated the room. Amelia saw his arousal strain against his formsuit as he stared at her vulnerable openings. His fingertips skimmed up her legs and stroked

her furred sex. She moaned, wriggling against her bonds in an effort to get her clitoris closer to his touch. He captured the aching bud between a thumb and forefinger. Her sex gushed warmth. He raised eyes dark with desire to hers.

"I want you," Amelia gasped, needing him with desperation. "But we don't have time. The general might come back at any moment and catch you."

Breft grinned. "He will be busy for awhile. Rajhir, Flencik and Israla distract the Earthers. Besides, this time I will not take long. I am aching to be inside you. I feared--," his voice caught. He couldn't voice the pain of nearly losing her.

He freed his penises from the formsuit and mounted Amelia. He pressed deep within her, soothing the flesh abused by Joyner. She moaned and arched against the straps that held her helpless and open to him. He filled her to bursting, yet she wanted more. Breft pulled back until only the tips of his organs remained inside then he slid back into her womb, letting her feel his entire length. He moved with care, loving her with gentle thoroughness. She received each thrust with gratitude.

Amelia tossed her head from side to side, the only part of her free to express the rising heat in her belly. She saw the nurse staring at Breft pumping his sex deep into her. The other woman's chest heaved, and she rubbed her thighs together. Her eyes gave away her yearning. Being watched by the aroused woman, knowing the nurse wanted to be the one receiving Breft's eager flesh, excited Amelia even more.

Breft grabbed her hips, pressing his fingers into her skin as his rhythm quickened. Now his organs were battering rams within her, pounding until she cried out in release. He groaned deep in his throat as he shot his seed into her belly.

Breft stood between her legs, his chest heaving, his eyes closed. Amelia watched him bask in the afterglow, loving how the sharp planes of his face relaxed.

His eyes slid open, and he smiled at her. "I told you I would not be long. My joy to have you back made me eager. I am glad you were able to find your pleasure too." He pulled free while untying her ankles.

He was right; their coupling had lasted barely minutes. Amelia watched him as he freed her, not quite able to speak. The emotion welling inside her choked off anything she might say.

And what does the condemned say when the execution is halted at the last possible second? There are no words, she decided.

"We move quickly now," he said as he freed her from the table. He lifted her in his arms and carried her across the room to the vent. "I will be right behind you." He boosted her up into the shaft. She moved forward a few feet and waited while he climbed climbed up to join her.

Amelia didn't hear the nurse speak, but Breft turned to the drugged woman before leaping into the shaft. "I cannot, dear one. Go to the Saucin. See what she can do for you."

Then he was in the vent with Amelia, prodding her to move forward. "Quietly," he breathed. "But fast. I do not know how long before those two recover enough to go for help."

Amelia obeyed, following Breft's instructions through the twisting maze of ductwork.

Chapter Twenty Four

The thumps of running feet inside the transport alerted Ramon in time to resume his proper position. No one except Copeland noticed he had left his post.

Dr. Joyner hurtled down the ramp, his eyes glazed and hair standing on end. He dragged the pretty, dark-haired nurse Ramon had noticed before by the hand. Her expression was rapturous, as if she'd seen the Promised Land. Ramon was so startled by their disparate expressions that it took him a few moments to notice the blood trickling from the doctor's forehead.

"The nurse and I've been attacked! A Kalquorian has taken the Ryan woman!"

Croft gaped at him, his argument with the two huge aliens ending abruptly. "That's not possible! There's only one way onto the transport and I have guards posted." Ramon cringed as the general charged over to confront him and Copeland. "Have you let anyone board this ship since I disembarked?"

Ramon exchanged a frightened glance with the other guard. "I've seen no one fitting the description of a Kalquorian besides those two, sir. No one has attempted to board the transport."

Joyner looked at the glaring aliens standing in the transport's shadow. "Two Kalquorians? Where's the third of the clan?" He whipped around, his eyes bulging at Croft. "Kalquorian males group in threes, not pairs. General, where's the third?"

Croft's face paled. His mouth hung open. "No one told me clans were made up of three men. What kind of woman would do such a thing?"

Joyner nodded, a look of grim satisfaction settling over his face. "I see. You didn't bother to research your enemy before you encountered them. Your incompetence has allowed a criminal and our research specimen to escape."

"No." Croft breathed the word, then spoke louder. "No, she hasn't. She and the Kalquorian are still on board, or those two wouldn't still be here causing a distraction."

The doctor stepped close to the general. Despite Joyner's whip-thin frame, the threat in his posture was unmistakable. "You'd better hope so," he murmured, low enough so Ramon had to strain to hear.

"There's a court martial in your future. Recovering Ryan and capturing that Kalquorian might go a long way to keeping you out of prison."

He strode back up the ramp, leaving Croft seething. The general unleashed his fury at his underlings.

He *screamed* the orders. "Everyone search the transport for the woman and the alien! They'd better be found." He glared at the assembled platoon, marking every face. His hand clenched at his sidearm. "If I go down because they escaped, you'd better believe I'm taking every last one of you sorry bastards with me. Now move!"

Everyone raced up the ramp past Croft, Ramon, and the dreamy-eyed nurse as if running for their lives. Even Copeland scurried from his post and onto the ship to escape Croft's wrath. After a moment's confusion, Ramon decided he'd follow his lead.

Instead, the general grabbed a fistful of Ramon's collar, yanking him close until they stood nose to nose. Ramon fought an urge to retch at the general's sour breath. "Don't you move, boy," Croft growled. "You let that slimeball alien on my transport. If you value your life as well as your career, you'll not let that slut leave this ship." His deadly gaze shifted towards the Kalquorians where they stood with Israla. "Damn the diplomatic relations. If they make a move towards the ship, or their companion shows his ugly face, kill them. You got me? The Kalquorians and their nasty whore. Blow their damn brains out. That's an order."

Croft stormed up the ramp without hearing Ramon squeak, "Yes sir."

* * * *

Rajhir folded his arms across his chest and contemplated his next move. Before he could order his thoughts properly, the nurse, who still stood on the Earther transport's entry ramp, giggled. The sound seemed unique to Earther females. He'd only heard his sweet Amelia utter anything similar. The thought brought his anxiety up another notch. Breft had found her; that much was certain. Would he be able to get them off the ship now that the alarm was sounded?

To no one in particular the beaming nurse said, "The general has serious anger issues."

Rajhir studied her face and fought off a smile. The two tiny trails of blood running down her collarbone confirmed his suspicions. He whispered so only Israla and Flencik could hear, "Breft has been biting the enemy."

Flencik, despite his worried expression, managed a chuckle, and it attracted the female's attention. "Kalquorians," she breathed. She shuffled a couple of drunken steps toward them. She offered a hopeful smile. "Are you part of that Ryan girl's clan?"

"Yes." Flencik darted a glance at Rajhir, who shrugged.

Her happiness dimmed a little. "That's too bad. I want to go to Kalquor. Are there any free clans running around Plasius?"

The soldier guarding the entrance started. He shifted his avid gaze from Israla's nearly nude body to the nurse.

"There is no room left on our transport," Rajhir told Israla.

"Then in the interest of good relations between our people, allow me to keep her until a clan can claim her." Israla approached the woman, who blinked at the guard staring at her.

"Are you going to tell on me?" she was asking him. Her eyes were wide with sweet entreaty.

"He won't say a word, will you my young friend?" Israla flowed up the ramp toward the Earthers.

"Is this a good idea?" Flencik muttered to his clanmate. "If he decides to shoot the Saucin, we can't stop him in time."

"Shooting her is the very last thing on that boy's mind. He can't take his eyes off Israla." Rajhir kept watch on the transport's entrance, willing Breft and Amelia to appear. *What is taking so long?*

"I still can't believe she's chancing it just to help an Earther female."

"It's not the female Israla is focused on."

"You mean——" Another nervous chuckle. "I know she likes them young, but he's barely done suckling his mother. 'In the interest of good relations' indeed!"

Rajhir flicked his gaze to the unlikely trio on the ramp. Israla whispered into the red-faced soldier's ear while simultaneously gesturing for the nurse to join them. All smiles, the intoxicated female came close enough for the Saucin to take her hand.

Tracing the tense jaw of the boy with one long finger, Israla raised her voice just enough for Rajhir to hear. "I'll be back in a moment. Think about what I've told you." With that, Israla drifted away, pulling the other woman with her.

The soldier watched them walk to Israla's aide, his expression dazed, his erection tenting the front of his olive green pants. He glanced at Rajhir, his confusion plain to read. He glanced back at the open entrance of the transport, no doubt to make sure no one had seen him allowing the nurse to leave. His eyes settled back on Israla, now deep in conversation with her aide and the nurse. That's where his lost stare remained, his lips parted, his tongue peeking out from time to time to wet them.

All amusement fled as Rajhir watched and worried. *Amelia and Breft, where are you?*

Chapter Twenty Five

Amelia soon lost her bearings in the twists and turns of the transport's ventilation system. Only Breft's assured directions convinced her they'd find their way out.

A large mesh-covered opening appeared to one side, and Amelia slowed.

"Stop," Breft whispered. "Make no sound."

Amelia obeyed. Her breath seemed loud to her own ears. She opened her mouth to let air flow into her lungs silently. She shivered as she crouched, still as a statue. Her naked skin bumped into gooseflesh.

A voice bellowed, making its way into the shaft by way of the vent opening. "Check the storage bins! Scan the air vents! The moment you have a reading, relay it to all and surround them! I want that Kalquorian bastard and his slut found now!"

Amelia recognized the grating voice and whimpered. "It's Croft." Behind her, Breft placed a warm hand over her buttock. She quieted, comforted by his unspoken promise. The Nobek would not let the Earthers capture her again.

Breft pressed his hand in the small of her back, and she lay flat on her belly. Silent as a cat, Breft eased up to crouch over her. He peered through the mesh.

Thudding steps thundered to a crescendo outside the vent, echoing until it seemed an army of thousands charged by. Finally the noise faded. The steps receded to distant parts of the transport, becoming the far off rumble of an angry beast.

Amelia thought all the soldiers had moved on until she heard the gravely muttering begin. Her heart froze to hear Croft so close.

"I'll kill them all. I'll kill that Ryan slut and her nasty alien freaks. I'll kill those stupid guards who let the Kalquorian on the ship. I'll kill that fucking pompous doctor too. They'll pay for this shit. They'll all pay."

Amelia looked up at Breft who continued to watch the man below them. She touched his arm to get his attention. When he looked down at her, she mouthed, "Don't let him see you. He's crazy."

"They're all dead," Croft continued to growl. Footsteps sounded; he was pacing back and forth.

Breft's eyes narrowed as he looked down into her face. He looked through the grate again.

"All dead."

Breft looked at her again. His cat eyes widened, and he touched her bruised, swollen cheek.

"Especially *her*."

Breft's lips twisted into a snarl, showing his fangs. Amelia knew he'd realized Croft was responsible for her injuries. She grabbed his wrist in a desperate attempt to stop him.

She might as well have been clutching wind. Breft was a blur, smashing through the vent cover and diving out head first with supernatural speed. The cover clattered to the floor below. Croft uttered a gasp but nothing more. There were a few thumps.

Breft's angry voice hissed, "No one harms my Matara." Then Amelia heard a wet, tearing sound, followed by more thumps and a whistling, drawn-out gurgle.

She didn't want to know. She really didn't. But it was as if an invisible hand pulled her head up to look down on the men below.

Blood had sprayed in an arc across the far wall. Breft stood over Croft, breathing hard, his back to Amelia. The general lay on the floor, his eyes still just glazing over as his last whistling breath ended. His throat was torn out.

Without looking at her, Breft said, "Do not look, Amelia. This is not fit for your eyes."

Amelia slid back, her eyes squeezed shut against the nausea that threatened momentarily. Below her, Breft muttered to the dead man, "You got off easy, *gurluck*."

He suddenly reappeared in the shaft, bringing the vent cover with him to snap into place. Once that was done, he smoothed Amelia's hair from her face. His expression was one of concern. "Are you all right? I did not mean for you to see that."

Amelia drew a shaky breath. "You have blood on your mouth."

He wiped his lips clean on his sleeve. "I am sorry."

"No." She felt a little shocked at the surge of savage joy she felt. "That bastard threatened to tear our child out of my body. I'm glad he's dead. I'm glad you did it."

His predatory grin appeared. "My clan is safe from that one. Now we leave. Follow me."

He crawled ahead of her, looking back often as if to reassure himself she still followed. Amelia stayed on his heels, her ears straining. Any moment she expected Croft's gruesome death to be discovered. Then the soldiers would really come after them. They wouldn't bother to take them prisoner now; they'd shoot to kill if they found her and Breft.

The shaft seemed to go on forever. Amelia realized she was close to panic but couldn't stop her heart from pounding or her breath from sobbing loud and fast. The walls of the shaft closed in, making air harder to find. Breft must have taken a wrong turn somewhere. They'd never get out in time. Surely the general's body had been found by now.

When the Nobek stopped abruptly, her racing heart skipped a beat. A wall blocked further advance; no other passage branched off from this one. Only a vent opening shining light into the dim confines provided exit.

Breft grasped the vent grate and pushed. It popped out with just a slight whine of metal against metal, but Amelia cringed anyway. Every sound amplified; that tiny shiver of the grate giving way shrieked in her ears. Her own breathing blew a hurricane.

Breft eased his head out of the vent and scanned the transport's corridor. He slid farther out of the duct until he leaned out from the waist up. Amelia squeezed her eyes shut, certain at any moment she would hear a shout of detection.

Instead, Breft drew back in unseen. "The way off the transport is across the corridor," he said. "Only one guard remains just outside the exit."

"We're trapped," Amelia moaned.

"Not for long. Rajhir and Flencik are out there with the Saucin." Amelia heard the smile in his voice. "Israla could distract one hundred guards."

"We can't be caught. If you knew what Earth has planned for me and the baby—"

"The Earthers will not take my Matara." All amusement fled his tone. His fingers raked her hair. "They do not dare."

The cold menace left no doubt in Amelia's mind of his exact meaning. A thrill of fear ran down her spine. He'd already proven once he'd kill for her without conscience. After the demonstration of his speed and visciousness Amelia actually feared more for their enemies than for Breft.

* * * *

Ramon felt himself go hot and cold at the same time. The beautiful Saucin Israla was looking at him again. He swallowed and dropped his eyes under her intense gaze.

The things she'd whispered to him earlier! Things she said she wished to do to him! Of course he knew it was all a ploy to get him to let the nurse escape. There was no way a woman of Israla's beauty and power could want a childish nobody like him. Still, he'd let the woman go, envying her the sexual freedom she was heading for. As oppressed as Ramon had felt on Earth when it came to his sexuality, he knew women had it the worst. He didn't begrudge the nurse her chance at a better life.

Besides, he'd have sacrificed anything to hear the Saucin whisper the deliciously naughty things she had. In those few precious seconds she'd described wonders he'd never even imagined a man and a woman might do together. It had been worth the court martial he undoubtedly faced to know the possibilities of unbridled love and lust. If only he was free to partake in them!

A movement brought his eyes back up. The Saucin's aide was leading the nurse away. The Earther woman's face was alight with euphoria.

Ramon barely registered this because he only had eyes for his beautiful tormentor. A whimper escaped his throat. Israla slunk towards him. Came right up to him. Stood before him. Surrounded him with her musky scent. Stared down at him from her greater height with black marbled eyes. Her lips parted. Dear God, was she deigning to speak to him again, to lowly Private Ramon?

"Hello once more, Earther. I told you I'd return." Her words spread over him like honey.

"Yes ma'am, you did." His voice was breathless.

"What is your name?" She spread her long-fingered hand on his chest as if to feel his drumming heart. He felt her warmth through his shirt.

He felt incapable of speech, but the undercurrent of command in Israla's voice forced a reply nonetheless. "Ramon, ma'am. Juan Ramon."

"Hhhwahn," the Plasian breathed. Ramon's heart double beat at the silky sound of his name from her lips. She tasted it. She savored it.

Israla stepped closer. She looked him up and down. He felt the heat from her nearly-naked body coming at him in waves. "You're very young, aren't you? An innocent, perhaps?"

This time, nothing could bring his voice back. He nodded his head, his eyes locked on hers.

"I am curious about Earther males. Young Earther males." Her bronze lips parted to let her golden tongue wet them. "I want to know about you."

Good Lord, how could he respond to that?

She didn't give him time to. Her slim fingers slid over his crotch, seeking. She found him hard. He couldn't believe the strength of her touch. For one so willowy and fragile looking, she possessed power beyond reckoning.

She smiled at his gasp. "Plasians are not — how do you say — shy? Tell me, has this known a woman's warmth, boy?"

His head shook despite fearing she wouldn't want a virgin. He didn't dare to lie to her.

Instead of walking away, she smiled and fondled him more energetically than before. He groaned as his manhood stiffened further in response, and she trilled laughter. "Good Earther boy. You have a strong *fralis*. I am pleased to know it. Show these people this fine thing you offer Israla."

He dimly recalled the other aliens that had gathered around the ship when all the drama of the Ryan woman's arrival began, and how more still arrived to watch the Kalquorians confront Croft. He couldn't tear his attention from the Saucin to check if they still watched. He and Israla must be giving them radically different entertainment from Earth versus Kalquor.

The Kalquorians! He'd forgotten about them. He jerked his eyes from the trap of Israla's gaze to check on the enemy — and more importantly, what they were looking at.

Among the tittering crowd, the clan alone paid no attention to him and Israla at all. Their attention riveted on the transport's entrance.

Israla strengthened her powerful grip on his groin. His body responded and he moaned, spurring her to stroke his aching need hungrily.

"I must experience this strength of yours." Her voice lowered to a throaty growl. "I want you for myself, Earther. I want to teach you the pleasures of love."

A thrill shot through his gut. She wanted him! She wanted the very thing he'd sell his soul for; to instruct him in the mysteries of sex.

This couldn't really be happening, could it? He must be dreaming. He'd better wake up before Croft returned. He tried to back away from Israla, but his legs refused to obey. The heat in his groin sapped his will to resist.

As if reading his mind, Israla said, "You go nowhere except with me." She circled the hand not busy with his cock to grasp his buttocks. She kneaded his flesh expertly. He groaned again, unable to defend himself. Chuckles from the crowd broke through the roaring in his ears. "Lucky boy," he heard someone say.

Israla sensed his helplessness and moved in for the kill. She pulled close, pressing the softness of her body against him. He fought the urge to fall to his knees and suckle at her breast like a baby.

Her mouth drifted close to his. His lips parted, and he tasted her breath as she spoke. "I desire your youth, your strength. You will stay with me, here on Plasius."

He finally found his voice and sobbed with need. "I can't. General Croft is a psychopath. He'd hunt me down, tear me to shreds and throw what's left in the brig for eternity." All this came out in a child's whine.

Israla stiffened, and her grip on his penis tightened until he almost did fall to his knees. "You deny me nothing, boy. Croft has no power here. I rule Plasius. I command all here including you. You obey me. I am the Saucin."

Yes, she was the Saucin, his goddess, his master. He bowed his head in submission.

A movement at the corner of his eye tweaked enough of his attention to make him glance that way.

A Kalquorian stalked by, the redheaded Ryan woman naked in his arms. A collected gasp issued from the crowd. Israla's two Kalquorian escorts rushed to them.

The clan looked at him, the woman fearful, and the men cold with threat. The one holding the woman handed her off to the biggest of the clan. He stepped forward, putting himself between Ramon and the others. His lips wrinkled back in a snarl, exposing long fangs. There was no fear in this man's face, only the silent promise of death. He waited for Ramon's reaction.

Israla's lips burned against his ear. "You will let them go. She is with those she belongs to. As are you."

Ramon returned his desperate gaze to her face. "I can really stay with you? Because the general would kill me. I'm not kidding. This is my life you're talking about."

"The general is dead," the Ryan woman said. "Take your chance and run."

Israla gave her a startled glance. She recovered and returned her attention to Ramon. "You *will* stay with me. Croft cannot touch you anymore." She backed down the ramp, pulling him along by the crotch. He followed, a puppy on a leash, dimly aware that the Kalquorians raced to another transport nearby. The crowd applauded. A few aliens patted him on the shoulder and shouted congratulations as Israla led him away.

"Come Juan," Israla said. A chauffeured shuttle pulled to a stop before them. The back door swung open, and she pushed him in. The moment the door shut, the shuttle raced away from the docking bay. Ramon heard the roar of a transport taking off.

He had no chance to reflect on Amelia Ryan's escape. The Saucin was all over him. She removed Ramon's clothes at an astonishing speed, simultaneously peeling and unwrapping the strip of cloth that barely concealed her own treasures. Ramon's young body, muscular but still unfinished, was suddenly bare for Israla's eyes, hands, and mouth to feast upon.

"Please," Ramon said. He held his hands up as if to ward her off even as his cock strained towards her hairless sex.

"No need to wait, my sweet young Earther." Her black marble eyes dark with desire, Israla straddled him and pushed against his shoulders. Despite outweighing the Plasian by at least 100 pounds, Ramon fell back.

"I'll show you what I want." She mounted him, sliding his turgid member into the tight sleeve of her sex. She threw her head back and cried out as she filled herself with him. Her nails raked his chest. The shallow tears in his flesh burned. He gripped the seat cushions, his knuckles turning white as he fought to hold back orgasm.

He moaned as he entered the enfolding warmth of the womb. Murmuring encouragement even as she administered stinging slaps to discipline his overly eager flesh, Israla began Juan Ramon's education. She proved every bit the stern teacher he desired.

Chapter Twenty Six

The captain of the transport the Kalquorians had booked passage on wanted no confrontation with Earth's military. The moment the Kalquorians boarded, the small ship took off.

As they flew for the safety of Kalquor, Rajhir led the clan down the transport's corridor. Breft flanked Flencik carrying Amelia, his hand clutching hers as if he'd never let go again. His grip hurt her damaged hand, but she wouldn't have him release it for anything.

"Did you find Vrill?" she asked, her voice trembling on the edge of a sob.

"She should be on her feet again within a few days," Flencik said.

Amelia screamed her joy. "She's alive? Oh thank God!"

Breft chuckled. "Thank Flencik too. He saved her life."

"Have I told you how wonderful I think you are?"

Flencik smirked. "I will let you show me after I treat your injuries and check the baby."

Amelia grinned at him. "You lech."

"What is 'lech'?"

"A man who thinks very naughty thoughts about his Matara. It's short for lecherous."

"Yes, I am lech."

Rajhir stopped before a closed door. He shook his head at them but smiled broadly. He barked a command in his own guttural language. The door clicked open and the clan went in.

The room possessed little space to walk, but what it lacked in size it made up for in luxury. A bed, sized for an entire Kalquorian clan including a Matara, stretched almost wall to wall. Amelia could tell just by looking that the linens were of the highest quality. The walls glowed golden, illuminating the billowy swells of the bed. Shelves lining the walls were stocked with intoxicants to enhance the senses, toys to tease private body parts, lotions to massage, and lubricants to ease entry into tight spaces. The room was made for pleasure.

"Oh boy," Amelia breathed. "Do we have time to try out everything?"

The three men laughed heartily as Flencik set her on the bed. The day's tension and fear seemed to vanish at last.

"We will see what we can do," Rajhir promised. "But for the

moment, let Flencik take care of your poor face."

"Do I look completely awful?" Amelia fretted.

"You could never look awful," said Flencik at his most soothing. "But you are bruised and swollen. Let me see what I can do to make it better."

He clicked a button on the wall, and a storage compartment opened. He brought out a container that held his carefully packed medicines and surgical implements.

Amelia sighed and let herself sink into the bed. "My arms and hands ache too. I think it'll be full-blown pain before long."

"I will keep that from happening," Flencik said. "Sit up so I can make it all better."

The bed was too comfortable for her to muster the energy, so Rajhir and Breft propped her between themselves. Neither was able to keep their hands from exploring her body. Amelia giggled and squirmed as they found places ticklish and sensitive.

Flencik yelled at his clanmates. "Hands off! I am trying to treat her injuries."

"Hurry up!" they roared back in unison.

Rajhir turned serious as he spoke to Breft. "You killed the general?"

"Yes."

"I told you to not waste time on retribution."

"He was next to a vent opening. We could not pass without his knowledge." Breft's face went dangerous. "He is the one who put these marks on Amelia."

"Did you kill him in front of her?" Rajhir's tone was full of threat despite his quiet voice.

"She did not see his death. She saw him after."

"And I approved," Amelia added. "I only wish he had suffered more."

Rajhir looked at her. He brushed fingers against her bruised throat and grimaced. "I wish he had too," he finally said. "But there will be real trouble between Earth and Kalquor now. This could lead to war."

Breft bowed his head. "I am sorry. I accept any punishment deemed necessary."

"Punishment? Rajhir, no!" Amelia pulled at the Dramok. "Croft was a real threat to my life and our child's too. Breft did what he had to."

"Perhaps." Rajhir patted her shoulder. "We will discuss this later. Now is not the time."

"You mean when I'm not around."

Rajhir cocked an eyebrow at her. "It is hard to concentrate on such serious matters when you are near, my little one." He grinned, and his face lost all its sternness. "Especially when you are naked."

Breft chuckled. "Rajhir is lech too. Are you still not done, Flencik?"

"Patience," Flencik muttered, still concentrating on Amelia's injuries. "Get out of my way!" He slapped Rajhir's hand away from her breast to their high amusement.

They managed to control themselves while Flencik salved, stitched, and injected medication, but Rajhir and Breft kept a whispered commentary on the pleasures they would inflict on Amelia as soon as the Imdiko finished his ministrations. Warm juices flowed from between her thighs at their teasing.

At last Flencik put his implements away. "Feel better?"

"Much. Thank you," Amelia sighed.

"Good. Now we celebrate your return," Rajhir said, shedding his clothing. His penises jutted toward her sex. Amelia eagerly fell back and spread herself open for him. She moaned as he entered her, his hard thrusts welcoming her back to her rightful place.

Flencik crouched over her mouth. She suckled hungrily, inhaling his scent as she lapped at one organ, then the other.

She felt Breft's hands close over her breasts. He touched them gently at first, his palms cupping each mound as his tongue swirled over each nipple in turn. Then he became deliciously cruel, pinching and slapping them, giving the nipples punishing nips of pleasure with his teeth.

Earth and Kalquor had nothing to do with home, Amelia realized as the clan brought her to the brink. As long as she was with Rajhir, Flencik, and Breft she already was home.

The End

Made in the USA
Lexington, KY
24 July 2011